MW00931954

Sweetness

Book One

The Sweetest Thing Series

by

Sierra Hill

Sierra Hill

Sweetness

Cover Design: RBA Designs

Photography: K. Keeton Designs

Models: Nathan Weller and Kerrigan Brianne

ISBN: **1535382929**
ISBN-13: **978-1535382922**

Be soft.
Do not let the world make you hard.
Do not let pain make you hate.
Do not let the bitterness steal your sweetness.
Take pride that even though the rest of the world
may disagree, you still believe it to be a beautiful
place.

- Kurt Vonnegut, Jr.

I'm still running away
Won't play your hide and seek game.
I was spinning free
with a little sweet and simple numbing me.
What a dizzy dance
This sweetness will not be concerned with me.
No the sweetness will not be concerned with me.

- Jimmy Eats World, Sweetness

Sweetness

Contents

Chapter 1
AINSLEY

It's a dry heat, my ass.

That's all I've heard from the moment I moved to Phoenix seven months ago, on yet another one of my mother's crazy-ass, hasty whims. Granted, moving from Idaho to Arizona in the dead of winter wasn't the worst idea my mother's ever had. But damn, it's hot.

A balmy, seventy-two degrees certainly beats Boise single digits during the dreary months of January and February. What twenty-one-year-old female doesn't prefer to hang out by the pool in a bikini versus schlepping through snow-covered parking lots and walkways, bundled up in an old hand-me-down parka that has more holes in it than buttons?

Not this girl.

Unfortunately, I haven't had the chance to sip spiked lemonade on a lounge chair, because as it so happens, I have responsibilities. Things that prevent me from ever knowing such luxuries of downtime. Or the joys of shopping for fun.

Or the possibilities of dating boys. Yeah, I'm not bitter. Not a bit.

I sigh wistfully, adjusting the strap of my messenger bag over my shoulder and step out of the air-conditioned bus, where I'm immediately blasted with a heat so intense it feels like my lungs have been ripped from my body and thrown across a Pampered Chef baking stone to bake at four-hundred and twenty degrees.

Holy balls, Batman. It's hot out.

As I trek down the street, the light weight material of my bright pink medical uniform immediately transforms into an unbearable prison cell of cursed confinement. Small pools of perspiration cling to my breasts, turning my durable sports bra into a sponge, hosting ringlets of sweat in its cotton material. So much for the claim that it *"wicks away wetness"*. Stupid false advertising. Apparently, the manufacturer did not do their product testing in the middle of summer in the hottest place on the map.

Thank goodness the grueling nine-hour shift I have ahead of me is indoors in an air conditioned house, where I won't be stuck in sticky, sweaty clothes. I love my new job and am so thankful to have found it so soon after obtaining my certification.

Passing a variety of people on the suburban sidewalk - some young boys skateboarding and a young mother pushing a stroller with a sleeping child - I smile to myself at the thought of where my life is at this moment. It might be hotter than Hades, but things have recently turned out really good - better than I could have ever expected.

Good is not how it's always been for me. To say I'm a testament to the resilience factor is no understatement. My life has been one thing after another, enough drama to fill a high school year-book. If you'd witnessed the hell my sister and I have been through during our short lives, you might understand my skepticism. It hasn't always been sunny skies for us.

Here in Phoenix, away from the mess of a life that once was mine, the sun shines bright three-hundred-sixty-five days, and my mother is actually happy and doing well for the first time in years. I had my doubts at first, for obvious reasons, and knew from experience that it wouldn't last long. It never does. Living with someone with mental illness is a rollercoaster after eating a shitload of cotton candy and sweets. You get the sugar rush and experience the joy and thrill of the fun. And then you go through a dip – fast and furious – and your stomach drops out. The sick feeling rises in your throat. You scream and yell, scared out of your mind and frightened that you're going to lose it all over the person in front of you.

But at least this time I've reached the 'Must Be This Tall to Ride' measurement, and have plans in place for the future in the event it all comes crashing down.

I've worked hard so I can stand on my own two feet. To support me and my sister with something more than just a minimum wage job.

This time, I'll be able to manage on my own, without being dragged from one town to the next by a woman who thought moving was an answer to everything. This time, I can plant roots to stay behind when she decides there is something bigger and better elsewhere. My mother seems to think a new place will, by some miracle, change our lives. She's an unrealistic optimist in that respect. But I know better, so as soon as we settled into our new apartment, I'd enrolled and was accepted into the Medical Training Institute. And I had soon become a Certified Nursing Assistant.

I'd been slowly adding to my savings throughout high school, whenever I had a little extra from my part-time jobs, wisely setting aside money so I could enroll in school when the time came. It was baby steps in the long-term goal of someday becoming a Registered Nurse. Nursing school was the end goal

— the whole enchilada. With the CNA, I was able to get a job where I could work in the field and earn enough money to attend nursing school.

And then it finally happened. My hard work paid off when I successfully passed my board certification exam and was hired almost immediately at Ethel Estates, the small, ten-patient adult living facility just a short bus ride from my apartment.

My job is everything I could have ever hoped for. My boss, Deacon, and his wife Gail, who are the co-owners, are wonderful to me. I've never met a couple who showed so such genuine care and concern for their patients, their staff, and each other. They've given me flexibility in my hours because they know about Anika, my sister, as well as my studies and other job. Oh yeah. No rest for the weary. I have another part-time job at a café.

Thankfully, Deacon and Gail have been more than accommodating. I've watched them over the last few months and I want what they have someday. If I ever end up in a long-term relationship, I want to emulate what I see every day between those two. They met in high school and after graduation he joined the military, both of them nurses. Now some twenty-five years later, Deacon is retired from the Army, and they've been running this place for a few years now.

I smile gratefully, getting a strange look from a guy on the corner who is also waiting for the pedestrian light to change. In this very moment I couldn't be happier. Well, I could be if I didn't have pools of sweat cloistered in my cleavage. But we can't have everything all the time, right?

As I round the corner, just a half block down the street from the residential house, my phone pings with a text message alert. An instinctive bodily cringe slithers up my spine, something like a Pavlovian dog's response, which drives me to worry over what the incoming message might reveal. It's never anything good, in my book.

I've always dreaded the sound of my phone notifications, because in the past it's only meant one thing – trouble with a capital T. It meant that either my sister was left at home, scared and alone, without any adult supervision because my mother went on one of her typical binges. Or it was someone contacting me about said binge.

Pulling the phone out of my bag, I take a deep breath and slip my cheap Wal-Mart sunglasses to the top of my head, peering down at the message. The sun is so bright I have to use my hand to shield the screen so I can see over the glare.

Anika: *Hey. Can I sleep over at Danielle's tonight?*

Me: *Where's mom? Did you ask her?*

I look down during the pause in the conversation and step off the curb, veering into the driveway of the large, ranch-style home on a quiet cul-de-sac in the Mesa subdivision.

Anika: *She's not here. I left her a vm, but no response yet.*

Me: *Fine. Just make sure to leave a note on the table with her number in case mom wants to check in.*

Anika: *Sweet. Love ya. TTYL.*

Me: *Love ya back, A. See you tomorrow.*

A twinge of worry creeps in as I slide my phone back into the bag pouch, stuffing it in the mess at the bottom of the bag. Although I'm glad my sister has made a friend since moving to Phoenix, there's still some residual guilt that I couldn't stop yet another move. Over the last year or so, she's become more and more withdrawn. She is naturally a shy girl, but it has caused me to worry about her ability to cope and interact socially. We've moved so much over the last ten years I know it hits her hard every single time.

I love my sister more than life itself and would do – *have done* – anything to make sure she is happy and safe. Although there is a fairly sizeable age gap between us, we have a special bond. She in many ways is my best friend- my only friend - because we've only had each other to rely on over the years of constant moving around. But things have changed recently, and she's definitely at that age where she's turning into be a pretty willful and secretive teenager. And it kind of scares me.

While I was never a rule breaker or acted out in any way as a teen, the truth is, Anika is a lot more like my mom then me, and shares the same wild and free tendencies. Which is yet another source of concern and keeps me up at night.

I let out a sigh as I open the front door and step inside, letting go of that tension. I'm immediately assaulted with the scent I've become all too familiar with in the last few months – that of pungent household cleaner, urine, and old people smell. I know that's not a very kind thought and I would never voice it out loud, but come on, you know what I'm talking about. There's just something about that smell. It's not a BO, per se, or anything that makes you want to gag - like rancid trash, or dead fish – but it permeates their flesh in a cloak of odiferous stench.

It also doesn't help that patients have died in this home on more than one occasion. And believe me when I tell you that death has a smell. It reeks of anger. Heartbreak. Disease. Death is selfish because it takes the gentle part of a person's soul, leaving the decaying flesh of the body behind.

I've become familiar with this stench over the last two plus months that I've worked at Ethel's. The sad smell reminds me of well-read book, when you flip through the pages of a novel that you've carried around with you for years. There are parts of that book that puts you in your happy place when you read your favorite passages. That's what this smell does to me. It's familiar and worn. Tattered and torn. And it feels like where I belong and where I can make a difference.

And just like that, I'm comforted knowing that I am making some sort of difference in these well-lived lives. These seniors have so many stories to tell – and often do – about their biggest accomplishments, their saddest regrets, and their most cherished loves. I just hope that when I'm at this point someday in my life, I'll experience the same generosity from others.

I place my bag down on the dining room table and take stock of what's happening in the five-bedroom ranch-style house. Glenna, the day-time RN and house manager, is in the kitchen dolling out the prescribed meds for one of the live-ins. Clark Newsom, Mr. Ornery, as I prefer to call him, is over in one of the three recliner rockers with his feet up, a blanket over his lap, and the newspaper spread out before him. He's mumbling something about the Cardinals, but I have no idea what that's about. Clark is early-onset dementia, and also suffers from Type 1 diabetes.

I don't see Dimitri, John, Dwayne or Simon. They may be napping at this time of day or may be out on the back covered patio with Adriane, who I'll be relieving shortly. They never mind it out in the heat, mainly because they are tough old men and aren't afraid of a little heat.

As I head down the hallway that connects the bedroom and baths, I trot by the room where my favorite patient resides. Mr. Simon Forsberg. With his snowy-white cap of full hair that most men would be jealous of, and his warm, generous smile, Simon is the grandfather I never had. The moment we met months before, I fell head-over-heels in love with the man. If I were only about fifty years older and he wasn't still pining for his late wife Martha...well, then we would be a match made in heaven.

When I peek through the cracked door, the room at first appears empty. The bed is neatly made and everything is in its place. However, just as I am about to move on toward the laundry room, where I'll start some wash for the day, I hear a low grunt and then a loud *thump*.

Pivoting on my heel, I quickly turn around and push the door open. My heart beats frantically in my chest when I see a body lying on the floor. No! Please don't let this happen, I pray.

Rushing over to his prone position, I find Mr. Forsberg lying on his side, his cane propped up against the wall out of his reach. A large photo box is open in front of him on the floor. Pictures, letters and other memorabilia are strewn across the carpet, as he appears to be trying to push himself back up to a sitting position.

Rushing to his side, I bend down to reach for his elbow.

"Mr. Forsberg," I softy scold, trying to hide the alarm in my voice. "Here, let me help you. Are you all right?"

Unlike other members of the household, Mr. Forsberg is perfectly capable in most situations and knows his own limitations. He's never refused my help, accepting assistance when necessary. Although, come to think of it, this was the first time I've ever had to help him in any capacity. Even though he is nearing eighty-years-old, and has been walking with a cane after the stroke he suffered a year ago, the older man is in otherwise great shape.

I carefully cradle his hips against mine, shoving my arms underneath his armpits and gently support and lift his body to an upright position. A whoosh of breath leaves his lungs –

maybe more from frustration than exertion. He braces himself on his hands behind him and leans forward, his legs haphazardly stretched in front of him.

Simon sighs heavily, rubbing a spot on his right hip which likely took the brunt of the fall.

Uncertain if anything is seriously injured or if it's just his pride that's hurt, I try to lighten the mood. It'll probably be necessary to conduct a medical exam to make sure nothing was broken in the fall.

"Mr. Forsberg, you know I would've been your dance partner if you'd only just asked me. But no…you're just too impatient when those toes of yours get to tapping, aren't you? You just can't help yourself, can you?" I jest, giving him the biggest, cheesiest grin I can muster so he knows I'm playing with him. Of course he knows I'm kidding, because I've never once caught Mr. Forsberg dancing. "That's for lunatics and little girls," I'd heard him say once before.

The old man chuckles a throaty cackle, his wild, bushy eyebrows narrowing in toward his large bulbous nose in embarrassment.

"Oh, if only that were true, my dear." He raises his head and arm, gesturing that he wants help up to his chair next to his bedroom window.

Once I know he's comfortable, I do a quick once over, checking for any bones out of place, or need for an ambulance. As my hands move over his legs, hips, knees in a visual assessment, I take his arms in my hands, smoothing over the wrinkled and puckered skin of his elbows. I tilt my head up and gaze into his eyes dusty blue eyes. They are a cloudy haze, due to the gradual glaucoma settling into his vision, but still full of life and love.

"Does anything hurt, Mr. Forsberg?"

Again, another chuckle.

"Nothing but my pride, Ainsley. Nothing but my pride." He shifts back into the chair as I let him reclaim his personal space, scooting back on my knees to begin picking up the scattered pictures that have spilled out.

I once saw a high school production of *Hello, Dolly*, so for some reason the open hatbox that lay on the floor brings back the images of a woman in her young teens, dancing around with a parasol and a bright floral hat. I can totally imagine Mr. Forsberg's wife all prettied up, ready to be courted. I'm sure he was a very handsome man in his late teens, early twenties. Heck, he is handsome right now.

Simon still stands tall, probably six foot, with broad shoulders that look like he carried a lot of responsibility in his younger years, and has a strong chin. Firm, but not aggressive. He still shaves every day, but I see he missed a few spots of the white scruff on the lower part of his jawline.

As I sift through some of the photos, trying to place them back in some semblance of order, Mr. Forsberg points down to them.

"I'm missing my Martha today," he murmurs, by way of explanation to the overturned box of memories. "It would have been our sixtieth wedding anniversary today. I was looking for the picture on our wedding day. My beautiful, young bride. She made me the envy of every man in our town. Martha could have had anyone – and any of them far more handsome than me. But for some reason, she chose me. Made me the happiest man alive for fifty-five years."

I keep my head down, sorting through the pile in search of a picture of their wedding day. I don't want Simon to see me with tears in my eyes. His sweet words, so full of love and adoration, make my heart ache for something. I just don't know what. I have no idea what that emotion even feels like, because I've never had it. But Simon experienced it while Martha was alive on this earth, and now knows the anguish of loss.

I've never seen a love like that before. Never heard a man speak of a woman with such reverence. I've never been in love, nor have I seen it firsthand. My mother never had a boyfriend or husband long enough to even celebrate a six-month anniversary. We had food in our fridge that lasted longer than most of her relationships. And certainly none of those losers would have ever expressed such tender emotions toward her.

Simon's sentiments made me realize that maybe there were men out there that did have a heart. Who possessed strength in character. Who treated a woman the way she deserved to be treated.

Not that it makes any difference to me.

I don't want a man. I'm just fine with how things are in my life, and the last thing I have time for is some stupid boy.

Chapter 2
CADE

I literally got busted with my pants down.

The situation is a massive shit show and there is no two-ways about it. I fucked up. Royally. And it is much bigger than any of the other stupid stuff I've pulled over the last three years of college. This was possibly the biggest mistake of my life, that could cost me everything I'd worked so hard to achieve since I was ten-years-old.

My future education, my college basketball career, and maybe even my undetermined professional life, is now lying in the hands of a judge and jury – the Maricopa County Court judge, the Dean of Students, my parents, and Coach Welby.

It had all started three nights ago, on Tuesday night, when Carver coaxed me into going out for a pre-birthday dinner, because my twenty-first was in six days. I'd initially told him no, because I wasn't feeling much like partying with the mounds of schoolwork already sitting untouched on my desk. It's still early in the school year, and I already feel behind. I was fairly certain I had a bio-chem test the next day, and a paper due in a week. I really couldn't afford another night out.

But it was Twofer-Tuesday at Casa de Frida, the little Mexican hole-in-the-wall down the street from our off-campus apartment. It was kind of a tradition that Carver and Lance, my two roommates, and I shared. So I gave in to Carver's incessant whining and we went to grab some chips and salsa, burritos and margaritas. It started out just the three of us, but before I realized it, we had a group of fifteen friends, and a plethora of chicks, all throwing back shots of tequila. And from the third shot on, things go a little fuzzy.

I had started chatting up this chick, Calista. I think that was her name. She had sidled up to me at the table and was a pretty blonde with really big tits. Had we been anywhere other than a restaurant, I might have insisted on doing body shots between her boobs. That would've been hot as fuck.

Anyway, since me and my pals are all starting seniors on the men's basketball team, we draw a lot of attention. Which means, a lot of pretty pussy. So there I was, talking to Calista – or maybe it was Calinda. Well, whatever. She was laughing. We were all drinking. Having a great time. And then I felt her hand make its way down the front of my gym shorts, and just like that, I was sporting wood. She leaned in, tilted her head up to my ear ('cause I'm six-five), and told me she wants to blow me.

Now, I'm not an idiot. Well, not usually. Truth is, I've hooked up with plenty of hoops hunnies at parties and other gatherings in my time. So I'm not unaccustomed to this type of come on. When a hot chick says she wants to give you a blowjob, you don't ask questions. You don't think too hard about it. You just get right on that shit. What drunk dude is gonna say no to that?

Not this one.

We stumbled out of the booth, I wrapped my arm around her tiny waist to keep her from falling, and we went out to my parked car in the restaurant lot.

Not too classy, I'll admit, but I'm not a sleazy asshole. Not usually. I could've taken her to my apartment a few blocks away, but I knew better than to drive in my condition. I was just feeling pretty fucking happy that I had a car in the lot at all, because at least it would afford us a little privacy, even if it was in the middle of a dimly lit parking lot. I wasn't overly bothered by the location or being seen by passers-by because it was late and my windows were tinted. My initial scan of the lot proved that I was right – no one around. Score. My raging hard on was quite pleased, so life was good.

I opened the door and let what's-her-face get cozy in the front seat. She started going at it – slipping her hand down my shorts, pulling out my hard cock, and bending over my lap to suck me deep inside her mouth. I remember looking down at the top of her head, watching her slide my dick in and out between her lips, thinking that it was really hot.

Not sexy-hot, but heat-hot. It was hotter than a brick oven inside my car. I couldn't roll the windows down, as to not compromise our privacy, so I stuck the keys in the ignition and turned on the air to cool things down.

At this point, I was totally in my happy place. Getting my knob polished by a young, eager hoops hunny, feeling a great buzz humming through my veins from the alcohol (or maybe it was from the little throaty hum that the chick had going on) – and I was settling back because things were just getting good. I could feel my balls tightening up, signaling the oncoming orgasm - that sweet little tingle of bliss as my cock goes rigid. I was just about to blow my load down this girl's throat when a bright light hits me square in the face from the driver's side of my car.

My eyes flew open in a disgruntled rage. At first, I was pissed as hell that one of my buddies thought it would be funny to take a video of the action going down in my car. I was just about to let them have it when I hear the *tap, tap, tap* on the window glass, and the loud booming voice that's attached to it.

"This is the Tempe PD. Please turn off engine and step out of the car with your hands up."

Everything in that moment turned to slow mo. Like the instant replay during a televised basketball game. You know the one – where the player goes up for a dunk and comes down wrong. ESPN plays the loop over and over again, as you watch with scrutinized empathy as the guy holds onto his leg, his face is contorted in agony. And that's exactly what it had felt like in my car in that moment.

The girl dropped my cock out of her mouth like it was on fire, jerking back into her seat with a garbled shriek of terror. I turned my head first toward her, where she was taking in large quantities of air as if she'd just run five miles. Then I dropped my head to my pants, where my exposed, semi-hard dick dangled in confusion over what was going on.

Holy shit. This is not good.

I somehow complied with the officer's orders to turn off my car engine and opened the door handle to get out.

"Get out of the car nice and easy, sir."

Jesus, did this guy think I was going to jump him, and clobber him with my dick as a line of defense? The thought had me wanting to burst out in laughter. But I didn't, because this was some serious shit.

I moved as slowly as I could, but also took haste in sticking my dick back in my pants and straightening up to my full height. Cowering isn't my style.

A pair of strong hands took hold of my shoulders, turned me around and shoved me down to the hood of my car. My head collapsed against the hot metal, my cheek burning against the heat. The officer kicked at my ankles to spread my legs.

I let out a grunt of displeasure. One minute I had been just about to come down a girl's throat, and the next I was spread eagle being frisked by an intimidating civil servant.

"Do you have any concealed weapons on you, sir?"

I stammered, but it came out slurred. "N-noooo, sir."

"Have you been drinking tonight?"

Okay, the first response that popped into my head had been a very drunken, sarcastic one. Luckily, I wasn't too far gone that I couldn't stop myself from making a complete fool of myself.

During that minute, a thousand thoughts ran through my head. And none of them were bound to end well for me.

I had been drinking, in a public restaurant and I wasn't of legal drinking age yet.

I was in the possession of a fake ID.

I was in the midst of receiving a blow job in the front seat of my car. In a public parking lot.

Could it get any worse?

Yes…yes it could.

Turns out, I'd broken more than a few laws that night. FML.

"Sir, you're under arrest for public indecency, as well as driving under the influence and underage consumption."

So here I sit, three days later, in a courtroom in the Maricopa County courthouse, waiting the fate that will be handed down to me for my error in judgment and utter stupidity that one night.

I want to blame Carver for making me go out. I want to be pissed at that girl Clarissa (shit, see? I'm no good with names), for being so easy. I want to confront the officer who busted me and ask him why me? Why'd he choose me to make an example of, when there were rapists, criminals and jay walkers to go after?

But in truth, the only one to blame is me. And now I await the punishment and consequences of my actions.

I look to my right, where my lawyer, Gerry Winger, is sitting in his thousand-dollar custom suit, shuffling some papers. He looks confident and self-assured based on the smug smirk he has across his mouth.

Just behind the attorney sit my mom and dad. My mother, Kristine, looks elegant as always in her crisp lavender blouse with her pearl necklace - a standard accessory - draped around her neck. If it weren't for the look of complete and utter helplessness, she'd seem like she belonged there. Part of the scenery. Blending in and becoming whatever she needed to be for her family.

Poor mom. Her only son – her golden boy – has gone and tarnished his image. And this time it had nothing to do with trying to make her and my dad look bad. Although that's exactly the reason my father thinks I did it. To get back at him for leaving us.

My dad, Allen, sits next to my mother, his body tensed tightly in his own custom-made pinstripe. He's aged in the last two years. More gray hair and small lines across his forehead showing his age. He wears the same stern and serious look he normally does. The one that tells everyone 'Don't fuck with me. I'll eat you for breakfast.'

Not a lot of love lost there. Maybe he loved me at some point in my life. Liked me even. But somewhere between moving from boy to manhood, my dad got it in his head that every dumb thing I did was intentionally done to humiliate him – t make him look bad – in front of his friends, his neighbors, his colleagues. Like I even thought about his lame-ass co-workers when I pulled the crap I did. It was laughable that he thinks I have anyone else on my mind other than myself most of the time. For that matter, I'm a pretty typical, self-involved, college guy.

When I called my father from jail that Tuesday night, I was prepared for yelling and screaming, ranting over my idiocy and juvenile behavior. Instead, I got the silent treatment. He went right into protective-mode, calling in favors with his lawyer partners and co-workers, to bust me out on bail. And before I was even out of the slammer, my dad had contacted my basketball coach, the Dean of Students, my frat president – and I wouldn't be surprised to hear even my Bible school teacher was notified. The man is nothing if not efficient, I'll give him that.

And thank God he has the connections that he does. As an attorney himself, he knows the right people. And the right guy is sitting next to me, looking cool as a cucumber.

Gerry leans over the side of his chair and whispers in my ear. Even though he's counseled me on everything I needed to know before we got into the courtroom, I guess he figures a dumb twenty-year old jock wouldn't remember the courtesies that are required to be extended in a court of law.

"Just as a reminder, Kincaid. You'll stand when the judge comes in, and remain standing until she gives you the go-ahead to take a seat. And then, you'll only speak when she asks you a direct question. And you'll always address her as Your Honor, or Judge. Got all that, son?"

Son? What do I look like – a five-year-old Boy Scout? Fine, I'll show him I can play nice.

"Yes, sir. I think I've got it."

I take a quick glance around the room and upfront where the court reporter and court clerk are both seated.

Just then, a young man I assume is the law clerk walks in and the bailiff calls the court to order.

"Please rise. The court of Maricopa County of the State of Arizona is now in session. The Honorable Judge Hawkins presiding."

I rise to my feet, my eyes set squarely on the distinguished older woman – probably in her mid-sixties judging by her graying hair – as she exits her chambers, and walks up to her little perch above the courtroom. It's just like a scene from Law & Order. Except the consequences are a helluva lot more dire and personal.

Perspiration drips from my armpits and down my back, my hands grow clammy, and my knees feel like they are about to cave in from nerves. I haven't felt this nervous since we made it to the Sweet Sixteen last year and played the unbeatable Gonzaga.

"You may be seated."

There are a few moments of silent pause as the Judge places her glasses on and reviews what I assume are my transcripts and court docs. I don't move. I'm not even sure I'm breathing.

"Mr. Griffin." Her voice is strong and loud, surprising me a little because she's so short.

"I've reviewed the charges against you by the County. I've also read through your exemplary history and school records which have been provided to me by your attorney. I'm saddened to see such an unnecessary, and regretful, lapse in judgment by such a promising young man."

My head hangs low. Talk about kicking me when I'm down. Does she think I don't already feel like an ass over my mistake? That I wasn't already filled with remorse over my actions?

But in all fairness, the charges are bogus, and hardly a serious offense if you ask me. It's not like I drove drunk and killed someone. Christ, I'd never do that. And I didn't rob a bank or pull a gun and shoot a group of students. There are far more heinous crimes being committed at this very moment than my measly, stupid public indecency.

In my humble opinion, the problem with the charges against me is that they don't adequately describe what really happened that night. Well, not all of it, at least.

The judge continues her verbal scrutiny of my case.

"I see here that on the night of August Twenty-first, you were charged with public indecency, a DUI, a first-offence, I understand, as well as underage consumption" Judge Hawkins looks up at me from behind her wire-rimmed glasses and I don't know if I'm supposed to answer her or not. My attorney doesn't say anything, so I guess it was rhetorical.

She continues. "Driving under the influence is a serious offense, Mr. Griffin. It could have led to an accident, or worse yet, a fatality. Vehicular homicide."

I want to jump in. To explain that I wasn't even driving. I had no intentions of driving the car until I sobered up. But under the Arizona law on driving under the influence, because I was intoxicated over the legal limit of .08, and was behind the wheel with the car's ignition on and in control of the car, it constitutes as driving. Under the influence. It definitely sucks.

My dad had never been a stickler with drinking. He knew me and my buddies in high school and college drank. And he may have even laughed off the public indecency rap, based on the 'boys will be boys' motto. But an underage DUI was well over his tolerance for forgivable. And the way the Judge leans on her elbows, her nose scrunched like she's smelled the inside of the guys' locker room after a game, she may not find it forgivable either.

And lest we forget I was using my fake ID while drinking that night. Six mother-fucking days before my twenty-first, and I get caught. All those years using it to get into bars, to clubs.

Going to concerts. To sporting events. To frat parties. I'd never gotten busted for drinking. Until now.

Gerry pokes me in the side. I jerk my head and look at him with pleading eyes. Shit. I wasn't listening.

"Mr. Griffin, I asked if you understood the ramifications of the charges against you? The underage DUI and the public indecency?"

I nod my head, and Gerry speaks on my behalf.

"Your Honor. Mr. Griffin is sincerely regretful for his undeniably irresponsible behavior and reprehensible actions from the night in question. As you may know, Judge Hawkins, Mr. Griffin is a respected athlete, an All-American basketball player, and is in his senior year at ASU. He has a 3.5 grade point average and is slated to graduate this spring with a degree in biomedical engineering. We are prepared to call upon a number of character witnesses to provide testimony related to his unblemished character and moral rectitude."

Gerry places a well-manicured hand on my shoulder and squeezes. "If it pleases the court, Your Honor, Mr. Griffin had no intentions of operating his vehicle on the roads that night. He was parked in a lot of the restaurant with a female friend, where he had been celebrating the beginning of their final year of school, as well as his upcoming birthday."

Well, that much is true. I hope the Judge doesn't ask what we were doing to celebrate.

"Mr. Winger, I'm well aware that Mr. Griffin has yet to turn twenty-one. That alone, in my opinion, is enough to sentence him to probation. However, I do not think there is need to bring in the character testimony for Mr. Griffin. I have several other cases to hear today, and I don't want to waste the court's time. But I think it would serve the court well if Mr. Griffin could speak to the choices he made that night. Why he was in the vehicle in the first place. Or for that matter, why he chose to drink and drive."

I gulp, taking in a long swallow of air. My hands tremble, so I place them in my jacket pockets. Gerry and I had spoken about this and drafted up my statement of apology. Even though I didn't wrong any particular person, my statement is aimed to hopefully prove to the Judge that I am sincerely remorseful for my actions. And that I promise never to do something that stupid, ever again.

I'd memorized the words. I'd practiced it more times than I can count. But now that I am standing in front of a Judge, my family and a courtroom of people – most of whom I'd never met – I have stage fright. I have a flash of panic that grabs my chest and twists it like a Red Vine licorice stick. I'm uncertain whether she will be able to hear the sincerity in my voice. I'm not sure I can remember what I'm supposed to say. If anything would even come out of my dry mouth, except maybe a weak croak.

Licking my lips and taking a deep breath in through my nostrils, I exhaled slowly, nodding my head in acknowledgement. It' now or never.

"Your Honor," I say, voice shaky and about two octaves higher. I sound like Screech from that *Saved by the Bell* show. "I make no excuse for my behavior and poor judgment the other night. My actions were reprehensible, and unbecoming of a member of this community. I disgraced my family – my parents. I embarrassed my Coaches and my teammates – who look up to me as a senior member of our team. I've let down my fans, for whom I should be acting as a role model. I acted disrespectfully to the woman I was with." My mouth goes dry and I suck in a stream of air.

This is harder than I thought it would be. I reach for the cup of water in front of me and take a small swig, getting my nerves back under control.

"Your Honor, I realize I broke the law. I was drinking, but I had no intentions of ever driving in my condition. I realize that will always be an unknown, but I know who I am and what

I'm capable of doing. I know my limits and would never put anyone else in jeopardy. The future is too important."

I pause for a moment. One, because this is what my attorney suggested I do. It helps that I appear thoughtful – remorseful.

Although the pause was intentional, I really did need it to gather my courage. It feels like I have a thousand butterflies stuck in my throat.

"Your Honor, I ask for the court's leniency in my case. I will prove to be a law-abiding citizen going forward. I will do whatever is necessary to ensure this kind of thing doesn't happen to any of my friends or other athletes. I'm ashamed of my behavior and am deeply sorry that my juvenile actions brought us here today. I'm prepared to accept the consequences."

This last part of my statement still scares the shit out of me. My attorney had warned me that the Judge has the right to sentence me up to six months in county jail, fine me a maximum of $2500, take away my license for a year, and throw community service on top, along with probation. My future and my life is literally in the hands of the Judge.

Gerry clamps his unusually strong hand on the top of my shoulder again, squeezing it as if to say, "You done good, kid."

We are all standing facing the Judge. Facing the consequences of my poor decisions. She seems to reflect over my testimony and nods her head a few times, her lips pursed in a tight scowl, rubbing her temple, as if a tempest is raging inside her head. Maybe it is and I'm the catalyst of the storm.

"Very well, Mr. Griffin. I appreciate your candor. It seems you've put a lot of thought and consideration into what grave consequences your actions could have resulted in, and for that, I do thank you. In light of the evidence in this case, your testimony, and the fact that there was no serious harm done and – being that it's your first offense, I'm here by giving you three months of community service, a $250 fine, and one-year of probation."

My jaw drops as I vaguely register a collective sigh of relief from my parents behind me. My ears buzz and my brain is fuzzy as I try to wrap my head around what she just said. The sentence she's given me.

And then her stern voice fills the room once again. "But if I so much as see your name on any of my court dockets again, Mr. Griffin, you better believe that I will be handing down the toughest penalty there is to administer. Do you understand me?"

I nod, and then remember I'm supposed to address her. "Yes, your Honor. Thank you."

"Mr. Griffin, I trust that you'll make good on your commitments and I will not see you in my court room again. Court adjourned." The judge announces this with a bang of her gavel before she stands. The bailiff once again commands everyone to stand, and I stare as Judge Hawkins departs to her chambers.

My relief is so great, I nearly stumble back into the chair, falling into the cushioned seat below me. The shock of what transpired over the last three days, along with the anxiety that's built up in my body, has left me shivering from the impact.

Gerry grasps my hand with a strong handshake, then turns to my father, who is waiting with a pleased smile on his fact to congratulate my attorney on his win. I guess that's what lawyers do. My mother, who has been toying with her strand of pearls the entire time, now stands and wraps her thin arms around my waist and hugs me tight.

I don't know what all of this means – the community service, the probation – but I definitely know I've dodged what could be a nasty, death-sentence of a bullet.

Now I just need to meet with Coach Welby to find out my fate for the final season on the team.

And that could be a much tougher penalty than anything else I've experienced so far.

Chapter 3
Ainsley

To anyone living in the Tempe vicinity, and certainly to all ASU students, Mill Avenue is known as party-central of the campus. Regardless of the time of day, the street is crowded with students, faculty, shoppers, business people, and civil servants who work in the courts or city offices. There's also a plethora of vagrants and homeless people milling around the streets, looking for handouts from passers-by.

It's especially bad around the Tempe Transportation Center, my bus stop on campus. I'm usually hit up for spare change a minimum of three times from the short walk from the bus stop to Bristol's, the small café I've been working at since we've moved here. Most of the panhandlers are relatively nice, and I've gotten to know a few of them – like Crockett.

I watch people on the street from inside the restaurant. Crockett and his dog, Tubs, sit in their usual morning spot on the curb facing the café's entrance, asking people for handouts. He's one of the nicer homeless men on the street, and offers me up a smile and a little good-tiding every time I see him. I tried to talk with him once about his life, but he just evaded the questions, turning the conversation into some nonsense about alien abductions and the corruption of the Catholic church.

I've been on shift since six-thirty this morning, when we open the doors. It's generally pretty slow until seven-thirty, when a lot of the county administrative staff, court personnel, attorneys and legal professionals will wander in for coffee and pastries before heading into the City Municipal court building right around the corner. And from that point on, the breakfast rush grows in number, usually in a steady stream until I leave for the day at three p.m.

I chose this job for the location, planning in advance that once I enrolled in my nursing program at ASU, I'd need a job close by. This was also before I got my job at Ethel's. Thankfully, I've been able to work my schedule around the needs of both employers, who have also been very accommodating to my needs as well.

I'm interrupted from my mindless staring by my manager, Kimmi.

"So what do you have planned this weekend?" Kimmi asks, her blue eyes wide in question. I'm surprised she even has to ask me because she's known me long enough to know I don't have a life.

Kimmi's a great boss and has an even busier life than me. A few years older than me, Kimmi's in a graduate program for civil engineering, and has an eighteen-month old baby boy named DJ, after his father.

I give her a playful eye roll. "You do know it's me you're talking to, right?"

Kimmi chuckles, shrugging her shoulders.

"Well, I figure maybe someday I'll ask you and you'll surprise me with an answer other than work and homework."

If only.

"Sorry to disappoint, but today's not the day. After my shift here, I've got some reading to do for my physiology class and some diagrams to study and memorize. Then it's over to Ethel's for my overnight shift and right back there again on Sunday morning. Winner-winner, chicken dinner." I give her a double thumbs-up and a goofy grin that would make even the Joker jealous.

"And how about you? Aren't you and David celebrating his promotion this weekend?"

David, her fiancé, had recently been promoted to Assistant Designer at the architectural firm he's worked at for over the last four years, ever since he graduated with his degree. Kimmi was so excited, because it would mean more income for their small family, and would afford them a babysitter once a month so they could go out on date nights.

She sweeps up some crumbs from underneath a table as I hold the dust pan handle to collect the mess.

"Yes, we are going out to celebrate tonight and David won't tell me where we're going or what we're doing. All he's told me is that I have to wear the dress he likes and some" – she glances around surreptitiously and whispers – "*sexy underwear.*" Kimmi giggles, turning a cute shade of pink.

I make a grab for the broom she clutches in her hand and turn toward the sound of the bell over the door. Sparing a quick glance, I notice it's a party of three adults. Kimmi starts to head off in their direction to get them seated at my table, but not before I have a chance to tell her what I think about her date.

"You deserve it, Kim. And I can't wait to hear all about it."

I walk toward the kitchen closet to store the cleaning supplies and wash my hands at the sink. I grab my notepad and pen, along with a tray of water glasses, and head back to the table where she's seated them.

Over the years, and especially working where I work, I've become rather adept at understanding body language. Within seconds, I can observe and make quick assessments of what people are thinking or how they're feeling based on the tells of their facial expressions. This breakfast trio is no different. It's written all over their faces.

The older of the two men and the woman sit stiffly across from one another. There seems to be a familiarity there – maybe a couple, but not a loving one. She mindlessly plays with her strand of pearls and looks out the window while he's talking in a clipped tone at the younger guy sitting next to the woman. They both wear a look of stern weariness, with a hint of relief. Interesting.

My gaze now wanders to the third person at the table. His face is hidden because he's hunched over the table, head in hands. You'd think he was a five-year old being disciplined for stealing a cookie before dinner with the way he's postured, along with the stern talking to he's receiving. As I step in, I plaster a welcoming smile across my face, hoping I don't get sucked into the vortex of tension that surrounds them.

"Good morning. Welcome to Bristol's," I say in my practiced cheery, I-just-love-waiting-on-people tone. "Here's some water to get you started, but can I grab something else for you to drink this morning?"

The woman is the only one who looks at me and she gives me a tight grin. The older man finishes what he's saying and the guy mumbles something in return, huffing out a grunt of displeasure. I'm looking directly at the woman, since she's the only one who seems to notice my existence. The two men's heads are buried in their menus.

"Oh, yes please. A small glass of grapefruit juice for me, and two large orange juices for them. And three coffees, also."

Easy, peasy, cool-n-breezy.

"Absolutely. Cream with that?"

"Oh yes, for me. Thank you. Kincaid? Do you take cream?"

The guy – or Kincaid – lifts his head up peering through his lashes. I place the third water glass down in front of him and his eyes snap to mine. They are the same shade of blue-green as the woman's, but so intense it looks like a tempest is brewing in them. His face is blank, but I can see the anger within him – he's like a bomb ready to detonate.

A snarl appears on his mouth. "Cream. And lots of sugar. I like it *sweet*."

I almost stumble back from the force of the double entendre he lobs out. The comment alone wouldn't be cause for alarm if it wasn't for the way he said it. With both spite and sexual deviance.

He pushes himself upright and leans his back against the booth giving me a smirk. As if he's waiting for me to say something in defense. And normally I would. I have a feisty tongue. But for some reason, I feel trapped in his snare, unable to do anything about it. Even with eyes that hold the intensity of a serial killer, he's incredibly good-looking. Gorgeous, in fact.

It's rare that I even notice the opposite sex. I either don't have the time or the inclination, because really, what would become of it? Nothing. My life is busier than Grand Central station at rush hour. And I'm not one of those single girls who just hooks up or has one-nighters. That's my mother's style, and I am definitely not my mother.

"You're staring at me," he says with a low chuckle, leaning forward now on his forearms, the smirk not yet vanished from his cocky mouth. "It's okay. A lot of people recognize me."

"Excuse me?" I tilt my head to the side, totally confused over what he's talking about. Recognize him? Should I? No clue.

He narrows his eyes on me, his eyebrows pinched as he assesses my response like he's confused too.

"Number 23."

Like that clears everything up.

I'm still confused. My gaze darts from him to the two others at the table, who are clearly uninterested and talking amongst themselves in a hushed whisper. I drop the hand that's holding the tray to my side and bite down on my lip and take a good look at his face for any sort of recognition.

Nope. None whatsoever.

I shake my head and shrug my shoulders in a quick jerk.

The guy laughs out a huff.

"Not a basketball fan, then. Well, that's okay. I'm sure you have other redeeming qualities."

Geez, thanks. I'll give you a redeeming quality right up your asshole. *Asshole.* If only I could say what's really on my mind sometimes. Like Donald Trump does.

But instead of letting my honest and unfiltered response fly, I give him a tight-lipped smile, adjusting my facial expression to appear apologetic.

"Uh, nope. Sorry. Not any kind of sports fan. But I'm great at table-hockey."

He seems to think about this for a second, letting his eyes rove up and down the length of my body. My uniform is not a sexy little waitress outfit. It's a pair of khaki shorts and a collared shirt. So I see nothing that could possibly attract him to me. But something flickers in his eyes, as they turn a deep shade of turquoise, that creates a flutter of excitement in my belly.

"Well, that's a good talent to have. Means you have quick reflexes and you like it fast and hard." He winks.

OHHHH. EMMMM. GEEEE. Was that his attempt at a come on? I don't know what to say, so instead of saying anything, I whirl around on my heels and set off to get their drinks. I can hear his low chuckle as I walk away and wonder who the hell this guy thinks he is…and why his comment has me fired up.

***

I'm literally sucking down a 16-oz iced-latte and rubbing my feet on the little stool back in the kitchen. It's Friday afternoon and I've just finished my nine-hour shift at Bristol's, one that kept getting busier and busier as the day went on.

The lunch rush was insane and because Lacy called in sick, I had to cover for part of her shift. Don't get me wrong, I'm glad for the extra money but annoyed because I still have a full shift ahead of me tonight at Ethel's. I'll barely make it home in time to shower, change, make a quick dinner for Anika, and then hop back on the bus to head over to the nursing home.

My poor feet ache, and unless it's a quiet shift at the house, I'll be working on them all night. I groan as I rub the balls of my feet, ready to throw myself a pity-party. But really, what good would it do? After witnessing the threesome in my booth earlier this morning and hearing even a small portion of their heated conversation, I want to throttle all stupid, rich kids that get away with everything and aren't grateful for a single thing they have.

Every time I stopped by their table, all I heard was the guy lamenting over whatever his parents were chastising him about.

"Kincaid," the man had warned in a hushed tone. "You have one year left before you're out on your own. You're a smart boy, so why do you insist on screwing around? Get your act together, son."

"Why, Dad? Because it's hurting your image? Because your son didn't make the Dean's List? And you can't tell me that you didn't screw around when you were in college." His tone had dripped with venom and attitude.

I'd only heard bits and pieces of their conversation, but enough to learn a few things about them. One, his parents were extremely disappointed in him. Two, whatever he'd screwed up doing, it was pretty bad. And three, they needed him to do something about getting on the straight and narrow.

The guy seemed to think he was God's gift to the world. Make the arrogant bastard suffer. Though, this kid…man-child – douchebag – admittedly was easy on the eyes. He had this boyish, broody Ryan Phillipe thing going on. His dark wavy hair cropped close at the ears with a mop of curls on the top, styled with some sort of product that still made it look soft to the touch. His eyebrows were a little on the thick side and prominently displayed his moss green eyes, which hinted flecks of gold.

An angular jaw covered by a nice day's growth of facial hair. I don't know what it is, but facial hair always does me in. It just makes a guy look so virile and masculine. Maybe Kincaid used the scruff to hide his boyish features. But his obvious pubescent attitude wasn't masked by the beard. If I ever saw Kincaid again, I think I might be tempted to smack him in his face for being a whiny little bitch. Or run straight into his arms. Which alarms me to no end. Because I shouldn't be attracted to this guy. He isn't a grown-up. And when I fall for a guy, it's going to be one with character, integrity and maturity.

I slip on my sandals, loving the feel of the airy open-toes which have my feet singing the theme song from *The Sound of Music*. I swing the strap of my messenger bag over my shoulder, grab the doggie bag of food, and walk out the door into the late afternoon sunshine.

I'm immediately assaulted with the heat that chokes me like a boa. But my greeting from Crockett turns things around.

"Well, there's my sweetness. How was your day, Ainsley?"

I hand him the food bag - just a leftover meatloaf sandwich and a piece of peach pie that I know he'll share with Tubs. He gives me a toothless grin of thanks as I squat down to scratch the top of Tubs' bristly, mangy head. I overlook their unwashed selves in favor of showing affection. Everyone – and everything – in this life is deserving of some form of human kindness.

Even guys like Kincaid? The unbidden thought comes out of nowhere and I groan inwardly.

Instead of dwelling on that dweeb, I give Crockett a big sigh and a so-so hand gesture, flipping my hand from side-to-side. I stand up and check Tubs' water dish to make sure he has enough water.

"Another day another dollar, Crockett. So that's good." I smile and give him a little wave as I begin walking toward the street corner. When I'm a few feet away I turn back around and say goodbye to him. "See you on Monday, Crock. Make sure you both stay hydrated. And by that, I mean *water.*"

Crockett gives me a snort of agreement and crosses his heart with his fingers as I turn back in the direction of the transit station, hoping he keeps his promise. I worry about him between shifts, since I'm never really sure if I'll see him again. Once a few months ago, he and Tubs were gone for two weeks. I had no idea what happened to him and had asked around to some of the other regular street guys. It turned out that Crockett had been attacked one night in an alley and had to recuperate from his punctured lungs and cracked ribs at Valley General.

I'd been both relieved and angry when he finally returned to his spot in front of the café. After that, I made him carry my contact number in his personal belongings so that the EMT or ER nurses would have someone to call if he needed something. Poor guy had no family and no one to care about his well-being.

And while he would never accept anything from me other than the few scraps of food I'd offer him after my shifts, at least he allowed me to be his emergency contact.

I know what it means to be homeless. And if there was one thing I could do to never forget my past, it would be to remind Crockett that he always had someone to count on.

Chapter 4
CADE

I'm so freaking mad right now I can't see straight. And that may be the reason I don't notice her coming around the corner until I smack right into her. All I see is red, then black, then hear a loud clatter as books go flying everywhere.

"Watch the fuck where you're walking." I rail, snorting out a loud curse as I rub my arm where the girl plowed into me. "Keep your eyes on where you're fucking going."

My anger shouldn't be taken out on this innocent by-stander, but in the mood I'm in right now, I don't care. I've just left the arena where I had a meeting with my coach and the news is not good. I don't know what I was expecting, but it wasn't that.

Almost in slow motion, the girl staggers to her left from the impact of our collision, and reaches a hand out to the brick wall to maintain her balance. My own hand instinctively darts out to grab hold of her opposite arm, tugging her upright to keep her on her feet. She squirms, trying to get out of my hold, her shoulder jerking back from my hand.

Fine, be that way.

Now that she seems to have her balance, she gives me the scariest death glare I've ever seen on a chick. Her eyes bore a hole in me and she looks like she's casting a spell to make my dick shrivel up and fall off. I shudder at the thought.

Although I'm pissed off over this interruption, and from the ass reaming I just go from Coach, my brain can't help but take in the scene in front of me. The girl is on her knees now picking up her tossed books – giving me a moment to check her out - starting at the top of her head, down her chest, to her legs, and then back up again.

I take note of a few things while I do this. The girl seems somewhat familiar, but I can't quite place her. Maybe I hooked up with her a few years back. Even with the *"I'm about to gouge your eyes out"* glint and obvious angry expression on her face, she's really hot.

Her dark, raven hair is pulled back in a shiny and sleek pony tail. Her face appears make-up free and those wide, angry eyes of hers are a brilliant blue, like a stormy sea, with thick black eyelashes that fan across her cheeks.

As she rises to her feet and lifts her head back up to me, I now see a wave of hostility sweep over her face. She's ready to unleash that storm. I'm not sure if I should cover my nuts or be turned on. The girl is beautiful.

"Excuse me?" she chokes out, taking a steady step toward me, her finger poking me in the middle of my chest, the sharp edge of her nail digging into my pecs. It's kind of a turn on, to be honest. She's feisty and I can't help that my mouth edges up into a smirk.

Probably not the reaction I should give her right at this moment if I want to keep on breathing. Or have children one day.

"You are the one that plowed into me, asshole. *You* are the one not looking where you were going. God, you arrogant prick." She lets out a loud huff, like a petite, fire-breathing dragon, dropping her hand from my chest.

She mumbles something about '*Goddamn jocks*' and then walks around me, giving me a wide berth, toward the street as I stand there in complete rapt.

All of a sudden I want her to stay. I can't let her leave. Something in my memory is triggered, and I remember now where I know her from. My hand darts out to wraps around her small wrist bringing her progress to a halt.

"Hey, I know you...we've met before. You were my waitress at that restaurant last Friday."

Honestly, I can't recall the name of the place where we ate. In fact, I don't remember much after the weekend I spent trying to forget it all. I was clearly in a fog that entire morning and it seeped into my weekend, making me a miserable and ornery bastard.

I spent Friday and Saturday night holed up in the apartment I share with Lance and Carver on the edge of campus. We'd have normally made an appearance at one of the frats or out at one of the local bars on Mill Ave, but because I was on lock-down from any place where I could get caught in violation of the terms of my probation, I stayed home. The guys were actually pretty supportive and we sat around all weekend playing video games and watching sports on TV.

And then today I had my meeting with Coach. He literally ripped me a new asshole over the last hour. It was the shittiest, most humiliating part of this whole ordeal. Even getting caught in the act, being recognized by the cops, wasn't as mortifying as listening to the Coach and assistant coach lecture me. They went on and on about how I've embarrassed the team, impacted the reputation of the program, and just plain acted like a stupid juvenile idiot. Yeah, tell me something I don't already know.

I didn't expect him to go soft on me or do me any favors just because of who I am to the team, but I wasn't expecting to be made an example of. Coach told me that he was going to make my "stupid lapse in judgment to serve as a 'teaching moment' for the younger guys on the team."

Just great.

You break the law? Or get caught doing anything that disrespects the team and the values of the program? You face the consequences and you get hung out to dry.

So to say I'm in a pretty fucking shitty mood right now is an understatement. And now, to compound matters even more, this beautiful girl makes it clear she doesn't even know who I am, and also blew me off when I tried to flirt with her the other day. And now she's insulting me.

This chick is a total ego-killer. Yet for some strange reason, it makes me want her more. To reveal myself to her, showing her every part of me. Letting her get to know the true me.

I don't even know her name and she's glaring at me like I'm a piece of dirt. A bug. Lower than a snake. Her head is cocked to the side and she's wearing an incredulous expression on her face, her bee-stung lips tightly pinched in disgust.

Shoving her book inside her bag that's strapped across her chest (which for the record makes her rather large breasts stand out enough to be ogled – but I don't fall for it), her hands land on her hips as she responds to my comment.

"First off, it's called Bristol's Café. And second, you don't know me or anything about me. I'm not one of your *fans*, Number 23. And I'm not going to bow down and worship at your feet like some fangirl groupie. Now, please let go of me so I can go. I'm already late as it is."

Not going to lie. I get a slight thrill knowing she remembered my number. That tells me she was a little bit interested in who I am. Maybe she even Googled me. Read through my stats. Gawked at my images plastered all over the internet. That thought makes me smile. Oops, maybe poor timing, as I watch her glower at me with angered scrutiny.

Reluctantly I drop her arm and she wiggles away from me, turning without another word or glance as she hustles away. I watch her jog across the cross-walk to the other side of the street. My eyes track her impatient movements. She looks down at her phone, then to her watch, her body in constant motion, shifting from one foot to another. I soon lose sight of her as a bus pulls up blocking my view. The moment it pulls from the curb, I'm disappointed to find she's no longer standing there.

A foreign feeling takes residence in my body - creeping up my limbs like ivy wrapping around a fence post, ready to overpower anything in its path. I've never felt this before. If I'd have to put a name to it, I'd say it's longing. Or amusement. Or just plain astonishment. Because this girl – this nameless girl whom I'm only seen twice - has somehow managed to not only ruffle my feathers by taking me down a few notches, but intrigue me in a way no other girl has done before.

In a weird way, this encounter with the girl seems to have doused my anger and turned around my negative mood. I'm still pissed off, but I don't have the need to pummel the next guy that I cross paths with.

Speaking of which, as I turn around to head back the other direction, my buddy Van heads me off at the pass.

He gives me the typical guy-greeting – our fists bumping before exploding open. "Yo, Griff. How's it going, bro?"

As teammates, we all call each other by a nickname. Hence, mine is Griff, short for my last name. His real name is Donavan Gerard. So we've shortened his name to Van. It's another jock thing, I guess.

As he stands there waiting for my response to his question, I'm weary of what everyone has heard so far about the trouble I got myself into. So I decide to keep things vague in my reply. Plus, Coach asked that I not share this publicly, as the court papers were sealed to shield my identity. I guess that was a favor called upon by my honorable father.

"Eh, you know. It's going." I shrug nonchalantly. "Got a pretty full load this semester and I need to stay ahead of things before the season starts, ya know?"

Van gives me a quizzical look like he's about to say something else, but then laughs, tugging at the loose-fitting beany on his head.

"Yeah, it's crazy, man. Can't believe we're seniors. Time flies."

Van glances around, his gray eyes darting around before landing back on me again. He shifts uncomfortably on his feet and his cheeks color up like a Paint-by-Numbers water color picture. His voice goes low and soft.

"So, listen man. I heard you might not be back on the team this year. Is that true?"

Well, I guess that the rumor mill is in operation if he's heard about my problem. But fuck, word travels fast considering I just got out of Coach's office fifteen minutes ago. The rumor he's heard, though, is a bit more over-exaggerated than what really went down.

I shake my head, wondering where he heard this from, but decide not to interrogate him or appear like I'm looking for the rat. It really doesn't matter, as long as Coach Welby sticks with the plan he outlined so vehemently to me in his office. It still sucks that I'm benched for the first three pre-season games, but the good news is I'll still get to practice with the team when they start-up in a month and it won't ruin the entire final season for me.

"Nah, dude. It's nothing like that. I'm still on the team. Just can't start the first three games."

Van gives me a grumble of solidarity. Good man. His loyalty has me marveling at the true bonds I have with my teammates. Even though we aren't tight as some of the other guys, Van's still got my back and vice versa. That's what I love about playing. You never lose that connection, even after the game is done.

"Well shit. That sucks. But glad to know you'll still be on the court this year. We need your skills, dude. Gotta get back to the championship our final year."

"Yeah, no doubt. We're going to crush Duke and Kansas."

I've always liked Van, ever since I met him playing in the high school prep school leagues. He stands a little taller than me, and is now sporting a dark-haired man-bun, which is usually held back by a headband of some sort. While I think the long hair would be a hassle on the court, I won't give him any crap about his girly-look. I'm sure the guy gets plenty of action for it.

In fact, out of the corner of my eye I see a trio of girls watching us and clucking like little groupies, but he seems oblivious. Come to think of it, Van has been dating the same girl since high school. So loyalty seems to be in his true nature.

I give the girls a quick wave and smile. Any other day I'd be all over those girls, giving them exactly what they are looking for. To hang and score with a hoops player. But not today. I've got other things on my mind.

Van lifts his hand in front of us and I lean in and grasp it in my fist, as we go in for the dude hug. That's how we roll.

"You know it, bro. So you gonna be at the gym tomorrow morning for the workout and scrimmage? Sounds like Wagner is putting his money where his mouth is and betting he'll crush

Lancaster. I've got my bets on Lan." He laughs, suggesting what I already know. Which is that Christian Lancaster, our nearly seven-foot center, is gonna crush the ever-living shit out of small forward Scott Wagner. Easy bet.

I shake my head in agreement before adding, "Yeah, I'll be in the weight room at seven a.m."

"Cool. Listen, I gotta take off. I got a Stats study group at the campus lounge. I'll see ya later, Griff."

"Yeah," I say, glimpsing one more time over my shoulder toward the bus stop, hoping for a miraculous sighting of the girl again. But I'm sadly disappointed. "See ya."

As I head off to my next class, my thoughts immediately return to the girl.

If I had been in the right frame of mind today, I wouldn't have let her leave. We would at this moment be grabbing some ice cream or drinks over at Reggie's. And after a few hours of flirting and eye-fucking, I'd have her naked in my bed. Or maybe we'd skip all the foreplay and just head straight to fucking.

But I'm not easily discouraged. It may not have happened today. But it will.

Mark my words.

That girl will be all over me the next time I see her.

Chapter 5
AINSLEY

"You're looking a little tired today, Ainsley. Everything going okay with school?"

My boss, Gail, looks me over like a mother-hen, probably wondering if I wore blue and black paint under my eyes today. Because I am beat. I don't blame her for her worried expression. I was pretty shocked when I glanced in the mirror at my reflection this morning. And that was over five hours ago when I got out of bed at six a.m.

I open up a can of fruit cocktail and pour the contents in a large bowl, spooning the juices around to evenly coat the fruit. I add a few cut-up banana slices and fresh pineapple because I know Mr. Forsberg absolutely loves the pineapple chunks. It's nearly time for lunch and my job today is to prep the meal and then help get whoever wants to eat set up at the table.

Throwing the empty can away, I turn back to Gail, who is sitting at a side table doing a crossword with Mr. Parker.

"Thanks for asking. I'm just exhausted. I had to pull an all-night study session last night. I got home around six, made dinner for Anika and helped her with her homework, then had to study for my Anatomy and Physiology exam. It's tomorrow and I'm not sure I'm ready for it."

Gail lets out a little laugh, her shoulders lift and jerk in movement. "You say that every time, Ains. And yet you always do well. You're too hard on yourself, you know that?"

I know she means to be humorous, but she's right. I have to be hard on myself. To push myself farther because no one else will do it for me. Certainly not my mother. And I don't have a father to support me, either. Anika has my back but she's only fifteen and her head is in the clouds most of the time.

She's not built the same way I am. Anika's the dreamer, like my mom, and I'm the boring pragmatic. Determined to make it on my own. To support myself one day in the future because that's the way it has to be.

I shrug my shoulders as I place the lunch plates and silverware down on the table, setting five places for the residents. Just as I do, Mr. Forsberg comes limping in slowly on his cane, giving me a bright, cheery smile.

"Did you have a good nap, Mr. Forsberg?" I stop what I'm doing and usher him into his seat at the table. "You're just in time for your lunch and I've got something special for you."

I lightly pat him on the back and wink, turning back to the kitchen to grab the soup, sandwiches and fruit bowl.

"I like the sound of that. Is it my favorite, Lemon Meringue pie? My Martha used to make the best pie in the county. That meringue was so light and fluffy, it melted on my tongue." His tongue makes an effort to lick his dry lips.

"Well, I'm sorry for getting your hopes up, Simon. But it's definitely not pie. But it *is* extra pineapple in your fruit salad. Hopefully that will suffice for now."

He looks down to the table and then back up to me, his bushy white eyebrows nearly disappearing into his head of hair.

"I do like my pineapple, dear." He winks. Such a cute man. Everything about him is kind and generous. It makes me wonder why he never has any visitors or family coming by to see him. I know he has a daughter and a few grandchildren, based on the pictures I saw the other day. But maybe they don't live in the area.

"Do you mind adding another place setting for lunch today, Ainsley?"

I whip around to face him again and see the pure happiness brighten his wrinkled face.

"Of course. Who will be joining you for lunch?" I ask, eager to find out about Simon's friends and family.

Simon places the folded paper napkin in his lap and looks down at his watch.

"My grandson said he'd be dropping by around eleven thirty today. I'm so happy he's coming to visit. I haven't seen him...well, in a long time."

This much I know is true. I've been working at Ethel's Estates for several months and not once has Simon had any visitors. At least not while I've been on duty. So I want to do everything I can to make this visit extra special for him. He deserves it.

"That's wonderful! Would you like to wait for him before you eat?"

Just as the question slips out of my mouth, the front doorbell chimes, announcing the visitor.

"That must be him now!" He exclaims in an animated voice that has me smiling over his excitement.

Because we are a family home and some of our patients are early-stage dementia, we are required to keep doors locked and a security alarm armed twenty-four hours a day. That ensures the safety of all our patients and staff. All visitors, even if they are daily drop-ins like Dimitri's wife, must be escorted in by a staff member.

Since Gail is on the other side of the room still helping Mr. Parker with the crossword, and I'm closest to the door, I announce I'll get it. I give a gentle squeeze to a still-smiling Simon's shoulder and head toward the door.

My own smile is still strung across my face as I enter the alarm code and open the door.

And just like that, my smile dies a quick death.

Standing on the front porch, towering over me like a real-life version of Marvel's Captain America, is *him*.

Number 23.

I'm in such a shocked stupor that I just stand there, my mouth gaping open like a Monk fish, staring up into the face of that giant asshole.

I see a flicker of amusement light his eyes and he cocks his head and smiles.

To his credit, he takes a small step backwards, probably for fear I might reach out and slap him. Or better yet, kick him in the balls. He seems to read my unsaid thoughts and his hand moves across his thigh to protect himself where it counts. I want to laugh, but his presence is too much for me to fully comprehend.

Everything around me fades away and I'm left utterly speechless. If you asked me my name, rank, and serial number right now, I wouldn't be able to tell you. My brain is cluttered with too many questions. With curiosity over his appearance. And animosity toward him for being such an entitled dickhead.

It doesn't register why he's standing here at my place of employment. At first I think he's stalking me, but then I hear Simon call out from behind me.

"Kincaid! My boy! Come in and let your old gramps get a good look at you."

My muddled brain processes what I've just heard. Kincaid? His grandson? There is no way this arrogant jock could be in any way related to Simon Forsberg. No. Freaking. Way.

Our eyes are tethered to one another, his blue-green eyes locked fervently on my blue ones, neither of us wanting to be the first to look away.

But I'm not interested in winning any staring competition with him. I just want to get back to work and then home so I can study in peace. Away from the likes of Kincaid.

His name alone clearly depicts his born-with-a-silver-spoon in his mouth spoiled attitude. Entitled. Arrogant. My-daddy-can-fix-everything with his wallet.

I despise him even more.

The only thing going for him is that he's related to Simon.

Okay, that's a lie.

There may be one other desirable asset that I notice as soon as he walks past me toward his grandfather. His ass is covered in thin nylon basketball shorts, and is so tight you could bounce quarters off it.

I'm still standing with the door held wide open when he turns suddenly and watches with cocky interest as my eyes dart from his butt back up to his face.

Shit. I am so busted.

I can feel my cheeks burning with embarrassment as he begins backtracking toward me. When he's a chin length away, he reaches out his hand to introduce himself. Formally. Like a gentleman. But I know the truth. He's a prick.

"Cade Griffin." he divulges, his voice pouring over me like whisky and chocolate.

I awkwardly stick my hand out and he grabs it gently, pulling me in like a wild rabbit in a snare. I can't help but look down to where we're connected, amazed at the sheer size of his hand.

Gigantic. He could crush every single bone in my right hand without breaking a sweat. Yet I feel enveloped in warmth, the gentle rub of his calluses doing funny things to the inside of my tummy.

"And you are?"

Suddenly Mr. Forsberg appears from behind Cade, slapping his grandson's back in welcome.

"This is the beautiful Ainsley Locker. My nurse. She sure is a looker, isn't she?" He winks, his bushy white eyebrows arching upward and his hand clamps down on Cade's shoulder.

Oh my god. Can I die now? Did he really just call me a looker like I'm some sort of 1940's pin-up girl? Embarrassment floods my cheeks again and I'm sure I'm as red as Rosie the Riveter's bandana. It's as if these two men want to outdo each other in a game of '*who can embarrass Ainsley the most.*'

I try to get Cade to drop my hand, but instead, his middle finger begins drawing little circles into my palm.

Ew. Really, dude? Can he be any less subtle? Boys in the sixth grade tried doing that to me on the playground when they thought it was cool. And it never worked. So why Cade thinks it's a great come-on tactic is beyond me.

Giving a swift jerk of my hand, I pull away forcefully and turn around to re-enter the house code on the door.

That's when I glance down at my bright pink scrubs. The ones with the penguins on them. Oh God. This day keeps getting better.

"She is indeed," Cade replies to Simon, his eyes roving over me salaciously. "Looking good, Ainsley. It's like serendipity to run into you again, isn't it?"

Serendipity? More like just plain shitty luck.

77

I did not want to ever see this guy again. I don't understand his game. I don't need a rich, cocky jock trying to make a play to get into my pants. And he's putting more effort into flirting with me than he needs to. 'Cause it ain't gonna happen.

I give a sigh of resignation before plastering on a fake smile for Simon. It's not fair to get him stuck in the crosshairs of this little strange exchange between his grandson and me.

"Yeah, what an *awesome* coinky dink running into you twice in one week, *Kincaid*. Small world, huh?" You'd have to be deaf not to catch the sarcasm dripping from my tone. "If I didn't know any better, I'd think you were stalking me or something."

Either he ignores this comment or is hard of hearing, because Simon grins from ear-to-ear, looking excitedly between Cade and me, as if he's watching some dating show with hopes that Cade will land a mate. Not in this lifetime, buddy.

"Do you two know each other from school?"

Cade and I both respond together at the same time.

"Yes."

"No." I say emphatically.

But it just goes right over Simon's head. "How wonderful! Let's go in for lunch, Cade, and you can tell me all about it."

Simon shuffles into the dining room, using his walker with the tennis balls on the wheels and leaves Cade and me to follow him. Just out of earshot, Cade leans down, his breath warm against my face and he murmurs in my ear.

"I have to say. I've never seen penguins look as sexy as they do on you, Ainsley."

I snort – loudly – at his horrible attempt to charm me. I tip my head up and sneer at him.

"Does that sort of thing work on other girls, Cade? Because if you're going for originality or sincerity, that sucked. Big time."

I roll my eyes and leave him standing there looking a bit flabbergasted by his crash and burn. I snicker inwardly because that's probably the first and only time he's ever been turned down.

Returning to the kitchen, I open the kitchen cupboard and pull out two glasses. Then I grab an Ensure drink from the fridge for Simon and fill up the empty glasses with water. It's when I walk back to the table that I notice Cade is staring at me over Simon's shoulder, as Simon eats his lunch, oblivious to the strange vibe going on around him.

It's a bit sad to think that this is the first time I've heard of Cade coming to visit him. Simon is everything I could ever imagine in a grandfather. Kind, generous, sweet-natured. And it makes me a curious to know why. And maybe I'm also looking for a way to get in some jabs at Cade.

I'd taken an instant dislike to him and his arrogant demeanor and full-of-himself attitude. I've had all of two previous interactions with him, so I honestly can't say I know him at all, but so far everything leads me to believe he's just a vain, self-important douchebag. And nothing like his grandfather.

I slam down the glass of water a little harder than I mean to, gaining curious stares from both men at the table. Cade gives me a lopsided grin, which for all intents and purposes should make my insides all gooey, but instead have me wanting to dump the glass contents all over his perfectly coifed curls.

A good defense is a good offense. Isn't that what they say in sports lingo? So I decide to go on the offensive attack.

In the sweetest, most innocent tone I can muster, I ask my pointed question.

"So tell me, Cade...Why is this the first time you've come to see your grandfather? I didn't even know Mr. Forsberg had a grandson."

There, that should hit him where it hurts.

I didn't count on Cade being such a good defensive player. He picks up the ball I just hurled at him and lobs it back at me. His smile goes from lopsided to full-on blinding white teeth.

"Well, Ainsley. I've been gone most of the summer coaching at a basketball camp for kids in Tucson. And I just got back a week before school started. So I haven't had much time in between school work and informal basketball practices. But I did call you a few times this summer, didn't I gramps?"

Simon raises his arm to pat his grandson on the shoulder, his loving smile enough to break my heart. What I wouldn't give for a family like that.

"Did I tell you, Ainsley, that Kincaid was an All-American in high school? And is studying to become a biomedical engineer? I'm so proud of this boy."

Geez. Now I feel like a complete bitch for cutting him down in front of Simon, who is clearly enamored with the success of his grandson. It's like the sun shines from this kid's ass and Simon doesn't mind the smell of bullshit.

Cade gives his grandfather a smile and a head nod before turning to grin at me again. I'm not a mind-reader, but the look Cade shoots me basically says, "*Good try. Want another go at the champ?*"

It becomes painfully obvious that I won't win the battle because of the high-regard Simon has for Cade, but that doesn't mean I can't win the war. So I decide it's time for me to return to my job and assist the other patients with their lunches, leaving them to have some time together.

"Enjoy your lunch, gentleman. Let me know if I can do anything else for you."

Just as I'm about to walk down the hall toward the bedrooms, Cade calls after me.

"Thanks, Ainsley. I'll be sure to let you know if there's anything else *you* can do for me."

Ugh.

Game.

On.

Chapter 6
CADE

Spending time with my grandfather wasn't as bad as I thought it might be. I'd actually had a lot of fun. The stories he told, although they veered off into some crazy tangents at times, were full of interesting aspects of his life.

Gramps was a pretty fun guy and I feel closer to him than anyone else in my family right now. We also have a lot in common. He told me that before the war he served in, he was recruited to play for Penn State and that's where he met my grandma, Martha. I really miss my grandma. She was this beautiful wrinkled woman with the softest skin. She always smelled like baby powder and made the best pies.

I've been kicking myself for not visiting more often. And now it's a condition of my probation. I'm required to serve three-months of community service. My attorney easily finessed a deal that allows me to continue working with the local Boys and Girls Club afterschool basketball program, which I already do. My parents' condition is that I would spend time with my grandfather a minimum of once a week.

But the piece de resistance in all of this is that I not only enjoy both these stipulations, but I'm also secretly enjoying watching Ainsley work. There's no win-win in a basketball game, but there definitely is in this deal.

Ainsley has an inner beauty that goes well beyond anyone I know. She's youthful, but holds a degree of maturity I've not seen in other females my age. I had to hold myself back on more than one occasion from slipping my fingers through her dark, inky hair and untying it from the low-hanging ponytail she wore it in. I wanted to feel the texture of it, because it looked so soft, and let it hang across her face to accentuate her alabaster skin, the curve of her long graceful neck, and the strong, stubborn chin that jut out with determination.

She'd tried hard to ignore me during my four-hour visit, but she couldn't avoid interacting with my grandfather or the other patients. I could sense she didn't like me there. Or like me in general, actually, which leaves me utterly confused.

What did I ever do to this girl that would make her detest me so much? I figured out early on that we hadn't hooked up. That much was clear. I would have remembered a body like hers. Did I do or say something rude when I met her at the café? There's no doubt that I was riding a roller coaster of emotion that morning and my dad was reading me the riot act, which made me angry and obstinate, but I don't think I said anything nasty to her.

But the more I observed Ainsley work, and the way she carried herself, I knew she would never be one of those girls I banged at a party. What I saw in her was enough to convince me that this girl was the real deal.

Her smile, when given freely, is as bright as the sun and does something weird to my insides. It packs a punch. The sweet charm she uses on the male patients, which as far as I can tell are the only occupants in the home, is easygoing and natural. She embodies a sweetness so genuine that even the grumpy octogenarians couldn't resist laughing or smiling back at her.

The funny thing is, I don't normally go for the sweet girls. They don't interest me. Sweet girls always want something I'm not willing to give them and aren't willing to give me what I want. I am a horny-all-the-time nearly twenty-one-year-old male. Getting into a girl's panties has been top of my list of priorities since I was fifteen. That and basketball. Oh, and food. Food is a big priority, too.

Just as that thought entered my brain, my stomach growls, reminding me that I have to grab something before my practice later this evening. Officially, team practices couldn't begin until mid-October. But we players have to stay in shape and limber all year long. Many of us play the entire summer on various squads. As for me, I coach high-school kids at The Boys and Girls Club, and also play on a traveling team. I live and breathe the sport of basketball.

My grandfather gives me a sad smile as I begin packing up the deck of cards we'd been using the last hour playing gin rummy.

His shaky, wrinkled hand stretches out to touch mine. "I'm glad you came to visit me, Kincaid. I had a good time today, even though you whooped my ass in gin. I'd be penny broke if we'd been playing for real money."

I laugh, but feel a stab of guilt wash over me. My grandfather doesn't know the real reason behind my visit. As Ainsley pointed out earlier, I haven't been by to see him since…well, since my mom, my sisters and I came to visit him last Christmas. I am pretty certain my mom didn't mention the reason to him when she called him this week. Knowing him a little better now, I think he would be wounded to know about the trouble I've gotten myself into and that this visit, and others to come, were basically forced upon me. So, yeah. I'm not about to burst his bubble with the truth.

"Gramps, you better start boning up on your playing skills for the next time, because I plan to kick your butt more often."

I stand up and lean in to grasp his shoulder, giving him a tender squeeze.

He places his trembling hand over mine, patting me in a loving gesture. Glancing up through his bushy eyebrows, he wears an amused look.

"Perhaps a certain nursing student has caught your eye?" He says it quietly and low enough for only me to hear. "I wouldn't blame you for wanting to visit more often. She is a cute little thing."

"Whoa, old man. Sounds like if I do, I might have some competition." I chuckle, wondering if he caught me giving her furtive glances. Because honestly, I can't keep my eyes off her. "I'm all good in that department, though. Plus, I've got too many other things to focus on right now. Don't have room for any cute things right now."

Admittedly, getting laid sometime soon might not be such a bad idea. It has been over two weeks and I am ready to bust a nut. But I'm not in the market for a relationship. And Ainsley, as far as I can assess, is not interested in me in any capacity.

"I gotta take off now, Gramps. Got practice in an hour and need to grab something to eat before I head over to campus. I'll see you soon, okay?"

"Goodbye, Kincaid. Thanks for the visit."

Feeling a bit awkward and uncertain about how to say goodbye, I ruffle the soft white mop of hair on top of his head and head toward the door. As soon as I reach it, I realize I need a code to open it.

Just as I turn around in search of someone to let me out, Ainsley rounds the corner, a messenger bag strapped across her chest. My eyes immediately gravitate toward her tits, which are accentuated from the binding of the straps pressed into the center between her breasts. I swallow hard, lifting my gaze to her bright sapphire eyes, which are wide in surprise.

I have plenty of one-liners I could put to good use in this moment as I'm caught checking out Ainsley's chest. But none of them come to mind. I just stand here stupidly. Her gaze lassoes me in, and my tongue is stuck to the roof of my mouth, my arms bolted to my sides.

"Trying to make your escape?" She quips.

She gracefully moves around me and enters the code on the alarm pad as I catch a whiff of her sweet orange blossom scent. Not overpowering, and with a hint of something I can't put a finger on. It it's soft and fragrant and sends a zap of interest to my dick. I can't help myself as my gaze travels down her backside. The scrubs she'd been wearing earlier during her shift have been replaced with a pair of cut-off jean shorts and a fitted blue and white striped T-shirt. As she bends over the keypad, the shirt rises an inch, exposing the small of her back.

I have to step back and will my hands to remain at my sides. Otherwise, I'm liable to let my desire get away from me and I'll reach out to touch her. To slide my fingers underneath the hem of that T-shirt, around her waist, to the front of those shorts where my hand can tease the soft flesh above her pelvic bone.

My lips press in a tight line. I probably look like a crazed lunatic, because she turns around with a confused visage, her eyes narrowed at me.

"I was just kidding," she said, the sound of her voice changing from sarcasm to sympathy. She opens the door and takes the first step out into the oppressively hot front porch. "And I just want to tell you that you made your grandfather a very happy man today. That was really sweet of you to visit."

I am once again mesmerized by the sight of her hands as they wrap around the fiber strap of her bag. Those fingers are touching the cotton material of her T-shirt in the center of her cleavage. My dick gets hard, envisioning those hands doing the

Sierra Hill

same thing to me and wrapping around my shaft. Stroking me hard.

Fuck, I need to get out of here.

I jerk in forward motion, my momentum accidentally butting against her shoulder as I brusquely step around her to head down the pathway to my car. As I open my car door, I glance across the roof of my car to find a shell shocked Ainsley.

I suppose I was a little abrupt, but damn, I can't trust myself to stand that close to her without losing my shit. And by that, I mean taking her by her shoulders, pressing her up against the side of the house and kissing her hard. Until we both can't breathe.

Instead, I snap out a curt goodbye and slide on my sunglasses. "I'll see you around, Ainsley."

My car engine starts with a low, tiger-like purr. It's a blue 228i BMW coupe. My dad bought it for me out of guilt two years ago when he and my mom announced they were divorcing. While I was pissed as hell at him, I gladly accepted the car, because what guy my age wouldn't?

This car has gotten me a lot of action. But it doesn't mean I forgive him. He's a bastard for leaving my mom. After twenty-three years of marriage and three kids, he just decides he doesn't love her any more. Fucker. While it was never truly clear why they separated, my gut says my dad screwed around on her. Cliché, no doubt. Since then, though, I know he's dated other women (I hear this from my sisters), but hasn't settled down with any one girlfriend. Which was fine by me. I don't need a twenty-four-year-old stepmom any time soon.

All relationships seem doomed, in my opinion. Why tie yourself down to one person for the rest of your life? It's seems like a recipe for disaster and eventual heartbreak. Though some of my teammates have girlfriends and seem to be okay. Like Van. I think he's been with the same girl since high school and they have a long-distance thing going on. That's just crazy to me, locking yourself down when you're in the prime of your life.

My thoughts on the subject evaporate as I lift my gaze from the steering wheel and watch Ainsley walk away down the street. At first, I'm not sure where she's going and why she doesn't have a car parked nearby. It's hotter than hell out here. August in Phoenix is a fucking oven and you don't want to be outside for more than a few minutes at a time.

I watch her turn the corner before I pull out of the driveway and slowly cruise down the street in the direction she walked. The nursing home is in a fairly quiet neighborhood, but a few blocks away is a main arterial that connects with all the major highways in the Tempe area.

I pull up to a red light and look down the street to the left. When I don't immediately see her, I turn to my right. There a few yards down the street is a bus stop, where several thug-looking dudes wearing black bandanas are clearly expressing their interest in the hot chick standing in their midst.

Ainsley.

Fuck that shit. Flipping on my blinker, I pull up next to the bus stop and roll down my passenger window. The guys stop their jawboning at the clearly disinterested Ainsley and glare at me. I'm not about to start anything with these guys. They could be packing. But I'm not about to let Ainsley stay out here by herself.

She has a pair of earbuds in her ear with her head buried in a book, her body language telling everyone in her vicinity to go the fuck away. I lay on the horn to get her to look up.

When she does, her eyes grow wide. Curious. Cautious.

I smile, liking how it makes me feel to know I've just scored her interest where the douchewads standing next to her couldn't even earn an eyebrow raise. Ainsley doesn't immediately move, though. She just stands there, her expression now one of growing wariness, like I've just interrupted something very important and she doesn't have time for my shit.

Huh. Wasn't expecting that.

Brushing off her impatience, I give her my best, most practiced panty-dropping grin and crook my finger. Her feet remain planted firmly until one of the thugs behind her says something I can't hear. Her body visibly stiffens and then she's stepping toward my car, bending down into the open window. The scent of orange blossom wafts through the front seat, filling my vehicle with the sensual fragrance that's all Ainsley. And it makes me hornier than fuck.

She's impatient when she speaks. "Yeah? What do you want, Cade?"

Impatient or not, I'm liking where things are headed right now. I'm counting my lucky stars for giving me this opportunity.

"Hop in," I demand softly. "I'll take you wherever you're headed."

Sucking in a breath, her face contorts like I'm causing her a considerable amount of discomfort. Or maybe it's the guys behind her, because they're getting louder, and I think they just said something about her joining them in a threesome. Her hand grips the door frame tight and then she sighs. Loudly. Apparently I'm the lesser of two evils, because she's made her decision. And my ride it is. Triumph whips through my body, as if I've just made the buzzer-beating shot in the championship game.

And I'm thrilled, because I wasn't about to beg this girl to get in my car. That's not how it works. Usually my crooked finger and my charming smirk can have a chick in the backseat of my car without breaking a sweat. But Ainsley is clearly resistant to my charms. And I have no idea why.

She settles herself in the passenger seat, setting her book bag on the floor between her Sketcher-clad feet. The jean shorts she wears inch their way up her supple thighs, which aren't as tan as most of the college girls I know. But the creaminess of her skin make my balls ache with want. My fingers twitch to skim the silkiness laid out before me.

As if she can read my thoughts, she drops her hands to the tops of her thighs, clasping her fingers together in prayer position. I hope she's saying a prayer for me. God give me strength…and all that.

She shifts under the weight of my stare and her impatient tone jerks me out of my reverie. "You said you'd give me a ride...now drive. I've got places to be."

"Yes, of course. At your service, Ms. Locker. Where am I taking you?"

I pull out into the road and wait for her directions.

"I'm going to campus. You can drop me near Memorial Union. I've got to grab something to eat before my class."

"Cool," I say and shrug noncommittally as I merge onto the 202. We drive a little while as an awkward silence descends over us. Ainsley is obviously trying to tune me out by typing away on her phone and I'm playing with the satellite radio like a nervous idiot. When I finally land on an old Beastie Boys tune, I turn it down a notch and quietly rap along to the lyrics. Not more than thirty seconds and I feel her gaze on me. I turn my head to find her head cocked to the side with an amused smirk on her face.

She snickers and shakes her head. "You're such a white guy."

"What? The Beasties are classic. Or would you rather I be rapping along with *In Her Mouth*?"

I knew I'd get a reaction out of that one. She throws out a disgusted expression, her lips tilted up in displeasure over Future's rap song, which is pretty raunchy. Now I'm worried that I may have just offended her. Because honestly, that is a pretty offensive tune. I've heard them play it a few times in the gym and at my frat at parties.

My eyes are back on the road when I hear her snicker. Deciding to be a gentleman, I offer up the song selection to her.

"Is there another station you'd prefer to listen to?"

"Anything you won't sing along to is going to be better." She snipes sarcastically.

Jumping in without hesitation, Ainsley takes over the airplay and lands on a classic rock station which is currently playing Lynryd Skynrd. I bite back my amusement as she begins humming along to *Sweet Home Alabama*. She has a pretty decent voice.

As we near campus, I'm curious to learn more about Ainsley. Aside from knowing she works two jobs, and that we go to the same school, I know very little else about her. Besides the fact that she's smoking hot and those legs, that are now tapping to the beat of an AC/DC song, are unbelievably sexy.

I don't even know what year she is. Or if she has a boyfriend. Or if she likes fuck-buddies, 'cause I'd be down for that.

I have to clear my throat and swallow down that question before it pops out.

"So, what year are you and what's your major?"

Not the best conversation opener I've ever had, but no one ever praised me over my conversational skills.

I dart a glance at her and watch the thoughts flick across her face. She'd be horrible at poker.

"Isn't it fairly obvious? Nursing. And I'm a third year transfer."

Snarky. I like this girl. She doesn't play dumb or coy, or say whatever she thinks I want to hear like most girls do.

"Where'd you transfer from?"

"The school of hard knocks."

My laughter comes barreling out, something akin to a snort and a grunt, because I wasn't expecting that answer. But when I don't hear any concurrent laughter and only silence surrounds us in the car, I tilt my head in her direction. She's wearing the most rebellious grin I've ever seen. And it's both blinding and erotic at the same time.

My body wars with my brain to just stop the car right now, lean over the console and wipe that smirk off her face with my tongue.

"Funny," I play along, nodding my head in consideration. "And what exactly did you learn at the school of hard knocks?"

She places a fingertip over her lips, which are puckered tight, one eye closed as if in serious thought. Then she turns to face me, her crystalline eyes bright with humor.

Yet the sound of her voice conveys a deep truth.

"To stay away from boys like you."

Chapter 7
AINSLEY

Accepting the ride from Cade was a grievous error on my part, and one that I am now paying dearly for.

I thought Cade would just drop me off on campus and be on his merry way. I could run to the union to get something for dinner, read up a little for my upcoming test, and then cruise on over to Neeb Hall for my four o'clock lecture.

That was far from what actually transpired.

Cade didn't drop me off. Instead, he parked in the lot closest to the union and walked with me as I tried to make my escape. I felt like I was in the presence of a king, or the Pope, by the number of people that greeted Cade along the campus corridor. If he wasn't high-fived, given an "atta-boy", whistled at, gawked at, or thrown a ball to catch by some gushing co-ed or sports fanatic, it was me who was being stared at like I was a virus in a petri dish. With apparent disapproval and disdain from every female in the vicinity.

If he is the king of the land, then I am his servant. And they are his court.

At this moment, the king is sitting across from me at a table in the student union, where I'm trying to eat my sandwich in peace, and he's just chatting away about everything and nothing. It's both endearing and annoying. Because I don't have time for this. But every attempt I've made to give him the brush off has been met with his dogged perseverance. The man cannot be swayed.

He's kind of like a cute Cocker Spaniel puppy. Everyone adores him and wants to pet him, but he just wants to sit on your lap and be loved.

And it pisses me off. Because I feel pulled into his little orbit. It's not exactly a hardship to be in the presence of Cade. He's pretty freaking hot. And if I'm being totally honest, he is sweet and charming. He has not one ounce of the whiny, stuck-up 'tude that he presented me with last Friday in the cafe.

This Cade is funny, a bit conceited, and highly entertaining. And he's made me smile more in the last hour than I think I've smiled in over a year.

So, he can't be all that bad, right?

Plus, he bought me my dinner. It was a nice trade-off.

"So what do you do for fun, Ainsley? Do you live in the dorms?"

I swallow the remaining piece of my sandwich and wash it down with the iced tea that's no longer filled with anything resembling ice. Even in the air conditioned building, it's sweltering hot. I shake my head to answer his question. It's yet another question out of the thousand it seems he's already asked me.

Cade wags his finger at me like he has it all figured out.

"Oh, I get it. You're a sorority girl?" He asks, once again trying to figure me out. Good luck, buddy.

He continues. "That's weird. You'd think I would have seen you at one of the parties this year." His moss-green eyes narrow in on me. "And trust me, I would have noticed you."

I almost choke, coughing loud enough to draw more unwanted attention. It's bad enough we are sitting in the middle of the union and I already feel like I'm in a fishbowl.

"Uh, that would be a negative. I'm definitely not a sorority girl. I live off campus." That's all I'm going to say on the subject, because I'm not about to share any personal details with him. I don't even know Cade, other than that he's Mr. Forsberg's grandson and apparently hot shit on the basketball court according to all his fans milling around us.

I decide to do the smart thing and move the spotlight from me and turn the tables to ask him a question.

"And how about you? Do you live at one of the frats?"

Just as I throw that out there, his eyes veer from mine and over my shoulder. Curiosity gets the best of me and I whip my head around to see what's caught his attention. I come face-to-face with a blonde bombshell.

I'm first assaulted with a large dose of richly scented perfume. You know the kind…that sweet cloistering smell that remains in a room long after the person has gone. It's not a horrible smell, but there's a lot of it.

As if I'm actually invisible, the girl leans over the table, her boobs spilling out over her top, pushing against my shoulder so that I have to bend to the right in order to have my personal space back.

Who does that?

"Hey Griff. Whatcha up to? Haven't seen you in a few weeks," she says, her voice alternating between a sultry song to something that resembles Minnie Mouse. I'm about to lose my lunch.

"Yeah, it's been a while. You're looking good, Hailey." He smiles that smile that has an effect on my girly parts.

Gah. Damn it. I don't want to like him!

My head moves side to side as if I'm watching a tennis match but have totally lost sight of the ball is. My brain can't quite compute what's going on between these two, but I'm pretty sure it's a heavy dose of syrupy sweet flirtation. And if by the tone of her voice, and now the angle of her very large assets dangling in front of Cade's face, there's no two ways about it. They've either been very intimate with each other, or she wants it to happen bad.

But seriously? I'm. Right. Here.

Part of me wants to raise my hands to the sky and yell, *"Yoo-Hoo! I'm here! There's another girl at the table, Miss Sorority Bimbo."*

And just as my thoughts center on that desire, I hear my name.

"Ainsley, this is Hailey Conrad. She's co-captain of the men's basketball cheering squad. Hailey, this is my friend, Ainsley."

Oh goodie. I'm now his *friend*. Should I be flattered by this descriptor? Should I fall down in front of him in worship and reverence, or faint at the high-regard Cade has just bestowed up me? Either that, or I'll just find the nearest trash receptacle to barf in.

I don't have time for any of that because Miss Perky O.C. Conrad turns and glares down at my sitting form. The two-thousand-dollar orthodontia smile she plasters on her face is so fake and plastic it would put Mickey Rourke's nips and tucks to shame. She pins me with the eyes of a viper. And I have a feeling I'm going to get stung.

This girl gives me the most practiced line I've ever heard.

"So nice to meet you, Annie. Any friend of Griff's is a friend of mine."

I try not to wince at the obvious passive-aggressive dig with calling me by the wrong name. Judging by her snide misuse of my name, she's not one to be trifled with. So I don't bother correcting her or even sticking around to say more. Instead, I give a tight smile and nod, gather up my trash and book bag, and stand up to leave.

As I'm practically hurling myself toward the exterior exit doors, I feel a hand gently wrap around my bicep, halting my progress just before I open it.

"Ainsley, wait. Where are you going?"

"I have to get to class," I spit out quickly, a little shaken by the exchange with Barbie and by the heat of Cade's touch. "I gotta go. But thanks for the ride and my dinner. See ya around."

"But-"

Cade seems shocked that anyone, especially a girl, would ever walk away from him. I think it's safe to assume most of the girls on campus would drop everything just to follow him around all day like googley-eyed sheep. But not me. I won't fall for his boyishly good looks, and his sweet charm. And his cute butt. And those cut biceps. They look like he chops wood every day because the grooves are so defined.

No sir. Not me.

His eyes follow mine as I look back over to Hailey, who's standing there with a shocked expression. "You better get back to Miss Cheerleader, Cade. She doesn't seem too happy that you just ditched her and her *Pom-Poms*."

I give him a piteous smile and nod toward Hailey's overexposed cleavage. He seems to know better than to push it with me and drops my arm to let me go as I walk out into the quad.

It's weird how just minutes ago all the attention was directed toward me – well, Cade, but I was cast in his glow – and now I'm as imperceptible as the gaseous air around me. And that's the way it should be. I don't want to be in the limelight. Or be noticed for anything outside my accomplishments. Cade Griffin is a super-hero to the people of this school. He's a celebrity in his own right. And everyone wants a piece of him. But not me. His spotlight is too hot. I'd scorch to death if I spent any time in his public eye.

I enjoy the walk through campus, with its pathways lined with palm trees, bright red bougainvillea, benches and open areas filled with clusters of students and faculty activity. But today I feel like something is missing. Although the sun shines bright, I feel a shiver of cold run through my spine, as if the rays are no longer strong enough to penetrate through my skin.

Cade's light feels hotter and more intense than even the ball of fire in the sky.

I chastise myself as I walk into the lecture hall and grab my seat in the top right corner. While this is the largest lecture theater on campus, the room is only half full with students at the moment. I'm about ten minutes early, so I pull out my study guide, notepad, pens and text book to review the most recent material I read. This is my Human Development lecture course, one of the upper-division humanities requirements, and part of the psychology aspects of the nursing program.

I really enjoy the professor. She is both a nurse practitioner and academic, so she understands the whole bedside manners dilemma when dealing with the ill and dying. Many professors have only been in the classroom and have no idea what it's like to show empathy for someone who can no longer speak because they have a breathing tube down their throat and can't communicate, or who is so angry at their lot in life because they can no longer bend over to put on their own socks.

Those are some of the things that I am good at. Where it comes from, I don't know, but I have a never ending supply of patience for those in my care. Not, however, for guys like Cade. Or for parents who are supposed to take care of their daughters but don't refill their medications and then fall into deep depression, drinking to stem the pain.

I'm remembering my mom's last binge when I hear my name being called and a hush of whispers echoes across the room. My head pops up and I look around the hall in confusion. Is the professor calling for me? I search her out but don't see her anywhere. And then I feel a strong hand on my shoulder and I tilt my head to find Cade standing in the aisle next to me.

Dizziness descends upon me from either his towering height, or from the uncomfortable feeling of once again being the center of attention as all eyes are on me right now.

Cade crouches down next to me, as a gigantic smile unfurls across his face.

"Glad I found you," he effuses in a rush of air. "Otherwise I'd have to resort to using a bull horn at the front of the class, which probably would've gotten me escorted out by campus security."

I roll my eyes and give him a *hmph* because he's absolutely crazy. "We can still make that happen."

He gives a low chuckle and I feel it down to my toes. Half of me is annoyed that he's bugging me and interrupting my class prep time. But the other half... my body is vibrating with a strange excitement. My nerve endings are firing off short charges of electricity that lights up my skin. Because Cade

Griffin came looking for me, for some unknown reason. And he's looking mighty fine.

My voice is a little shaky, tinged with antagonism and wonder. "What are you doing here, Cade? You need to leave before the professor gets here."

He moves his head side to side, scanning the lecture hall and shrugs his shoulders in defiance.

"This will only take me a second. I'm not worried." He casually points out, like he is above the law because of who he is.

Arrogant jerk.

"You rushed out of the union so fast, I didn't get to ask you my question."

My nose and forehead scrunch in confusion.

"What are you talking about?" I hiss back in a loud whisper. I want him to leave me alone, but now I'm curious. "What question?"

His grin grows unbelievably wider and I notice how straight his teeth are. His lips are full and look like they could devour a girl in a single kiss. His angular jaw and upper lip are covered with a fine layer of scruff, just like the other day. It's a little darker than his hair color and I have a sudden urge to reach my hand out and touch, to experience the rough abrasion against my palm.

I blink, trying to refocus my thoughts. He was about to ask me a question. *Right.*

"My birthday is tomorrow."

"That's not a question," I snidely remark. But I hate sounding bitchy, so I follow it with, "But happy early birthday, I guess."

Cade takes it all in stride, shrugs and smiles. Then he blows me away.

"My roommates are throwing a small birthday party for me. I want you to come."

For the record, that was not the question I was expecting. For one, I don't even know Cade Griffin. We've never hung out, had any classes together, or interacted in any other way outside the short expanse of time this past week. And second, I don't go to parties. I don't associate with his type of people. Jocks. Athletes. Frat brothers and sorority sisters. Campus celebrities.

And third, why in the world would Cade want me at his birthday party? I'm not the type of girl he'd want. Not that I know what type that might be, but from the little exchange I witnessed between cheerleader Barbie and him in the union, I'm definitely not of that crowd.

He must be amused by the look of sheer horror and panic across my face, because he lets go a booming laugh.

"Ainsley, it's just a party – not prison camp. I think you'd have fun. And I'd like to get to know you better."

"Why?" I squeak out, feeling everyone's eyes on me.

I don't know what my problem is around Cade, but I have no self-confidence around him. I just feel like we are in two different socioeconomic classes. I don't fit into his BMW-driving, sorority cheerleader life. While I learned early on in life never to compare myself to other girls, because that's self-destructive, it doesn't mean I'm meant to be in Cade's circle.

My mind flashes to my favorite teen movie, *Pretty in Pink*. I am the girl from the wrong side of the tracks and Cade is the richie athlete. And never the twain shall meet.

I quickly add an excuse. "No, I work that night. Sorry, can't go."

Cade blinks a few times, bites his lower lip, and then scratches his chin. Analyzing me. Looking for something that I can't quite name.

"I didn't even tell you what night the party is on. So how do you know you can't go?"

Well, shit. He has me there.

It doesn't matter what night. Even if I don't work, there's no way I'd be caught dead at his party.

"Whatever, Cade. I can't go. Let's just leave it at that."

He surprises me then when he sits down in the seat next to me. My eyes dart to the clock on the wall of the lecture hall and see that it's one minute to four. Crap, he's got to get out of here before the professor comes in.

"Tell you what," he says, his voice calm and collective. The gold flecks in his eyes glimmer like light reflecting off a gold wedding band. Kind of hypnotic. I feel pulled in to whatever he's about to say and I physically lean closer, to which he grins.

He crosses one foot over his knee and settles back in the theater-style chair. "I'm gonna plant my butt right here for the next hour during this lecture. At the end of the class, I'll give

112

you a ride home and you can quiz me on anything related to the topic. If I answer the questions correctly, then you have to show up at my party."

An odd noise of disbelief flies from my mouth. What little twisted game is he playing? Why is this even an option?

I plant my palm against my forehead and shake my head. "You are exasperatingly annoying. Why the hell are you doing this? Can't you find someone else who wants you to annoy them?"

Cade laughs and grabs for my text book, opening it up to where I have it bookmarked. I watch his eyes track over the page, his face contorts into thoughtful appraisal.

"The allostatic load theory of illness occurs when the patient is continually stressed and they are unable to return to a normal stress level, thereby increasing the stress demands on their bodies…" He reads from the book, flipping a few pages to read aloud again.

Tapping the book with his thumbs, he makes a humming noise. "Hmm, well, isn't this interesting? The biopsychosocial model is a model of health that integrates the effects of biological, behavioral, and social factors on health and illness…"

My hand grabs the book and I whip it off his lap, snapping it closed in a mini-tantrum of hysteria. It makes a rather loud sound and I see a few heads turn to see out what's going on.

My face is burning with mortification and frustration. I hate attention like this. I just want him to leave me alone. "Cade, just get the hell out of here. You're making a scene and you're acting like a child."

He turns his broad shoulders toward me and crosses his arms over his chest, making his pecs pop out like the Hulk. I have to turn away so my body doesn't betray me. Because that? That is too much man muscle to ignore and still stand my ground.

"Two choices here, Ainsley. You can either say yes right this minute and I'll leave you to your lecture. Or, I stay and get the most out of my educational experience, learning a little more about biopsychosocial models. And from the looks of it, my shenanigan will probably embarrass the hell out of you. Which, noting from your angry little tantrum, you don't like one bit."

I'm still facing away from him when his hand grabs my chin gently to turn my face back toward him. I want to remain mad at him for disrupting my day. But all of that is impossible when I look into his eyes and see sincerity. And then I just turn to mush out of sheer lack of self-preservation.

"Fine," I capitulate, jerking my chin out of his hand, which leaves a warm tingly feeling in its absence. "I'll come to your birthday party, as long as you leave now. But I won't be bringing you a present. And don't you dare expect this to be a hookup."

The whoop Cade lets out has now garnered the attention from everyone in the lecture hall, including Professor Lang who just walked in and dropped her notes on the podium. I drop my head to avoid any eye contact with anyone and let out a seething whisper.

"Now just go! Please…" I implore, fidgeting restlessly in my seat.

He grabs my cellphone in a flash of movement, types in some digits before handing it back, his face glowing in celebratory glee. And then, when I thought I couldn't be shocked any more than I already was, he leans over a places a kiss on my cheek.

"Your presence, Ainsley, will be the best present you can give me."

Then he stands up, turns, strides up the stairs two at a time and doesn't look back. I watch him leave in haze of incredulity.

What did I just get myself into?

Chapter 8
CADE

Saturday mornings around our apartment are usually pretty quiet. We're either all crashed out from a late night of partying, or my roommates aren't home. Between the three of us, Lance, Carver and myself, it's usually a given that at least one of us will wind up with a Friday night hookup.

That honor went to Carver last night. The noise and sex sounds emitted from his room told me he wasn't alone. I'm not sure what happened to Lance, though, as I lost track of his whereabouts after I left the party, and I don't think he ended up back home.

More often than not, when we do finally emerge from our bedrooms, or the bathroom floor, we are all suffering from some level of hangover. The giant Costco-sized bottle of aspirin on our kitchen counter is a pretty good indicator that this happens fairly frequently. We all suck at holding our liquor.

Today's my birthday, though, so I held things together last night at one of our teammates' parties. We'd played in a scrimmage game until six-thirty, came home, showered and ate, and then went over to Jake's apartment around nine. At that point, there were just a smattering of guys playing video games, some chicks hanging on their arms, and some music playing. By the time I left at one a.m., the party had blown up and people were busting out the doors.

I know Carver got laid last night, because I woke to the sounds of his bed squeaking in his room next door and the muffled moans of a female in the height of climax. When I rolled over to look at the clock, it was close to four in the morning. I was too tired to get horny from the noises they were making, so I rolled over and went back to sleep.

But now I'm awake from the incessant vibration of my phone on my nightstand, as several calls and text messages come rolling in. I mumble a low curse and reach over to grab the offending device to see who has the audacity to wake me at nine a.m. on a Saturday morning.

The first call came in at eight-fifteen and was from my mom. She left me a voice message that I'm not quite ready to listen to. I'm afraid she'll want me to come over to the house for brunch or something. Not that it would be a bad thing, but it's just weird being back home when it's only my mom living there now.

Once my dad moved out, and my twin sisters Kylah and Kadence left for school, my mom was completely alone. She took the separation and divorce hard. And now that both Ky and Kady are away at school, too, I'm the only one that lives close enough for her to lean on for support.

I've tried to be her shoulder to cry on, but the timing of it was…well, I was a sophomore going on junior in college at the time they divorced. I'm not a dick, but it isn't my forte and definitely not where I wanted to be. She was alone for the first time in over twenty years and I just wanted my freedom. We'd finally come to a mutually agreed upon compromise. I would come home every other weekend for brunch. She'd either make a huge spread at home, or we'd go to the country club.

And now that my sisters are both attending different colleges out of state, the responsibility still lands squarely on my shoulders. I look at the stream of birthday texts and see I have one from Kylah. That girl has probably been up since the crack of dawn studying this morning. She's definitely the more studious of the identical twins. Kady is the free-spirited wild one, who went off to the University of Colorado Boulder where she's an undecided major.

Kylah, the more reserved of the two, is attending Harvey Mudd College, the small liberal arts college in Claremount California where she's studying science. In that regard, Ky's a lot more like me academically. We both have dreams of someday developing lifesaving methods – me through the science of medical devices. Kylah through the true form of science to cure some disease.

I shoot a quick text back to Ky to say thanks and ask her when she'll be home next. She says she isn't sure.

Then I pull up the next unread text, this one from Ainsley. Her contact name is already stored in my list.

Before I left the lecture building the other day, I dialed my number from her phone, so she had my number. Plus, her number then popped up on my call list, so I could have it. I think she was still in shock that I followed her (or maybe stalked is a more apt representation) into the classroom that she didn't balk when I grabbed her phone for my stealthy tactics.

It took everything I had in me not to text her yesterday or last night. I don't know much about her, but I know I am pushing her limits with personal space. So I let her have it. The personal space, that is.

The weird and unique thing about my newfound interest in Ainsley is…I have a genuinely serious interest in her. And yet, she seems to be repelled by my actual living existence. It's perplexing. I can't wrap my brain around it. The more she seemed eager to get rid of me, the more insatiable I become.

It's like she puts out this vibe that worms its way under my skin and tickles my intrigue to want to know her. To find out what makes her tick.

Then there's also that little fact that I want to fuck her. She is hot as hell. But unlike the other girls I've hooked up with, she doesn't seem to know it. Or if she does, she definitely doesn't flaunt it. Not like fucking Hailey Conrad. God, I was so pissed at her for interrupting my conversation and dinner with Ainsley yesterday. And when Hailey acted like a bitch in heat, calling Ainsley by the wrong name, I wanted to say something to put her in her place.

And I was just about to, too, when Ainsley just up and left.

Ainsley was already reluctant to be in my company. And I couldn't have her thinking I was okay with Hailey's attitude. So I went to find her.

It wasn't hard. I saw the text book she was studying from at the cafeteria table, so I knew the class. I also was familiar with the arts and sciences buildings, so I traipsed over to Neeb hall and asked a few girls that were hanging out in the hallway. They were more than eager to show me what room it was in.

It was the highlight of my day to see the way Ainsley reacted when I asked her to come to my party. Her bright eyes rounded in shock and confusion. As if she couldn't possibly believe that I would be interested in going out with her. That thought gutted me.

If I were to have asked any of the other fifty or so girls that had been sitting in that classroom with Ainsley to come help me celebrate my birthday, every one of them would have jumped at the chance. I'm not trying to sound like a boastful motherfucker, or anything. It's just the way it is.

But not with Ainsley.

After the shock of seeing me in her class wore off, she was actually pissed. Then she had a serious case of embarrassment when I started making a scene by reading out loud from her text book. Honestly, I thought it was pretty cute. And then she practically shut down when I asked her to come to my party.

So here I am now, my legs stretched out and tangled in the light blue sheet covering my lower body thinking about Ainsley – which, by the way, is causing a serious tent under the covers with my morning wood. My dick grows increasingly harder when I see Ainsley's name pop up. I choose to ignore my erection and open up Ainsley's text.

Ainsley: *I need to know deets for tonight. For your stupid birthday party.*

I snort out a deep laugh because I can honestly see her throwing her hands on her hips and tilting her head to the side in exasperation.

Me: *What kind of deets? Like what you should wear? You better be prepared for my answer if you ask that.*

There's about a minute pause and I worry I may have crossed the line with the innuendo. But fuck, I can't help myself. That's how I flirt. I'm a dirty bastard. And she…well, she is sweet. And I can only imagine her wearing those teeny-tiny shorts like she had on the other day; my hand wandering up her toned thigh and underneath the frayed jean edge to find her wearing no panties. And no bra underneath a tight tank top that accentuates her full rack.

Fuck. That does not help the hard-on situation and my hand unconsciously moves down to give it a solid rub before I cup my balls in my hand.

But then I see the little ellipses start to appear and I wait, biting my lower lip with anticipation.

Ainsley: *Um…so here's the deal. I've never been to a college party and don't know what to wear. So don't be a dick and make fun of me.*

She's kidding, right? She can't be serious. She's twenty-one and is a third year transfer. I mean, I went to college parties and frat houses when I was a senior in high school. There's no way anyone as beautiful as Ainsley could be that sheltered. Maybe her parents were strict or something.

Me: *Are you fucking with me? You've never been to a campus party?*

Ainsley: *No. And again, I'd appreciate you not laughing at me. This is my first year on campus and I didn't go the traditional route. All I've done the last two years is studied, worked…and hell, why am I even explaining this to you? Just tell me what I should wear cuz I've got things to do today.*

And now, even more than ever, I want to hang out with her and find out her story. It's obvious there's something that draws me to her. I'm fascinated by everything about her. There's a connection that's been tugging at me and I want to see where it leads.

So instead of going the more flirtatious route, I decide to play it cool and simple. I realize she's making a big concession in coming tonight, and I don't want to scare her off.

Me: *Shorts and a T-shirt are fine. Nothing fancy. Do you drink beer? Or liquor?*

Again, all I can think about is her in the short-shorts as my hand absently strokes my aching cock waiting for her response. I don't expect anything sexually from Ainsley tonight, but just the potential that she'd be in my bed has my dirty thoughts on hyper-drive.

Just then my phone rings and my hand instinctively flies off my dick, as if whoever is on the other end has caught me in the act. I feel like a dirty bastard. There are some things I keep private, and jacking off is definitely one of them.

"Hello?" I say, my voice deeper and more gravely than usual - full of sleep and desire.

"Hey," she says quietly. I can hear sounds in the background and wonder if she's at work. "I need to clarify a few things before tonight." Her words are firm, but hesitant.

"Sure. Let me have it."

"I don't drink."

"Not a problem. I'll get you something else. Soda? Lemonade?"

"I like Dr. Pepper. But I'll bring my own…"

I nearly laugh, but think better of it. "You don't have to bring your own drink to the party I invited you to, Ainsley. I'll get you some."

She sighs and concedes. "Fine. Whatever. But I'll pour my own drinks. No one else touches it."

Ah. I get it now. She's leery about someone giving her a roofie or something. Smart girl. But she needs to know that would never happen on my watch.

"Ainsley. I know you don't know me very well. But I would never let anything happen to you. You're safe with me. You can trust me."

I hear a scoffing laugh across the line. I probably shouldn't have used those words. Girls hate it when a guy tells them to trust them. It's so cliché. But I'll do and say just about anything right now to make sure she shows up tonight without reservations. I just want to be with her.

"This is a bad idea, Cade. I don't understand why you want me to come to your party. I have nothing in common with any of your friends."

"You don't *know* any of my friends to even say you don't share any commonalities," I counter, hoping she'll listen to reason. "I will introduce you to everyone and I won't leave your side all night. My friends are cool guys and will like you. I promise."

There's a long, uncomfortable pause where I can hear her wheels turning. One thing I've learned about Ainsley thus far is that she is very skeptical of me. Which I don't understand fully. But that's not a deterrent because I'm one persistent motherfucker.

I've always set my goals high and worked hard to achieve them, even though most people see the opposite. They think everything comes easy for me. That I've been handed everything in my life on a silver platter. But I've had to bust my ass in basketball to get where I'm at. It takes immeasurable time and practice to become a strong competitor. You can't give up when you're hit with an obstacle. I like challenges.

And for some unknown reason that I can't quite comprehend, Ainsley represents a challenge.

"So, we cool, Ains? Will you show up for a little while tonight?"

Her exaggerated exhale says it all.

She's throwing in the towel.

Conceding to my request.

Letting me have my way.

"Fine," she says begrudgingly. "Give me your address. But I'm telling you, Cade. If I don't like it, I'm out of there. And there is no funny business. I'm not sleeping with you tonight. Got it?"

I know she's not one of those girls. Everything about her reads *"hands off"*, *"don't touch"*, *"you try, you die."* But even with all those warning signs, my attraction to her remains sky high. I'm willing to take it slow because that's how much I want to get to know this girl.

And that's a scary proposition because it's never been like that before. I'm a senior in college and not once have I ever been in a serious relationship. Sure, I've gone out on dates or brought a hookup to a few frat parties, but most of the time, it's been a one-night, one-and-done arrangement. No seconds.

But with Ainsley, there is no other choice. I have this gnawing need deep within me that has to have her. The circumstances with her are different, so I'm letting her set the tone and the pace, and throwing my usual playbook out the window.

I prattle off my address and tell her she can park in my car stall, number 16. Our apartment complex's visitor parking spots are few and far between, and there's no way I'll have her walking by herself at night down the street to get her car.

"That's okay. I don't need a spot. I take the bus."

"Oh, right. Well, text me when you get dropped off and I'll come meet you there."

"You don't have to…"

I interrupt immediately. "You're not walking by yourself. Just promise me you'll text me when you get there."

"Fine. I'll see you later."

I smile, feeling I'm making a little progress.

Winning!

"Later, Ainsley. I'm looking forward to it."

And I really am.

Sierra Hill

Chapter 9
ꓮꓲꓠꓢꓡꓰꓬ AINSLEY

Public transportation is normally not a problem during my day trips to and from work or campus, but it can become pretty sketch at night. There's a certain element of riff-raff that is prevalent on Valley Metro. I've just learned to be extra vigilant when riding at night. My pepper spray keychain is always in hand and at the ready. I may look disinterested, but I'm constantly on the alert.

I've been on the bus now for over thirty minutes, through three stops between Mesa and Tempe. Between the retched heat and my nerves, the back of my legs stick to the plastic seat of the bus, like I'm sitting on a film of honey. I squirm and shift uncomfortably trying not to let the sweat build up behind my knees. Car headlights and taillights zoom past outside the window as I watch from the loud confines of the bus. I'm still kicking myself for agreeing to this stupid idea.

I was a ball of indecision all day long, my mind was on nothing else besides Cade's party tonight. I screwed up half the orders I took at Bristol's this morning after speaking to him on the phone. It was a miracle I escaped unscathed when I absently reached barehanded for a hot plate the cook had placed on the warmer. Thank god he noticed my carelessness and yelled at me to stop before I burned a hole through my hand. I literally jerked to attention, wide-eyed and confused until he flapped an oven mitt in front of my face.

But who could blame me for my lack of focus? Didn't they realize that I was living in some third-dimensional Twilight Zone? Because how else could you explain a hot, sought after PAC-12 basketball player inviting me to his birthday party? It made zero sense.

The more I think about it, the more jumbled up I become. One theory I have as I sort through all the possible notions is that this is all a big frat joke. Like those movies where the stud athlete has to win over the loser geek girl and then she goes all Carrie on them at the prom when she finds out.

Or maybe that one of his friends bet Cade that he couldn't get some random girl into his bed before midnight. I don't know. That one seems highly implausible, because all Cade has to do to make that happen would be to simply snap his fingers and he'd get a girl to drop her panties.

So where did I fit in to all of this? When I told Cade that I was not an easy conquest, he didn't even bat an eye. It's not as if I wouldn't consider sleeping with him. I'm not a virgin, by any means. I've had a few short-lived relationships late in high school. I punched my V-card when I was nineteen to a guy named Denny, who I worked with at a camera store in Portland. I dated him for three months and finally decided to go for it. It wasn't love, but he was a really decent guy and treated me nicely.

Unfortunately, a week after I gave it up, my mom informed me we were moving yet again. That was the first time in my life that I was actually mad about having to move because I had to leave behind a guy. To his credit, Denny was pretty upset about it, too. He tried valiantly to stay in touch with me, but after a month, the texts and calls dwindled until we eventually lost touch.

Needless to say, I know there's an attraction between Cade and me. I feel it every time I'm with him. I'm not a prude and it's not like I'm saving myself for marriage or a ring. What I am saving myself from is getting caught up in a romance with a charming guy the same way my mother does. She is notorious for falling fast and hard for the wrong guy who winds up using her, cheating on her, and dumping her faster than yesterday's garbage.

No sir, not me. I have too much self-respect than to go all gaga over a little attention thrown at me like confetti by a star basketball player.

Granted, Cade has surprised me since I met him. He has been nothing but sweet up to this point, even though I've been more than a little snippy with him. Call it my "resting bitch face" reaction, but my suit-of-armor has been securely in place since I met him. My defenses seem to be on high-alert around Cade, almost as if my body knows there's danger lurking around the corner.

Not scary danger, like a maniac clown or anything. Simply the kind of danger that will crack open my heart and bleed it dry. I feel him chipping away at me, piece by piece, as he plies me with attention, making me feel like he's really interested in me. Making me feel special.

My thoughts are interrupted when the bus comes to a stop. This is my exit.

I gather up my small cross body purse, swinging it over my head and shoulder, and grab hold of the pole as I wait for the side doors to open up. Cade had asked me specifically to let him know when I'd arrived so he could come get me at the bus stop, but I figure his apartment is just a block down the street and I don't want to interrupt him in the middle of his own birthday party.

Just as I step off the last step and my feet hit the ground, I look up into the smiling face of Cade.

Holy shit.

He's here.

Waiting for *me*.

I'm momentarily stunned and don't even know what to say. He takes my breath away. Words are trapped in my throat. I think this is the sweetest gesture anyone has ever done for me. To say that my opinion of Cade has changed dramatically over the last week is an understatement.

Aside from the charming grin, he's wearing a dark colored polo shirt (very preppy) and camo cargo shorts. Flip-flops accompany his casual attire. He appears freshly showered with his curly hair still a little wet and as he steps toward me I get my first whiff of his soapy fresh scent, along with a hint of spicy deodorant. My nose immediately sends crazy-ass messages to my olfactory receptors, which in turn serve as the ignition to rev up my libido.

OMG, his masculine pheromones are doing a number on me already.

And then he speaks and my knees about give out. His voice is a low baritone, with a hint of boyish enthusiasm.

"There you are, beautiful."

Gulp.

I'm done for.

"Hey."

Not a super intelligent response, but the fact that I got one syllable out of my mouth is pretty damn impressive in my book.

He looks me over, not licentiously or anything, but appreciatively, his smile never wavering. When he reaches back to my eyes, I see the admiration in them.

"I didn't want you to have to wait for me here alone. So here I am." His arms fly out from his sides.

I nod my head. "Yep. Here you are."

My insides feel like they've turned into gelatinous goo. While it's still pretty hot outside, even at this time of night, my internal body temperature spikes to about one-hundred and twenty.

Cade takes another step toward me to close the gap, because I haven't moved an inch since I got off the bus. My feet stick to the hot pavement, and his hand reaches out to take hold of mine.

Sweetness

I don't even have time to register shock when he pulls me into his side, leans in and brushes his soft, warm lips over my cheek. Heat prickles on my skin where his lips leave a lasting mark.

"You look really pretty."

My brain and body are warring between themselves over how I should respond to this thoughtful compliment.

The brain is telling me it's exactly the type of thing that my mother's boyfriends would say to her to make her go all giggly and desperate for more attention. Like bait on a line.

My body, on the other hand, is screaming with girlish delight, saying "*YES*! I like that. MORE. MORE. MORE."

And my heart...well, let's just say it just seized up, did a few cartwheels, and possibly would have flopped right on out my body like a Tasmanian devil, had it not been encased within my ribs. I'll probably go into cardiac arrest right here on the sidewalk and never even make it to the party.

I'm ready to make a snarky comment, because that's who I am, when I look up into his face and see sincerity reflecting back at me.

"Um. Thank you." Nice. That's all I can think of to say.

"You're welcome," he says, gently guiding me down the street, his feet setting an easy pace. I'm wearing low-wedge sandals, so it's easy to keep up with his long strides. "I'm really glad you showed up tonight."

It surprises me that he doubted I would. I just nod my head and keep walking. I notice the small stucco houses that we pass along the street, all likely inhabited by college students or faculty, or others affiliated with the school since we're so close to campus. I also happen to notice the warmth of his hand and the gentle pressure as his palm cups mine. I glance down and can't even see my own hand, which is swallowed up by his big mitts. No doubt he can handle a basketball.

"Did you really think I'd stand you up like that?"

I can see the blush color his cheeks. "Well, you weren't that enthused at the prospect of coming. So, I had some doubts."

I don't know what to say to that, because he's right. So I try to change the subject, to show him that I do want to be here and I am interested in him.

"So tell me about your friends. Who am I going to meet?" I ask, trying to lose some of the edge I've been feeling all day.

This whole thing makes me nervous. Yet I'm also comforted by the way he holds my hand in his. Protective. Kind.

It just feels good. Right. Perfect.

We've known each other for over a week now, but I don't know anything about his friends. This is a good way to remedy that.

We walk a few more steps until he suddenly stops, tilts his head and narrows his eyes at me.

"What?" I ask, suddenly concerned I've said something wrong.

"Maybe I'm rethinking the idea of introducing you to my friends," he says, his hand clasping mine tighter.

Oh great. Here we go. I did all this primping tonight and he just now realizes that it's all a huge mistake. He's embarrassed to be seen with me because we aren't in the same social classes or circles, or whatever.

Well fine. That's his problem and all on him. I'm not about to beg for forgiveness or grovel at his feet to apologize for who I am. I'm on academic scholarship. I work two jobs. I support my mom and my sister. I'm not the upper one percent.

But I'm solid. And if he can't see that about me, then screw him.

"Why? Aren't I good enough for your boys?" My tone says I'm ready for a fight and I yank my hand out from his. His body does this jerky thing. I've definitely made him uncomfortable. Well too bad.

"What are you talking about? Not good enough? Jesus, Ainsley." Cade's hand flies to his head and he grips on it, looking like he's ready to tear it out. "My *boys*, as you call them, are going to realize you're too good for me the minute they meet you. And by the end of the night, at least two, probably more, will be tripping over each other to get your number. Mark my words."

"Oh." I lamely throw out there, completely stymied by his response. Wasn't expecting that.

To be honest, I've never been interested in the attention of boys. Guys. Men. Whatever. I just always had more pressing matters to deal with than chase after the affections of the male persuasion. I don't go out of my way for it. I wasn't a mall rat in high school like some of the other girls in my class. I didn't wear a lot of make-up or overly suggestive clothing. I didn't chase. Or call. Or put out to gain the attention of the boys. It just wasn't who I was or wanted to be.

Sweetness

To hear Cade tell me that he's worried other's will want me makes me honestly wonder what he sees in me. I gaze down at my ensemble that I wore tonight, trying to remember exactly what I picked out to wear. A pair of jean shorts, a white-peasant top with bright blue embroidered designs across the chest and edged collar. And a pair of beaded sandals.

I didn't even really do anything to my hair after my shower. I just pulled it back into a ponytail, leaving a few wisps of hair and my bangs falling across my cheeks and forehead. I did put a little extra effort into my make-up. Not overly ambitious, but some mascara, some pink shadow, a little swab of blush, and some shiny neutral colored lip gloss that Anika bought for me last Christmas from Sephora. It was practically unused.

My sister at fifteen knows more about the art of make-up than I do. She and my mother won't leave the house if they don't at least have falsies or mascara on their eyes. I'm happy if I've brushed out my hair before leaving sometimes.

Trying to identify what it is that Cade likes about me is just perplexing. Yes, I'm by some standards pretty. Maybe even beautiful sometimes. But why he, or his friends, would think I'm a catch is just difficult to fathom.

Cade gives a light tug on my hand and heads us toward a small, two-story apartment complex of maybe twelve units.

Then he reminds me that I'm going to meet his friends, who will apparently have it out for me. "Okay, you'll definitely meet my roommates, Lance and Carver. They are also on the basketball team with me. We've all been rooming together since freshman year, but started out in the dorms. And watch out for Carver."

When my eyebrows go up inquisitively, he just shrugs.

"He's team captain, point guard, and official ladies' man. The guy can get into a girl's panties faster than he can set a pick and roll."

"I have no idea what that means."

He cracks an adorable grin. "Eh. It's just a basketball play. The point is, don't fall for Carver. I'd be crushed. He always gets the girls."

I roll my eyes and laugh, because who is he kidding? I know without a doubt, Kincaid "Griff" Griffin, has gotten his fair share of the lasses. He then pulls my hand across his broad chest to his heart and gives me his best puppy dog eyes. God, what a flirt.

"Anyway, I think Van will be there, too, unless he went to visit his girlfriend this weekend. And let's see…who else? Drew, Casey, Darryl, Caleb, Matty, Bailey, Liv…"

"Okay, okay!" I exclaim, feeling a tad overwhelmed with all the names he's whipping through. "If I wasn't freaking out before, I am now."

His eyes widen incredulously. "You're nervous? Why? You seem the picture of confidence."

"Right." I snort indignantly.

"Nah, I'm serious. You just come across so sure of yourself most of the time."

I've always been confident in most areas of my life. I've had to be. I had to have balls to grow up the way I did. But that doesn't mean I can't be just as insecure as the next person. I'm just better at hiding it more than others.

"Well, thanks. I think…I guess it's just having to walk into a room not knowing anyone and knowing they are immediately going to judge me because I'm there with you."

I have to crane my neck to look him in his eyes as Cade leans in, his nose just inches from my face, dips his head closer to mine to gaze at me. It's a moment of clarity. Time stops.

The Earth's plates shift and move beneath us. Electricity shimmers between us, like fireflies in the dead of night. Buzzing. Crackling.

I think he's about to kiss me. And I don't know how I feel about that. Okay, I do know how I feel. I want him to kiss me really, really badly. The desire licks through my veins, sending small explosions of heat and blood whipping through my body. My heart beats faster. Louder. My breath tightens into short pulses of air. In. Out. In and out.

And then the moment is over and he pulls away, giving me back my personal space and room to breathe. And I realize I want him back in that space.

Cade shakes his head and places a hand on the doorknob of his apartment. I can feel the bass from the music vibrate against the bottom of my feet. Or maybe that's still the tingling sensation from Cade being so close to me.

"Believe me. The only person they are going to be judging tonight is me. They're going to be wondering why such a smoking hot, smart girl like you is hanging around with a guy like me."

And with that, he opens the front door to a chorus of celebratory shouts, music, and laughter.

Sweetness

I tamp down my trepidation and slap on a big smile. I take a steadying breath and tell myself I'm sure I can handle whatever the night has in store for me.

Chapter 10
CADE

I realize something the minute we walk into the party.

I don't want to be here with Ainsley. I have this overwhelming desire to walk right back out that door, Ainsley's hand in mine, and get as far away from everyone as possible. To just be alone with her, without the interruption of all my friends who are trying to shove drinks down my throat.

I'm pretty certain that I would be laid out naked and drunk in the bathtub tonight if it weren't for Ainsley. I don't mean to imply that she's a wet blanket, but I keep getting a glimpse of something flash in her eyes every time someone hands me another drink. Fear, maybe. Concern. I don't know, but I've been trying to pace myself, drinking lots of water in between games of nerf hoops and shots of tequila.

The last three hours have gone by quickly. I'm having a great birthday party and enjoying introducing Ainsley to my friends. Sure enough, within five minutes of arrival, Carver was hanging all over her, giving her cheesy compliments, talking up how great his three-point shot is — to which Ainsley literally made a gagging noise at. I doubled over belly laughing when she did that, because Carver was wearing the most ridiculous look of shock I've ever seen him wear.

And then Ainsley tried to placate him by patting him on the arm to assuage his ego. He took advantage of her patronizing gesture and wrapped an arm around her waist, yanking her to him.

I quickly went all caveman on his ass, giving the motherfucker a friendly drunken shove, which Carver protested loudly and pushed me right back. And then we were all laughing over our stupidity.

It was impressive to watch how easily Ainsley maneuvered through the crowd of people, chatting effortlessly to the people she didn't know, finding commonalities with each and every one. If I were going into politics, she would be a woman I'd want right by my side to ride the political circuits. Ainsley has brains, beauty and an unbelievable charm.

I'm sitting on my desk chair inside my bedroom now waiting for her to finish up in the bathroom. She was a little apprehensive when I said she could use the master bath in my bedroom, but saw the line outside the main bath in the hallway and decided her biological needs dictated the use of my private commode. Plus, I told her it was cleaned that morning, unlike the one Carver and Lance share. Who knows the last time they cleaned their toilet?

Had I mentioned going into my bedroom to use my master bathroom to any other girl, they would've jumped at the chance to find their way into my private quarters. And they'd probably use it as a ploy to get me back here and in my bed with them. Ainsley isn't like that.

Minus the hand holding and light brushes of our arms as we stood side-by-side tonight, I have yet to kiss or touch her otherwise. Don't get me wrong. I want to. Very badly. And the tequila I've been drinking has only increased that horniness factor. With or without the alcohol, though, I've wanted to kiss her since the moment she stepped off that bus.

Fuck, I knew I was a goner when I saw the look she gave me. Like I was some white knight or something. Her smile nearly brought me to my knees. There have been plenty of opportunities throughout the evening where I could have leaned down and touched her lips with mine. All night long she's been so close I can smell the sweet vanilla flavor of her lip gloss and it makes my dick ache to kiss it off her mouth. And I think she would have let me.

But I've resisted. I'm not willing to push this if it meant risking her stepping back. And that's a really weird sentiment coming from me. I usually don't care. I wouldn't tread this lightly or give a fuck if the girl I'm with wanted to or not. I'd just take, and if she gave it up, good for me. And if she didn't, then I'd find someone else. Hoops hunnies, or ball bunnies, come a dime a dozen for a college ball player. I'm not being cocky. That's just how it goes.

My eyes droop a little in the soft glow of the desk lamp as I see the bathroom light go out from underneath the bathroom door. And then the door opens and I watch Ainsley step inside my bedroom, stopping when her gaze lands on me. Waiting for her.

I can see what she is thinking as it flashes through her eyes. "I didn't want you to be in here alone, so I waited. I promised you I'd be by your side all night long."

That was true. I can see that she's quietly assessing my intentions. Smart girl. And if she could read my mind right now, she'd be gasping at the visuals.

"So you did," she whispers, her eyes taking in the walls of my bedroom, decorated in basketball awards, a shelf full of trophies, pendants and a signed team poster from last season. She walks over to the picture, turning her head to look at me over her shoulder.

"I'm sorry…but I've never asked you what position you play? You any good?" I can hear the humor in her voice, because even if she's never seen me play, she has to know I'm good. My gramps couldn't stop bragging about me the other day if that's any indication as to my skills.

I stand up and slowly walk toward her until I'm standing right behind her. And I can't help myself. Maybe it's the booze or maybe just my natural flirtatious behavior, but I lean down so my lips are right at her ear and whisper, "I'm *really* good."

I hear a small gasp escape her lips. She smells incredible. Soft. Sweet. Orange-spice. And up to now, I've been on the defense, trying to keep myself in check, giving her distance. Space. But in this moment, I let go of it all and let nature take over.

My mouth brushes the sensitive skin under her ear. It's exquisitely smooth. Like the silk edging on a blanket. My first kiss is just a nip and I feel her body instinctively stiffen. I go in for another, this time allowing my lips to linger and flit over the exposed skin. I feel her gasp before I hear it.

Her body relaxes and I take the opportunity to step in so my chest is pressed against her back, the top of her head just underneath my chin. The next kiss I use my tongue to lick a line from the base of her neck to her earlobe and then nip the cushiony lobe with my teeth. Whether she realizes it or not, Ainsley nestles her butt against my groin.

Goddamn. It's almost too much.

Almost.

My hands find her waist and I grab both hips, spinning her around to face me. Just before I take possession of her mouth with mine, I say, "Shooting guard."

I doubt she even takes notice of the answer I give her to the question about what position I play because she lets out the most fantastic moan when my lips meet hers in an open mouthed kiss. She tastes like Dr. Pepper and cinnamon. So delicious and delectable. I can't get enough.

My tongue plunders her mouth, in search of more from her. To taste her. To feed on her. To go wild on her. The heat of her body seeps into my pores. The soft texture of her smooth legs rub against my own, creating a friction that sends all my blood down south. I have to direct my hands up to her face, to cup her cheeks, otherwise they'd wind up on her ass where I'd pick her up and throw her down on the bed.

A low growl erupts from my chest when her own hands grasp my ass and she squeezes. Hard. Holy shit. That's so hot. I love it when a girl gets handsy.

We continue kissing, sucking on each other's lips, conquering one another's sounds and moans. I want this to go all night. Stop time and just kiss the ever-loving fuck out of Ainsley. Nothing else matters in this moment except touching her. She's all I've ever wanted.

My lips move down her jawline, placing small wet kisses on every part of her skin. I meet up with her earlobe again and pull it between my teeth and suck hard. The sexy gasp she makes is a perfect complement to the way her body suddenly conforms to mine, arching into me. I can't resist any longer. My arms swing behind her, my hands move to cup her ass and I pick her up. Her legs instinctively wrap around my waist for support as I press her against the wall to gain leverage, our bodies aligning so perfectly it hurts.

My cock is nestled between her legs, counting down the clock and readying itself to launch. The heat emitting from her center is glorious. I want to be inside that heat. Soon. I take advantage of our perfectly aligned symmetry and start to move. I don't even realize it, but my body knows what to do. I just keep kissing her neck, moving down to the scooped cut-out at her collarbone. Her skin tastes amazing. Like a sunrise breakfast in Hawaii.

As my brain begins calculating the fastest route to my bed, my bedroom door swings open, allowing a flood of sound and light to come pouring in.

"What the hell?" I grunt, turning my head to search out the offending perpetrator while keeping my palms planted firmly on Ainsley's ass. I'm about ready to unleash my fury.

And then I see Lance come stumbling in, oblivious to anything going on between me and Ainsley.

"Dude. Get the fuck out!"

His head pops up, mouth gaping open. "I gotta take a leak, man," he mumbles in a drunken stammer, his hand automatically cupping his dick. "And there's a line."

His eyes, half-lidded, seek mine before locking on Ainsley, who is ducking her head into the crook of my neck. I like the feel of her warm breath as she lets out a hysterical half laugh/groan.

"Impeccable timing, Lance." I tip my chin over to see Lance, who stops in his tracks as it seems to finally dawn on him what we're up to and he makes the most exaggerated hand gesture toward us.

"Oooooh…you guys are getting busy. Nice!" He yells out boisterously, practically loud enough for the entire apartment to hear his announcement. "You naughty, naughty kids."

Ainsley wiggles in my arms. "Oh my God…but I think that's my cue to leave. I've gotta get going. It's getting late."

I shake my head in denial. I don't want her to leave yet.

"No…not yet. Just wait until he's gone."

Lance makes it to the bathroom but doesn't even bother to shut the door behind him. Jesus. What an asswipe.

A loud belch and then a long, contented sigh follow. And then all we hear for the next minute is something close to the sound of a waterfall hitting the toilet water. Ainsley lifts her face to me and we simultaneously crack up.

"Geez can that guy pee." She says between bouts of giggles.

I take the moment to admire her face. Her cheeks are colored a sweet rosy shade, either from embarrassment or the heat that we had just been producing together. The smile she wears is carefree and natural, and it makes me want to see her like this all the time. She's happy right now. She's happy with me.

The bright blue of her eyes looks almost turquoise in the dim light. The same color as the water in the Caribbean. My parents took me there when I was fifteen for a family vacation and I will never forget the almost unreal hue that colored the ocean. I also remember the warmth that wrapped around my body as I swam and surfed during that week. It's the same warmth I feel in this moment as Ainsley smiles up at me.

I don't want to put her down. And I certainly don't want to let her go, but her laughter has dulled and she's squirming to get down as her feet dangle at my sides. The moment is gone, thanks to my drunken asshole roommate. The next chance I get I'm going to make him pay.

With as much grace as I can finesse, I slowly lower her down to the floor, but don't release her entirely. I move my hands to her lower back, pressing lightly so she has to arch her head back to look up at me.

She's probably average height, but because I'm nearly six foot five, there's a generous gap between us. But that doesn't stop me from pressing her into my torso and bending to plant quick kisses along her temple. I think it's safe to assume that our alone time for the evening is over, unless Ainsley wants to resume our make-out session, which I would have absolutely no problem with at all. Because there is nothing I want more than to get naked with her.

The promise I made to her was real, though. I'm not going to treat her like just another hookup. I invited her to my house so I could spend time with her. Get to know her. And that's what I did. Now I like her even more than I did before. I like her a lot. I'm not about to screw it up, all the progress I've made, by trying to press her just to get in her pants.

So I decide to lay it out on the table and let her know that the ball is literally in her court.

"Can I see you again?"

Ainsley shifts nervously between one foot and the other, but I don't give her a chance to pull away.

"When can I see you again?" I whisper as I continue kissing down to her ear. Then we hear the toilet flush and Lance comes out humming a Weezer song about getting high, a goofy grin sketched across his face.

I ignore him and go back to prodding an answer out of Ainsley, using my hands now to rub down her forearms.

"*I –* I don't know. I'm super busy with work and school."

"What's your schedule like at Ethel's? When are you there next? I can come visit both you and gramps at the same time."

What she doesn't know, and what I'm keeping from her, is that I'm required to go visit him weekly. I will tell her about it at some point, but not now. Not yet.

She shrugs. "It's not exactly the same set schedule every week. But I do work every Thursday night."

"Okay, good. Then I'll definitely come by Thursday."

I grab hold of her hand and we walk toward the door of my bedroom. It's well after midnight and I need to call her an Uber to take her home. There's no way I can drive, especially now with my record, and I'm not about to let her take the bus or light rail home by herself at this time of night.

Ainsley pulls back and hesitates a moment as I glance over my shoulder at her pensive expression.

"Well, um…maybe I could stay a little while longer. Unless you want me to go and have someone else lined up."

I whip around and yank her body into mine so fast she sucks in a deep breath. I know she can feel how hard I still am for her. I want her to know – to *feel* – how much I want her. And that there's no one else who I have my eyes set on.

"I was trying to be respectful," I explain, as I shove my dick into her crotch. "But if you don't want me to behave myself, then by all means, I'd love to finish what we started."

Ainsley gives me a good humored laugh and raises her eyebrows at me.

"Well, I have to admit, I'm a little torn. Because I would love to stay and have some more of that fabulous chip dip you got out there…"

In one swift move, I grab behind her legs and throw her over my shoulder in a fireman's hold, and dump her across my bed.

She lets out a loud shriek. "Hey!"

She scrambles to get up but I'm faster as I straddle her legs and pin her arms to keep her in place.

"Chip dip, huh? That's why you'd stay?"

Testing out my theory that all women are ticklish around their ribs, I start digging in with little jabs of my fingers along her sides. And sure enough, I found the spot.

Ainsley wiggles underneath me, and if my dick wasn't hard already, it's a fucking steel pole now. I will my cock to stand down, because unless she gives the go ahead, nothing is going to happen here tonight.

Nothing. At. All.

After a few minutes, I finally relent and we both catch our breath. Her hair has come undone and the black strands spill across my pillow. I lean over her and press my lips against hers. We kiss with pent up need, all that's been stored up since the first time I saw her. It's a heady feeling, wanting a girl this much and knowing that it won't come to fruition tonight.

Her hands, which were fisting my shirt, finally let go and she gives me a soft shove. Ainsley rolls to her side and props her head up on her elbow, staring down at me. It feels good to have her eyes on me. It's validation that she's as into me as I am of her.

"So in all seriousness," she says softly. "I'm not a virgin or a prude or anything. I'm just not sleeping with you tonight. And I do have to go. I've got to get up at the butt crack of dawn."

I prop myself up on my elbow to mimic her posture and push a strand of hair out of her face. Her jet black hair is silky and soft as it sifts through my fingers.

"Ainsley. I'm into you. I don't expect anything to happen tonight. Unless, of course, you want to give me a birthday blow job. That I wouldn't refuse, just so you know."

I wiggle my eyebrows so she knows I'm kidding. Although, it would definitely make my dreams come true. All I've dreamt about lately is her full lips wrapped around my dick. So getting one in real life would be pretty awesome, but not expected.

She slaps at my chest playfully and laughs. Then she gives me a long, thoughtful look, as if she might actually be considering the prospect of my dick in her mouth and my cock jumps in excitement.

"If I had time, I just might consider it, since it's your birthday, and all. I wouldn't want you to be deprived of your birthday wishes. But alas" – she shrugs apologetically – "I've got to get home before I turn into a pumpkin."

I groan and shove my face down into my pillow between us.

Popping my head back up, I put on the most charming, sexy smile I can muster, trying to hide my disappointment.

"I guess I'll have to take a raincheck on that, then."

Ainsley leans over so her lips hover above mine. I feel her warm, sweet breath mingle with mine. My buzz wore off over the last hour, as lust sobered me up, but the way she makes my body buzz lying next to me, gets me drunk. High on her.

"I guess you will."

Chapter 11
AINSLEY

"I don't want a sandwich again. Just give me some money so I can buy a salad."

I'm slathering the final layer of mayo on the sandwich when Anika walks into the kitchen and plops down at the table, dropping her book bag on the floor next to her with a *thump*. I give her a sidelong glance, watching her fill up her cereal bowl with Frosted Flakes. I'm getting pretty good at ignoring the teenage attitude she's been throwing off recently, trying to avoid needless arguments and petty fights. But today I'm tired and not really in the mood for her demands.

"I'm not going to give you money for something we already have in the fridge," I reply, letting the piece of bread flop down onto the counter. "If you want a salad, you can find it in the crisper drawer and all the fixings right alongside of it. You are totally capable of putting it together yourself."

She lets out the most dramatic of sighs, as if I've just told her she has to plant and harvest the lettuce herself.

"But I don't have time this morning." Her whine is three octaves higher and laden with angst. "I still have to do my hair, Ains. I just need ten dollars. What's the big deal?"

Ah. Now I see where she's going with this. Ani doesn't want the money for lunch. She needs it for something else. I just don't know what it is.

Since we've moved to Phoenix and she's become friends with this new girl, Danielle, she's become a lot more secretive and sullen, pulling away from me in an attempt to hide her feelings. I guess that's par for the course with most teen girls, but it makes me sad.

When we lived in Boise, we were really close. We shared everything. She told me about her friends, and the boys she liked, the teachers that annoyed her, her first kiss, the way Justin Lacid's breath smelled like mustard when he finally gave her tongue. But now, over the last few months, she's withdrawn.

It could be partially my fault. I haven't been around as much as I used to be. Between both jobs and school, I only see her a few nights a week, and some mornings like today. Weekend mornings she's still in bed sleeping when I leave and out and about somewhere when I return. My mom assures me she's looking after things with Ani and is always aware of Anika's whereabouts at any given time. I have to trust that, even though it's a tough pill to swallow.

My mom. She won't be winning any Mother of the Year awards anytime soon, that's for sure. The only upside is that since we've moved here, she's been trying to change things. She took a job at a hair salon just a few blocks away. It's a decent living, but she works long hours and on weekends, so she's not home often with Anika, either. Her moods have been tempered by the meds that she's been taking again. As long as she keeps on those, I feel safe in knowing we won't be going down that rocky road any time soon.

I turn and watch my beautiful younger sister eating her breakfast, gracelessly shoveling spoonful's of the sugary cereal into her mouth. Her dark long hair is still wet and clings to her back, wavy from hand drying it with her towel. In some ways we look similar, but Ani's hair color is much lighter than mine and the shape of our face and nose are different. We have different fathers. Neither of us ever knew either one of them because they never stuck around. Or maybe it was that my mother didn't stay with them. Who knows?

The one trait we do share is the color of our eyes. That we got from our mother. Sapphire blue with long, thick lashes that fan across our cheeks.

As I stare at Anika, I notice her frame appears to have become much thinner than it has been. I wonder if that's just a normal thing for a fifteen-year-old developing body, or if there's something else going on. We are naturally slim and willowy, although I carry much bigger breasts and a more cushioned ass than my mom.

Anika, on the other hand, is just plain thin. Had she ever been able to go to dance classes, she likely could have been a decent dancer. But mom never had the money for extracurricular activities for either one of us. Nor did we ever stay in one place long enough for her to join such activities. It never bothered me much, but now I worry Anika is missing out.

I'm also now curious as to what Anika isn't telling me. She's hiding something. I can feel it.

"What do you really need the money for, Ani?"

Her mouth stops chewing mid-bite and her head jerks to the side, eyes giving me the teen death glare. Telling me without words, "none of your business."

"Nothing," she shrugs, setting the spoon down in her bowl and pouring more cereal. "I just want to buy my lunch like my friends do. Is that a crime?"

"No, it's not a crime. But we don't have extra money for cafeteria food. We have food here that's perfectly acceptable."

Anika scoffs sarcastically.

"Whatevs. I'll just get it from mom then." The retort cuts me deep.

But now I know she needs the money for something other than just lunch, because Anika wouldn't resort to asking our mom for money. Not that our mother wouldn't give it to her if she had it, but we've just become so accustomed to taking care of ourselves for so long, we don't rely on our mother for anything outside of rent and medical costs.

I scoot the chair out next to Anika and sit down, leaning my face in is so close to the side of hers that if she turned, we'd bump noses.

"Ani, what's going on? Tell me what you really need the money for." I try not to sound desperate or needy, but I'm sure she can hear it in my voice. I'm worried. "You can tell me anything, you know. I love you and I will help you any way I can."

Her eyes flicker and shimmer, the impenetrable wall she's erected just about to fall. One more push and everything she's holding close will come rushing out. I see it in her expression, the softening of her face and the lines around her forehead. I touch the top of her wet head for good measure, stroking the strands reassuringly, hoping that will demonstrate my sincerity.

Instead, I'm surprised when she does the opposite. She snaps her head away and nearly jumps from her chair in a dash to empty her dish in the sink.

"Ani..."

"It's nothing, Ains. Just forget I asked. I'll eat the friggin sandwich, okay?" She turns away from the sink and throws all the lunch items in the paper bag, grabbing it to shove in her book bag.

Before she hits the hallway, she stops briefly, as if she's just remembered something.

"Thanks," she says in a rush. I honestly can't tell if she's being sincere or it's laced with sarcasm. But I choose to believe she means it, and I respond back.

"You're welcome. I love you. I hope you have a good day at school. I'm going to be late tonight, but I think mom will be home to fix you some dinner."

"Yeah, okay. See you later."

And then she closes the bathroom door and I'm left wondering how to get through to a fifteen-year-old who still has the innocence of a child, but the life experiences of an adult. I'm not sure what to say or do, but I know it will weigh heavily on my mind until I know the truth.

****

"Gin rummy," I hear Mr. Forsberg bellow from the kitchen table where he and Cade have been playing cards for the last two hours. It's Mr. Forsberg's favorite game, besides cribbage, which he's ruthlessly beaten me at nearly every time he's cornered me to play.

"Gramps, you're killing me!"

I smile to myself as I fish out the block of cheese from the fridge to make the grilled ham and cheese sandwiches. I'm on dinner duty while my co-worker, Adriane, is in with Mr. Ornery getting him bathed and dressed. Mr. Newsom has been suffering from a bladder infection and it's been doing a number on his system and his dementia. I've noticed that when he's sick, the dementia symptoms increase even further. Yesterday when I was on shift, he spoke to me as if I was his late wife, Marion, reminding me to go feed the chickens. He must've lived on a farm at some point in his life.

Out of all our current live-in patients, Simon was by far the healthiest, and most gracious, and charming of the group.

168

Now I see where Cade gets his charm. It's obviously a family trait.

This is the first time I've seen Cade since the night of his party last Saturday. We've been in daily communication though. Each morning, he sends me a sweet text to say hi and two nights ago we talked on the phone well past my bedtime. Laughter from their table has me glancing up from the cheese I'm slicing.

"Ainsley, dear," Mr. Forsberg calls over to me. "I think Kincaid may need some lessons on how to lose graciously. Perhaps you can provide him with some pointers."

I snort out a laugh at his backhanded compliment. He's a card shark to be sure.

"We all know you cheat, Mr. Forsberg. You don't fool me with your innocent comments about luck. I'm on to you." I give him the fingers-to-eyeballs signal.

Simon's eyes cast downward in meek playfulness and he shakes his head. "I don't know what you're talking about, my dear. I play fair and square."

Cade places his cards down on the table and lifts his hands above his head to stretch. He's facing toward me and my eyes catch a glimpse of the muscled planes of his abs and the sleek skin and V peeking out below his T-shirt.

My brain short circuits as I lose focus on what I'm doing. I can't help but stare at his body. Honest to God, I've never seen a guy's abs look as solid as Cade's. When I finally shake myself free from the snare his physique has me in, I look up to find him smirking at me.

Smugly smirking. He's caught me ogling him like a fool and now he knows what effect it has on me.

Jerk. I stick my tongue out at him and return to my attention to the cheese sandwiches.

Turning around to face the stove, I begin to grill the ham and cheese as I listen to Cade and his grandfather chit chatting. Simon asks him how everything is going with school and in preparation for the start of basketball season.

"When do I get to watch you play a basketball game?" Simon asks. "The last one I attended in person was a few years ago. Now you're some hot shot player."

Cade laughs boisterously. "Hardly, Gramps. Although, I have been starting the last two seasons. Our team's pretty good this year. Solid. We only lost two guys to the draft last year.

Most of my boys are returning and we feel good about our shot at the title."

Simon makes a humming sound at his grandson's proclamation. "That's wonderful. I'm so proud of you, Kincaid." I think it's sweet when he calls him by his full name.

There's a short stretch of silence before Cade continues. My ears instinctively perk up because his voice goes low and soft.

"I may not be playing the first few games, though. But we can get you some tickets to later in the season. Dad comes to most of the home games, not that you'd want to go with him. But maybe Ainsley can take you."

My head whirls over my shoulder and I raise my eyebrows at his comment. Me, attend a college sporting event? Unlikely. Admittedly, it would be kind of exciting to watch him out in his element. All hot and sweaty and out of breath…

Whoa. Don't even go there right now. Concentrate. Ham and cheese. Spatula. Tomato soup.

Cade sees my incredulous look, and probably reads the naughty thoughts all over my face, and his lips quirk up into that smug smile again because he knows he has me.

"Wouldn't you like to escort my gramps to one of my games, Ainsley?" He asks in an oh-so-innocent tone. "And I know *I'd* sure like it if you came to watch me play."

His tone reflects something not so innocent then and I can feel my cheeks flush. Damn him. Doesn't he realize that all I've been able to think about the last five days is how hot and jittery he left me last Saturday night? I've been keyed up ever since and unable to banish the lustful responses he awoke in me. I've been in a constant state of arousal.

Honestly, I wanted nothing more than to sleep with him that night. And I had secretly hoped that he'd put the moves on me so I didn't have a choice. But he didn't go back on his promise and was a complete gentleman, instead. Which pissed me off and made me happy at the same time. Spending time alone with him in his bedroom had my body shaking with need. I don't think I'd ever experienced that over another boy before.

To make matters worse, I had imagined my hands running over every single muscle in his chest, his back, his arms. He's like a living, breathing Hercules. Big and strong. And beautiful. I loved sifting my fingers through his soft mop of curls. And the rough abrasion of his short beard against my lips and neck when he kissed me. It lit me up in areas of my body that haven't gotten action for years.

Even when I said I had go, there was no pleading for me to stay. No promises that if I just laid back down he'd keep his hands to himself. He simply stood up, took my hand in his and walked me out to the front door where the Uber was waiting for me. And then kissed me senseless until the driver honked at us to get a move on.

Oh, an that. My heart clenches tightly even now to think about how he called and paid for the ride on my behalf. He wouldn't accept my money. Said it was the least he could do to make sure I got home safe, since he was in no state to drive.

Thoughtful. Sweet. And oh-so-gorgeous.

So tell me…how the hell am I supposed to say no to his request? His asking me to take Simon to watch him play basketball.

I'm just about to flip the grilled cheese sandwich over when I feel a very tall, hard body press against me from behind. Cade's hands land on my hips, his breath hot on my ear.

"You're looking especially gorgeous today, Ainsley."

His voice is like molten honey. Thick and rich. I want him to spread it all over my body and cocoon me in a prison of smooth silk.

I chuckle humorlessly as I look down at what I'm wearing. I'm in bright blue scrubs and my hair is pulled back in its usual pony tail. Nothing sexy or enticing, but I did spend a bit of time on my make-up since I knew I'd be seeing Cade.

"Flattery will get you nowhere. Look at me…I'm a frumpy-looking caregiver," I deadpan, stepping to the side and presenting my attire to him with an eye roll and a flap of my hand. "I probably smell like urine and bleach. If you think that's hot, you're nuts."

Cade looks over into the TV room and concludes that everyone, including his grandfather, is now watching a documentary and no one is paying us any attention.

"I want to kiss you so bad right now." His admission turns me on.

"Cade, I'm working." I say half-heartedly, hoping he won't care about that and do it anyway. To hell with the consequences of being seen.

He just gives me his killer grin and shrugs.

"So there's a rule that says you can't kiss on the job?"

I give him a snort of laughter because that's stupid. I'm sure there's nothing in my Employee Handbook about kissing while on duty. But I do take my role seriously and can't let my attention wander when I'm responsible for my patients.

"You're dumb," I lamely throw out at him. "Now go away, before I burn dinner."

He steps back to give me room and leans against the counter to watch me. His eyes roam over me, driven by lust and desire.

"I saw you checking me out earlier. Did you enjoy the show?"

Oh God. How embarrassing. I'm sure he's used to girls on campus gawking at his body all the time, and no doubt that he relishes in the fact that he is hotter than hell. But he's put me on the spot and I don't know how to respond.

Do I admit I liked it? Do I tell him that if I could, right this minute, I'd let my hands run up the length of his body and I'd use my tongue to lick up and down his totally-sculpted torso? Or do I act nonchalant about it, like if you've seen one, you've seen them all?

I decide to go with unimpressed. "Sure. It was okay."

His jaw locks tight, lips pinched and eyes narrow on me. "Just okay, huh? That's not what your drooling mouth told me when I caught you gawking."

"Gawking? I was not!" *Of course I was gawking.* "You are so full of yourself, Number 23. You think you're God's gift to women, don't you?" *Damn, you really are. And I want to unwrap you.*

"I don't think it. I *know* it, baby. And I also know what I saw. So even if you don't admit, I know the truth. You want me." His finger taps me on the nose with a little *thump*.

I place the sandwiches on the dinner plates and begin to fill the bowls of soup as a text message notification comes through on Cade's phone. Out of the corner of my eye I see him pull out his phone from his shorts pocket and look at it. Then he quickly puts it away.

"I gotta get going. Meeting up with the guys for a workout tonight."

"Oh, okay. Yeah, sure." I hope he doesn't hear the disappointment in my voice. I'm not sure what I expected, but I was hoping he'd be around for a little longer. My shift runs until ten tonight and it's only six o'clock right now. We barely had any time to talk and I can feel a small bloom of resentment in my heart. I'm a bit crestfallen.

Cade helps gather up the tray that I've just piled up with all the dinner plates and begins walking it to the dining area. I admire his fine ass with a frown as he walks ahead of me.

"You're checking me out again, aren't you?"

"Oh my God!" *I was absolutely checking him out.* "I'm just making sure you don't spill, idiot. Geez, you have such an ego."

Once we have everyone settled for dinner, Adriane comes back in and tells me to go take a break. I think she's done a pretty good job deducing that Cade and I are…well, I don't know what we are. Friends? Friends that make out? Whatever we are, she sees something between us. I give her a grateful smile and run to the restroom while Cade says goodbye to his grandfather.

We meet at the front door and step out onto the porch, and before I can even get the door closed behind me, Cade cups my cheeks and captures my mouth in an urgent, blistering kiss. Two quick kisses in succession follow and then I melt into him like an ice cube in the Sahara. His body isn't the only thing that's strong. Cade's lips are soft and full, yet strong in their command of my own mouth. He's demanding and thoroughly captivating.

And then it's over much too soon. Cade pulls away from me, leaving me bereft and wanting more. I want more of him. I don't want him to leave.

"I'll be back here to pick you up at ten."

Once again, Cade says and does something that I'm totally unprepared for. He just keeps throwing me for loops and doing the opposite of what I expect of him.

I cock my head to the side and meet his gaze. "What do you mean?"

His soft chuckle against my cheek tickles.

"It means I'm picking you up after your shift so you don't have to ride the bus home."

"Cade -" I warn, but he doesn't allow me a chance to refuse.

"No argument, Locker. I want to spend more time with you. Is that a problem for you?"

Yes. No... *Yes*, it is a problem. The more time I spend with him, the more I realize that he's almost too good to be true.

He's thoughtful, a gentleman, and extremely easy on the eyes. And he's like a human defibulator, because every time I'm around him he jumpstarts my heart.

So yeah, it is a huge problem that he's all these things and I'm unequivocally attracted to him to the point of no return.

What am I supposed to say to that? No Cade. Don't pick me up. I'd rather ride the Metro with all the seedy elements of Phoenix sitting right next to me, reeking of alcohol and their own shit or trying to grope me.

"*No*, it's a not a problem. But it's pretty presumptuous, don't you think? I've been fine on my own well before I met you...I don't need a chauffeur service." I say indignantly, but I fail at making my point when he just smiles down at me with a knowing grin.

Cade's lips brush my ear and sends shivers of excitement down my spine. He smells so good. A spicy intoxication of cologne with a hint of spearmint.

"Personally, I think it's more selfish than presumptuous because I need to see you again tonight. *Alone*. And I want to keep kissing you. And my hands want to touch you." As he says the words, his hands slide behind my back and rest just above my butt. If I wiggled just a little bit, his hands would fall to cover my ass. That wouldn't be a bad thing.

And then all I can do is agree with him. Because I need to see him again, too. He's very persuasive.

"Then I guess I'll see you later."

Chapter 12
CADE

"Dude, what's your rush? I thought we were all going out to Hungry Howie's tonight for wings and pizza?"

Carver is towel drying his hair, buck naked in the middle of the locker room where we're all getting showered and changed after our workout. Although practices haven't started yet for the season, the team unofficially practices together three nights a week. Afterwards, we usually go out for some form of nourishment and entertainment.

But tonight, I'm going to hang with Ainsley.

I don't know what it is about her, but I can't stop thinking about her. It's not something I ever thought I'd do. I actually chased her. I fucking sent her daily texts – just random, stupid shit over the last week to let her know she was on my mind. And then I called her the other night while I was lying in bed wondering what she was doing. It makes me sound like a pussy, but I don't care.

The problem is that we don't get to see each other much. I'm a busy guy, with school and basketball, but Ainsley's schedule is fucking insane. I don't know how she manages to always remain positive. Nothing seems to razzle her – especially not at the nursing home. I know I couldn't handle working there. She just has this way about her. Kind. Compassionate. Sweet.

She hasn't told me all that much about her family, but I've learned it's just her sister, her mom and Ainsley. When I told her about my twin sisters, she flipped her shit. Thought that was the coolest thing, which I found amusing. Although I'm fairly close to both of them, more so with Kylah than Kady, I do still find them slightly annoying at times. Even Ainsley admitted that while she has a strong relationship with her sister, Anika, she's dealing with the disgruntled teen attitude right now.

Even with that, she still seems completely devoted to her. It makes me like her all the more.

In the time that we have spent and gotten to know each other, there are still things I feel that has avoided talking about. She glosses over things about her life, speaking only in vague terms about her childhood. Like she has these dark places she's hiding and doesn't want me to know about.

But then again, I can't begrudge her since I haven't shared anything about my problems with the law or the reason for visiting my gramps so often. Part of me feels a twinge of guilt, but it's not exactly public knowledge at this point. Coach Welby promised it would be kept confidential, so unless someone digs into the public records of my arrest and court appearance, folks will stay none the wiser.

The only ones who know right now out of my friends are Carver and Lance. And I trust them to know they won't say anything. The rest of my team will know soon enough about my suspension when I don't get to play the first three games of the pre-season. I guess I'll cross that bridge when I come to it.

For now, it's business as usual. Except for my plans tonight. Ainsley is my plan for the night. And although I don't want it to appear that I'm rushing things, I definitely want more of her. Whether that leads to sex or not, I'm up for anything she'll let me do to her and with her. And my imagination is vast.

I try to steer my thoughts clear of getting Ainsley naked right now, considering I'm in a locker room of nude teammates. Pulling my gym shorts over my boxer briefs and slipping a T-shirt over my head, I reply to Carver about my skipping out on the night's activities.

"Sorry, bro. I got plans with someone a helluva lot prettier than you tonight."

Carver scoffs. "Doubtful, 'cause we all know I'm the prettiest of everyone." He poses in the body builder flex and kisses his right bicep. Good Lord, he's a vain dude.

"This happen to be that hot chick you had over last weekend? Goddamn, bro. She's got a pair of tits I'd like to fuck when you're done with her."

A flash of angry jealously floods my body and I whip my wet towel at his naked ass.

"Shut your fucking hole, douchewad," I scowl as he yelps from the slap of the cold material. "You're not getting anywhere near her tits. So don't even think about it."

I'm in no way interested in discussing my feelings toward Ainsley with Carver. At least not yet. The truth is, I don't really know what we have going on. Are we dating? A couple?

Defined relationships have never been my thing. I've always been too focused on partying and playing basketball to get serious with any one chick. But I have no reservations about seeing more of Ainsley. In fact, I crave it. It's an adrenaline rush, like the feeling I get when I'm dribbling down the court, my opponents surrounding me as I make the perfect jump shot.

Carver's sarcasm can sometimes be annoying.

"Oooh…someone's jealous over a chick. This must be serious, Griff," he shakes his dangling dick in front of my face as I lean over the bench to tie my shoes. "She got you by the gonads, bro? Have a magic pussy or something?" He laughs uncontrollably, making a few of the other guys turn their heads to see what's going on.

I push at his stomach so he stumbles against the locker. "Fuck you, Edwards. It's none of your fucking business. Now shut the fuck up."

Carver's easy-going attitude makes it hard to ever ruffle his feathers. He just snickers and struts back over to his gym bag and pulls out a pair of boxers, completely disregarding my outburst.

He's a great friend, and the biggest player I've ever known, both on and off the court. But he has a big mouth that's always yapping and giving shit. Typically, I can handle it, 'cause that's what guys do. We talk smack about each other, always looking for ways to rile one other up. On the court it's expected. It pumps you up, drives the competitor in you. Gives you the shot of adrenaline that's needed when you're playing.

When it comes to Ainsley, though, I'm a little less forgiving. It actually bothers me that he's talking about her like that. Sure, I've thought about her tits and her pussy. I'm a horny-ass motherfucker. But I'm not going to degrade her in front of my pals. That's not how I roll.

Pulling the strap of my gym bag over my shoulder, I turn to head out of the locker room, giving everyone a wave goodbye. When Carver says *"Toodles, twat-eater,"* I give him the finger and walk out the door with a grin.

I have about an hour before I have to pick up Ainsley, so I decide to run over to mom's and maybe eat whatever leftovers she has in the fridge and talk with her a little bit. I haven't seen her since my court hearing. In fact, I've avoided her calls and texts over the last two weeks, with the exception of my birthday and a few yes or no replies.

I'm a shitty son and she doesn't deserve that treatment. It's bad enough that she was walked all over and out on by my dad. So I hope me showing up unannounced will remind her that I do love her.

I pull into the driveway of my childhood home in Keirland, a suburb of Scottsdale. My dad is a prominent criminal attorney, which means I grew up in a wealthy, elite neighborhood. He was rarely ever home, always working or traveling, leaving my mom to dote on and raise the kids. She was loving, nurturing, and only occasionally would she smother me.

But I love her, regardless.

And she is a helluva a good cook. Although we could afford a housekeeper and cook, she always made our breakfasts, lunches and dinners on her own when she could. When I was in school, my friends and I would come home from basketball practice and scarf down the Snickerdoodle cookies (my favorite) and baked lemon bars she always had waiting for us. Everyone loved my mom.

It isn't just her skills in the home, though, that make her special. She is smart and extremely kind, unlike my friends' moms who were always gossiping about their neighbors, or trying to one-up each other with their clothes, and cars, and beauty regimens. She spends time volunteering at local charities and community events, and was always on the PTA and school booster organizations. In my mind, she is supermom.

She's also extremely intuitive and would always provide helpful advice to my boyhood problems - once she coaxed them out of me, of course. Part of me wonders if that's why I found my way home tonight. Maybe I secretly craved spilling my guts out about what I'm feeling for Ainsley. I need her advice because I feel like I'm in the deep end of an ocean and don't know how to swim.

"Hey mom!" I call out, stepping into the well-lit kitchen from the garage door. "Are you home?"

The smell of lasagna permeates the air and I check out the counter for food as I drop my bag of dirty clothes on the floor and round the corner. We have one of those great room kitchen floor plans where the room is divided by a ten-foot island in the middle. To the left is a large dining room with an eight-piece dining set, and to the right a couch and two chairs circling the stone fireplace.

It always seemed weird to have a fireplace in Arizona, but for people who live here their entire lives, the winters can get cold. Not for me, because I run hot, but my mom is always chilly and wrapped in a sweater indoors.

My eyes scan the dining room table first, taking in the burning taper candles and two place settings, the plates littered with half-eaten dinner. Two open bottles of wine are in the middle of the table, one completely empty and the other half full. Weird. She must've been entertaining tonight.

As I move further into the room, I see a pair of my mom's high-heeled pumps lying carelessly in the middle of the hallway. And right next to them, a pair of size thirteen men's loafers. What the hell? Is my dad here? I can't imagine he'd ever leave his shoes there. He's a total neat-freak.

I make my way down the hallway, now a little curious and anxious, passing the guest bathroom and my dad's former office. My parents' bedroom — *scratch that* — my mom's bedroom is on the main floor.

As I get closer, I hear moaning. Female moaning.

Oh shit. Is my mom sick?

My instincts kick in as I run the rest of the way down the hall and right through her bedroom door, which is ajar. What I find there concludes the reason for the moans. And they are certainly not brought on by an ill woman.

There, in my mother's California king bed is my mother - naked except for a bra - straddling an equally naked Mr. Roberts, our next door neighbor.

Holy fuck.

After a few seconds of shock, it finally dawns on me that I'm standing in my mother's bedroom watching her get it on with a man. She shrieks in panicked surprised as I blindly back out toward the door, shell shocked and utterly confused by what I've just witnessed.

When I do finally realize that I've just seen my own mother fucking Mr. Roberts, I nearly double over and vomit. That is not a scene any son ever wants to see his mother in.

I run back out to the kitchen, grab the half-full wine bottle and finish it in nearly two seconds flat, just as my mother comes running out, in the midst of tying up her bathrobe.

"Cade, what are you doing here?" Her voice is panicked hysteria.

I'm stunned and almost speechless. Almost.

Then an irrational anger sweeps over me and I feel the urge to hit something. Preferably Mr. Roberts.

"What am *I* doing here?" I practically spit out the accusatory question. "What the fuck is Mr. Roberts doing here, mom? Are you seriously fucking our neighbor? You might as well be fucking the pool boy, that's how cliché this is. Jesus Christ."

I open the wine fridge and pull out another bottle, uncorking it swiftly and taking a huge gulp. The warm acidity of the Pinot goes down smoothly and I start to feel a bit more in control of my emotions. But I'm still fucking pissed.

It's not like I expect my parents are ever getting back together. They've been divorced now for over a year. And I wouldn't want my dad to get that chance again. My mom is too good for him.

She's a very pretty woman. Tall, slender, with a sleek tawny-colored bob that lands at her shoulders. We have the same eyes, even though hers look much larger on her small face. She's what people call a classic beauty. And much to my frustration in high school, a MILF.

So I don't doubt that she gets the attention of the male persuasion. But it's not something I ever wanted to think about – much less see – when it came to my mom getting back on the old proverbial horse.

Ugh. Now I'm picturing her straddling Mr. Roberts again. Ew. My stomach churns the wine I just downed.

"Cade, let me explain," she pleads quietly, her hand placed gently on my bicep, which I shrug off.

"I don't want to hear it. It's none of my business."

"Honey. I don't know what you think it is, but John and I…well, we've been dating. For a while now. And he loves me."

My brain can't quite comprehend the words. Dating. A while. Loves me.

I'm an adult and understand the nature of human relationships, even though I've never been in one myself. But learning that your own mother is dating a new man, who is not your father, and fucking him in the same house your parents raised you, is just a difficult pill to swallow.

My mind goes back to all the past barbeques and block parties we've had in our neighborhood over the years. Did Mr. Roberts – *John* – have a thing for my mom even then? He's close to ten years older than my mom. Graying hair. Glasses. A little pooch of a belly. But overall, somewhat handsome for an older dude.

I recall that his wife died a few years back from lung cancer, even though she never smoked. I remember going to their house after the memorial service. John has two older daughters, both married and with kids. He seemed genuinely upset and saddened by his loss. I shrug off the thoughts that they had a married fling.

In a way, I wish she was fucking the pool boy. Then it wouldn't be so real, because from the sounds of it, this thing between them could be serious.

My throat is coated with the remnants of the wine, so I have to clear my throat before I speak. And I'm surprised by my own question.

"Do you love him, too?"

A small wisp of a smile adorns her face as she sits down on one of the bar stools.

"John's a lovely man. He's generous with his time, kind, a good father…"

I read between the lines. Your father was never around. Your father was a hard ass. Your father was an asshole.

"You didn't answer the question. Are you in love with him?"

She nods her head.

"He's asked me to marry him, Cade. I do love him. But, it will be an adjustment. I was going to wait until Christmas, when the twins are home to announce it then." She hangs her head in contemplation. I can see she feels guilty she's upset me. "I'm so sorry you had to find out this way. That was never my intention."

That's my mother for you. Always concerned about her kids, even now, she's trying to protect me from hurt. I can see it in her eyes how much she is holding back. She really does love him, yet she is worried about my ability to handle the truth.

I place a wine glass on the counter in front of her and fill it half-way, topping off my own next. Lifting it up, indicating she should do the same, I give her glass a clink.

"Well, here's to poorly kept secrets and new loves," I say, truly meaning it. My anger has dissipated now that I see the truth behind what's going on. "You deserve it, mom. And if he's good to you, then that's all that matters."

"Oh honey." She sniffles and wipes a tear that's running down her cheek.

A shuffling sound from behind me has me turning my head to find John slowly entering the kitchen, a weary expression on his face. He's quiet and reserved, obviously apprehensive as to what he might find going on in here. I could be a total dick about this and give him hell, but I man-up, and turn toward him and give him my hand instead.

"Mr. Roberts. Nice to see you."

"John, please," he says, giving me a solid handshake, his eyes lighting up in appreciation. I watch him move around the counter and stand behind my mother, his hands landing on top her shoulders with an affectionate squeeze.

Reflecting back, I don't think I ever saw my dad do that to my mom. Give her any sort of public displays of affection, not even in our own home. I'm not even sure they ever kissed in front of us, unless it was just a peck on the cheek. Weird. Funny how as a kid you never pay attention to your parents in that way.

"Cade, I'm very sorry you…uh, found out about your mother and I in this manner."

I give him a wave of my hand.

"Please, don't worry about it. I apologize that I stopped over unannounced and interrupted your…uh, date." We all laugh at my attempt to downplay the situation. It's not every day a son walks in on his mom doing the nasty with a guy.

My mom stands up and wraps her arms around me, hugging me tightly.

"Honey, you are welcome home any time, no matter what. This is still your home. And I love it when you come to visit me."

She then looks around as if in search of something.

"What?" I ask, following the direction of her eyes.

Shrugging, she sits back down.

"Well, usually you come accompanied by a load of dirty clothes. So I'm just surprised you don't have anything with you."

I cross my arms over my chest and give her my most appalled glare. "What? Can't a guy just come home to visit his mom once in a while because he loves her?"

My mom's no dummy. She knows it's something else, so I capitulate and come clean.

"Fine...I was hungry and was looking for some home cooked food."

Laughter fills the kitchen, leading into the next thirty minutes of discussion over the best damn lasagna and tiramisu I've ever had.

As I get ready to leave to go pick up Ainsley, my mom walks me to the front door.

"Thank you, Cade, for being so understanding of things. You've grown into such a fine young man."

"Mom..."

She places her hand on my cheek, her head back so she can look up at me. "No, really. I'm so proud of you. I realize that the last year, even though you have your own life at school, things have changed a lot. I'm sorry if you were hurt by your father's and my divorce."

Honestly, I was hurt at first. But I was more pissed and angry at my dad for his betrayal of my mom. I vowed that I would never, ever do that to the woman I loved. I don't want to become like him.

"I'm glad you found someone to love you. And screw dad for losing the best thing he ever had."

I lean down and place a kiss on her cheek and a brief hug.

When she steps back, her voice is quiet, but authoritative. "It wasn't just his fault, Cade. I made mistakes, too. But that's between the two of us. I just don't want you to hate your dad anymore. He's trying to be the best dad he knows how."

I grunt in opposition. "Yeah, sure."

"Was there another reason you stopped by today? Aside from food?"

Telling her about Ainsley would be so easy to do. She'd listen. And give me advice. But I know she has other things on her mind right now.

"Mom, are you sure you should wait 'til the holidays to tell Ky and Kady about Mr...er, John? You know especially how close Ky is to dad. Maybe waiting isn't such a good idea."

She gives it a moment to consider my position and nods her head.

"You're right. I'll consider telling them sooner, if the time is right."

"Okay." I grab the handle of the door as I'm about to leave. "I love you, mom. And thanks for the dinner."

She grins. "You're welcome, baby. I'm here whenever you want to stop by!"

I laugh and wave my hand in the air behind me as I walk out to my car. "Thanks, mom. But next time, I'll make sure to call ahead!"

Chapter 13
AINSLEY

"Are you hungry? Do you want to grab something to eat?"

I've just buckled myself in to Cade's sporty little car as he makes his way around to the driver's side. It's fairly late on a Thursday night, but I don't have to work tomorrow morning and my first class isn't until eleven a.m., so I have some leeway tonight to just go out and have fun with Cade.

In fact, not counting his birthday party, this is kind of our first date.

Cade slides in and starts the engine, which sends a sensual thrill down my spine at how masculine the roar of his engine sounds.

"You changed." He says offhandedly, switching topics on me.

I take a quick peek down at what I'm now wearing. Although I hadn't planned on going out tonight, I did bring an extra change of clothes with me. I don't like wearing my scrubs home because they're usually filthy.

I confirm that yes, indeed, I changed my clothes and then throw out the question on my mind.

"Are we on an actual date, Cade Griffin?" I add a sarcastic inflection in my voice so he knows I'm just playing with him.

He's easy to goof around with. It's funny to think back at what I thought of him when we first met. I thought he was such a jerk. Like total ego-maniac, full of himself, jerk. Now that I know him and have spent time with him, I've come to find that he's a really decent guy.

Cade shifts toward me in his seat and raises an eyebrow at me, along with a smirk.

"Why yes, Ainsley Locker, it is an actual date. So where would you like to go?"

I try to remember the last time I ate out. Aside from Bristol's Café, where I nibble on pastries during my breaks, I haven't eaten out for well over a year. A few times, I've picked up fast food for Anika on my way home from work, but an actual sit-down restaurant hasn't been on the radar. Or part of my budget.

"Can we go to the Mellow Mushroom? I haven't had pizza for such a long time."

Cade laughs and then gapes at me like I'm an alien that just plopped in his car.

"Are you for reals? If you don't eat pizza at least twice a day, then I don't believe you're actually a college student. You're an imposter!" He jokes.

I give him a shy smile and shrug my shoulders, acknowledging I know it's hard to believe.

"I guess I'm not your typical student."

Just as I finish my sentence, Cade's hand wraps around the back of my neck and pulls me toward him. And then his lips devour me.

The kiss takes my breath away.

I melt.

I soar.

I fall.

I wonder when I'm going to touch back down to Earth. Because this connection with Cade can't possibly last. It feels too good to be true.

"Ainsley," he murmurs into my lips. "I love that you're not typical."

We make the fifteen-minute drive and end up parking a block down the street from Mill Avenue. When we get to the restaurant, we find it's packed, brimming over with students. Since I don't get out – like ever - I'm surprised to see things so busy this late on a weeknight.

Cade has my hand clutched in his as we walk up to the hostess podium and I swear a hush goes over the crowd in the waiting area. They all know who he is and their whispers quickly make their way through the restaurant. A swarm of busy bees with craning necks and gawker stares.

There's no less than ten groups of people waiting for tables, so I'm more than a little shocked when the hostess, Amy, says she can get us seated right away. Cade just nods his head and drags me behind him, as I glance around with guilty eyes at the sea of faces we've just cut in front of in the waiting area.

Amy directs us to a small table on the upper deck in the corner. As we pass all the tables along the way, Cade is constantly greeted by people calling his name and giving him high-fives. It's just like the time in the cafeteria. It's so strange to be the center of attention like this. I make a mental note to ask him how he does it.

"Is this okay?" Cade asks me as we get seated at the table. I just nod in agreement, as I avert my eyes from everyone's stares.

The hostess hands us the menus and tells us our waiter will be right with us to get our drink orders.

I peruse the list of pizza variations for a few minutes and when I finally look up, I find Cade staring at me. Grinning like the cat who ate the canary.

"What? Why are you smiling at me?"

"This doesn't faze you, does it?" His hand makes a wide sweep of the room, toward all the people who are probably at this moment Tweeting or SnapChatting that Cade Griffin, star ASU basketball player, is 'in da houz'.

I shake my head. "Well, it is a little different. I can't say I've ever been a fan of attention. I have to keep checking that I'm wearing clothes, because it feels like I'm naked and everyone is staring at me like I'm some sort of freak."

Cade waggles his eyebrows suggestively.

"I wouldn't mind seeing that. And freak is not the word that comes to mind when I picture you naked."

"Perv." I give him an eye roll, but secretly I like it when he gets all flirty. It's his special gift.

"Seriously, though. Does it bother you that everywhere you go, people talk and stare?"

His expression tells me it's not even an issue.

"Nah. I guess I'm used to it. You've probably figured out by now that I'm kind of an attention whore," he grins and I laugh, because yeah, it's a pretty accurate description. He continues.

"I remember the first time I got asked for my autograph. It was after we won the Pac-12 division championship my sophomore year. This group of kids, probably no more than nine or ten years old, came rushing up to me after the game, all of them talking at once about how I made that three-pointer, or the turn-around fade away move I made in the game that sent us into overtime. They all looked up to me like I was some kind of hero. And since then, well...you just become accustomed to it. The press after the games. The fans outside the locker rooms..."

"The groupies." I cock my head to the side and raise my eyebrows.

He coughs into his hand, clearing his throat. "Yeah. Okay. Them, too. What can I say? Most girls just want to get with me because I'm recognizable. I'm not gonna lie, I've always gotten a hard-on for that. I like the celebrity of it. And I know it won't last forever, so I've enjoyed it while I can. But with you, Ainsley..."

He stops himself and reaches across the table to grab my hand in his. His eyes flash to mine, telling me without words that this is special. That I'm special to him.

"You don't care about who I am on the court or seek out the notoriety and fame" – he uses air quotes – "or my position, or my car. If I'm not mistaken, you might actually like me because of *me*. And I happen to like all of *you*."

Well damn. I can't argue that point.

I give him a half-shrug, lifting my chin to him. "Meh. You're okay."

Faster than I could blink, Cade grabs the bottom of my wooden chair and scoots it next to him so our legs touch. Then he leans in to my ear, brushing the hair that's fallen forward off my shoulder.

"Just okay, huh? We'll see about that. I have many more talents than just basketball playing." He skims a long finger down my neck, sending shivers scattering across my skin. Then he kisses my neck, sucking gently at the exposed flesh. The feeling is like nothing else and it lights me up like the Fourth of July night sky.

"Mmm," I murmur, not realizing it's me who made the sound. "Maybe you could show me those talents later."

He lets out a growl as our waiter descends upon our table. Before he's even able to say good evening, Cade jumps in.

"I think we've decided to place our order to go."

****

The smell of fresh, hot pizza permeates Cade's car with the most tantalizing aroma, but neither of us really care at the moment. We're sitting in his parked car in front of his apartment and the minute he turns off the engine, our hands and mouths are everywhere.

It's possible that I'm just really horny because it's been well over a year since I've messed around with a guy. Or, it could be that Cade is just irresistibly sexy and he makes me want to do very wicked things to him.

Cade's hand slips under my T-shirt and his thumb flicks over my sensitive nipple, covered by my lace bra. With that one simple touch I'm just about gone. Geez, the moan that comes out of my mouth would make a whore at a church on Sunday blush with embarrassment. Or maybe it was the sound he made. A frenzied groan. A deep, needy, beastly growl.

"God, Ainsley," he murmurs, attacking my neck with his lips. Taking ownership of my breast with his hand. Driving me wild with need. "I want you so bad."

You know in romance novels when the woman can only respond with *"Please"* because she's in such a bad state of arousal? Like it's the only word in the English language that she can possibly form in the heat of the moment? I always thought that was so stupid. Please *what*? What exactly is she asking for?

Now I understand it because it's the only word that can be used to articulate what it is that I want. *Please* take me inside. *Please* don't stop. *Please* do whatever you want to me. *Please* don't make me regret this.

So that's exactly what I say.

"Please."

It doesn't take us long to get from zero to one hundred and soon our breathing is a cacophony of inhales and exhales, with a mixture of moans and indecipherable words. I haven't even gotten my seat belt undone and Cade is leaning over the seat practically on my lap, covering me with his large frame.

"Take me inside." I command, as he releases me in agreement.

He's out the door and opening the passenger door faster than I can blink an eye. I've unfastened my seatbelt and grab my bag when he's taking my hand in his and leading me into the apartment.

I look back at the car as we hit the porch. "You forgot the pizza."

"Fuck the pizza," he laughs, opening the door and whisking me inside straight to his bedroom. I'm vaguely aware of his roommate, Lance, who is sitting on the couch with a drink in hand playing a video game. Cade doesn't even give him a second glance. He just grunts out a greeting as we walk by, as Lance hollers out a "*whoop whoop*".

I should be embarrassed by our rapid entrance and urgency to make it to the bedroom. It's fairly obvious what we are about to do. I doubt Lance would believe that I'm here to study. But he's a guy. And living with Cade, I'm sure he's very familiar with the type of entertaining that occurs in Cade's room. Just that single thought creates a lump in my throat that's hard to swallow.

I'm not the kind of girl that easily falls in bed with a guy. I'm not an easy lay. I take this seriously. And I want Cade to know it. But I don't want to ruin the mood, either. Such a conundrum.

Cade seems to sense my hesitation — maybe because my feet are glued to the floor just inside his bedroom door. He turns toward me, shutting and locking the door behind me, and then places his hands on my hips. He pulls me against him and I can feel the hard ridge of his erection against my thigh.

"We don't have to do anything you don't want to do, Ains. I swear. We don't..."

I place my fingers over his mouth, breaking off whatever else he was about to say. His eyes linger on my lips and I lean in on my tippy toes and trace his mouth with my tongue. He grants me access as my tongue slips into his mouth, and my lips explore the shape and texture of him.

My body buzzes with excitement, brimming over with unfulfilled desire. I want this. I want him.

I've never been bold when it comes to speaking my mind sexually. Maybe it's because I have limited experience or just never felt the same passion with my previous encounters. Those were somewhat awkward and lacked the type of passion I'm feeling right now. But something completely different happens when I'm with Cade. A type of sensual power courses through me, boosting my confidence like a shot of B-12.

I take a swipe at his lower lip before biting it between my teeth, yanking on it. My hands travel the length of his torso, down his ridged abs to the edge of his waistband. His mouth curves in a wicked grin against my lips and then I let go of his bottom lip.

"I want to do everything with you." My voice sounds hoarse. Husky.

Needing no further encouragement, Cade grabs the neck of his T-shirt from the back and yanks it over his head as I stand mesmerized. I'm assaulted visually by a wall of tanned and chiseled flesh. He's like my own personal mountain to climb. Cling to.

I don't know how long I stand there in a stupor, but his snicker brings me back to earth.

"You like what you see?" His voice is also husky. Gravely with desire.

I tip my head and roll my eyes, a common occurrence when I'm with him. He brings out my snarkiness.

"Do you even need to ask? You're kind of perfection."

He says nothing in return, but with one powerful arm, he curls me into him, his hands locking around my waist to hold me in place. As if I would consider going anywhere else.

I turn my face to the side and my cheek and breasts press up against his rock-hard chest. I inhale and my senses go haywire. He smells so sexy. Spicy sandalwood and something all Cade. There's a soft patch of chest hair that snakes down between his pecs and it tickles my face.

Cade's hands move down my back, lifting my shirt and my arms instinctively rise above my head to allow him to remove it. We're now skin-to-skin, the contact I crave, the warmth I need. The feeling is incredible. Heat wicks along my body, leaving a wake of sensation everywhere he touches me. I turn my head and my tongue darts out to lick his pecs, as I move along a path to find one of his tan, perfectly shaped nipples. He sucks in a breath as I spear the tip of my tongue over the small nub, my own body answering as my own nipples tingle with a sharp pull. I press a palm to his chest, rolling the nipple between my fingers.

His lips travel down my jawline, dipping into the curve of my neck, where his open-mouth kiss leaves me shuddering with a pulsing need between my legs. Cade's fingers thread through my hair, bringing me back to where he wants me as he kisses me again. He thrusts his tongue into my mouth again, and I'm dizzy from the heat. My panties are wet now and all I crave is his touch.

Speaking of panties…I'm so lost in the kisses he's given me that I barely registered Cade has been busy unbuttoning my shorts, slipping his hand past my belly button and down between my legs. Holy shit. He's stealthy good. I can feel my insides quivering as his finger slips underneath now soaked panties, touching me where no other man has been in a very long time.

I should be embarrassed by how wet I am. By how wet he's made me with just a few touches and kisses. But I'm not. I'm turned on beyond belief.

From the sound that escapes his throat, low and deep, he doesn't mind it, either.

"Ainsley," he says with a rasp.

I buck against his hand, my own body instinctively taking over to find the friction it requires. I arch my back and he bows on top of me, his heavy breath coming out in pants against my ear. And then he swings around me so my back is flush to his front, one hand still down the front of my pants, the other now cutting a path to cup my breast.

I shameless gyrate against him, his heavy erection pressing between my ass cheeks. He feels big. Like Superman big – steely hard - and I wonder what he'll look like. Is he cut or uncut? I've never seen an uncut cock before.

I slide my hand between us and palm his cock, rubbing it slowly against the thin cover of his shorts. Cade smothers a groan in my hair. I can feel him twitch and grow unbelievably harder and bigger. His lips find mine again, my head tilting up and back, as he takes ownership and removes all other thoughts past or future from my brain. All there is in this moment is the present.

Our bodies shift forward toward his bed in front of me. Just as my knees hit the edge, he whips me around and pushes me back so I land with a soft thud against his ginormous mattress.

His fingers find the belt loop of my shorts and give a hard yank, bringing them down past my ankles. I'm naked with the exception of my white lace bra and cotton panties. I raise my eyes to Cade towering over me, his bare chest on full display and his eyes heated with lust. I reach out to drag him down on top of me. Before he falls into place, he quickly removes his shorts, dragging them along with his briefs, down and off.

And that's when the truth is revealed and I see him in all his naked glory.

For all that's good and holy. Cade's fully extended cock is huge.

While he leans over to reach inside his bedside stand to grab a condom, I have the unobstructed view of his dick. His full length curves a little to the left and the mushroom tip nearly touches his belly button, which is an outie, by the way. I make a mental note to explore that later.

But first, all I want to do is reach out and touch him.

Because a cock like Cade's needs to be worshipped. And worshipped well.

Chapter 14
CADE

Holy fuck. My mouth promptly goes dry and my legs feel like they belong to a new foal.

Ainsley's hand is wrapped tight around the base of my cock as she begins stroking me into a semi-conscious state. I think I'm going to pass out from the pleasure she's giving me.

I bend my knee and place it on the bed next to her hip, closing my eyes so I can concentrate on her ministrations. The pleasure is too intense for me to even try to keep my eyes open – even though to watch her overcome with sensations is so hot.

Fighting the urge to let my leg fall and nestle on top of her, I imagine all the things I plan to do to her tonight. My dick swells in her grip and all I want in that moment is to sink deep inside her and take us both over the edge.

Don't get me wrong. I'm not a fast-shooter. I know how to pace myself when I'm with a woman. Learned early on that you always to take care of your partner first because it's one of the best aspects of the entire experience – to watch her come while you're fingering, eating, or fucking her.

And it would be so easy to just let her continue to jack me off until I come all over her hand and stomach. It would be fucking hot. The way Ainsley's small hand pumps my cock makes me want to lose my ever-loving mind. If she keeps at this, I'm going to explode in about ten seconds flat. So that's why I need to redirect things to keep myself under control.

She's propped up with one elbow on the bed, the other wrapped around my shaft. Reluctantly, I remove her hand, which feels fucking phenomenal, and reach around her back to undo her bra. Flicking the snaps open, I watch with rapt interest as the straps fall down shoulders, the cups slipping away to expose her gorgeous, supple tits.

Christ Almighty.

My breath catches.

I've seen a lot of tits in my experience — but none hold a candle to Ainsley's. They are perfect.

Engorged and generously full, but not oversized. The rosy pink nipples are peaked from arousal and the pink tips pucker teasingly, calling me to taste, suck and bite. And I do just that.

Leaning over her, I push her back watch her hair spill over the pillow as she falls to the bed. She licks her lips and I can't help but pin them with mine. We kiss for several minutes, allowing my hand to explore the map of her breast. Moving from her mouth, I take a nipple into my mouth, wetting it with my tongue that's still mingled with Ainsley's taste.

The flavor and feel of her breast has my head spinning. She bucks against me in response, as I suck and lick. She pushes her breast further into my mouth, moaning out as she does, giving me more to feast on. I lave my tongue over her sensitive flesh until I pull it tightly into my mouth and suck. Hard. Just the sound of her raspy moan has my dick practically ready to fuck the mattress.

I take the opportunity to move to the other breast, sliding my hand and tongue over that soft, fleshy globe. Playing with the hard nub with my fingers, I tweak and pinch, followed by a smooth lick from my tongue. I do this several times because she seems to love the variation of hard and soft. Rough and gentle.

Moving to my elbow on my side, my leg thrown high over her thigh to nudge her legs open, giving me more room so I can slip my hand under her waistband and into her panties. My mouth waters at the first touch – the wetness coating the cotton panel. I'm dying for a taste. To bury my nose in her pussy. She makes me so hungry to learn what turns her on.

Our bodies move simultaneously, tilting our hips for friction — using each other to get off. My hard shaft rubs against her thigh and her pelvis presses into my finger, poised to enter her cotton-covered entrance.

I slide my body down her side, shuddering at the softness of her hips and legs. My breath comes out in pants as I'm finally at my destination, the tip of my nose nudging the soft cleft covered by her underwear. She tenses for a second, her head flying off the pillow to look down at me. I smell her arousal. It's heady.

"I'm going to eat you out. And you're going to love it." I command. She flops back down, and I watch her belly button flatten and sink in with her inhale. She relaxes briefly as my fingers remove the imposing material hiding what I covet the most.

The scent of her has me dangerously close to losing it and I snap into focus, lingering over the banquet she's given me — a feast which fills my deep and urgent hunger for her. It's erotic. It's perfect. It's almost too much.

My tongue dips, testing to her readiness, pleased when I find her bare lips coated in arousal. Soft, silky, and wet. A breathy moan escapes her lips and her hips shoot up off the bed. I place my left palm across her pelvic bone to gently keep her in place. I nudge her thighs so she opens to me fully. Placing my right arm in the crook behind her knee, I bend it upward so I have the room to make her go wild.

"Cade…" she exhales, stiffening slightly. I read the uncertainty in her blue eyes.

"Let me in, baby. I want this so bad."

An almost inaudible "okay" comes out in a soft whisper. And I proceed to show her how wild she makes me.

Ainsley gasps and groans, thrashes and bucks. I fucking love how uninhibited she is. It's sexy as hell. I can tell she's getting close because her breathes get harsher, faster. I show no mercy. Once I'm started, I won't stop until the end. Until she's screaming my name and fucking my face.

I kick it up a notch, giving her long, concentrated licks up her center, dipping in her entrance and then sucking at her clit. And when I latch on to that swollen numb, I really suck it. Hard. And just like that, her body stiffens against my face and screams out like a wild banshee and comes long and hard against my mouth.

I take a peek up at her to find her hands gripping my bed cover above her head, and her face turned to the side, a blissed out expression across her face. Absolutely beautiful.

"Wow." She whispers softly, followed by a satisfied sigh. "That was…wow."

Being the cocky bastard that I am, I can only agree with her. "I know."

But sometimes I don't, because some girls are liars. Although I feel fairly confident that I've mastered my pussy eating techniques over the years, I know some chicks don't like being eaten out and instead of telling me that when I go down on them, they'll fake it.

The biggest turn on for me is the fact that I know Ainsley truly enjoyed herself. She let go and showed her vulnerability – and trust - by allowing me access to her body in this manner. And let me tell you – there's no greater feeling for a guy than making a girl orgasm. I feel like beating my chest and shouting out, "Me, Tarzan!" Because that's how you feel. And right now, I feel like a wild jungle beast.

I lean over the bed and unwrap the condom, sliding it over my thick shaft. I'm not gonna lie. I'm a big boy, in more ways than one. At six foot five, two-hundred pounds of muscle, my dick measures up. It's never been a disappointment to me or any of the girls I've slept with. I close my eyes as Ainsley's hand reaches down and closes over my shaft and gives me a good yank from base to tip. Fuck that feels really good.

Sweetness

When I open them, again, we lock eyes, her intense blue sapphires blazing with heat, as she rubs my cock in even, measured strokes. My body craves release, but I want to enjoy this sensation a little longer. And I need to confirm we're doing this before I go any further.

"Are you sure?"

She nods her head languidly, as I position myself at her entrance. I rub my latex covered-head between her slick folds a few times, using her arousal to lube me up good, because I know it may be a tight fit. And then I slowly push my way in. Straight to heaven.

We moan simultaneously as I enter her body. I feel her walls constrict and conform around my cock as she accommodates my girth and size. Once I'm to the hilt, I slowly pull out, back to her entrance, and then slam back in again. I do this several times in slow succession, and each time, she gasps like it's the best thing in the world.

And fuck. It is.

The. Best. Fucking. Thing. In. The. World.

Ainsley places her hands on my ass and digs into my cheeks with her nails, which are thankfully filed short. But it feels good. She moans every time I hit a spot deep inside her and I feel her tighten around me. My balls are already tightening and my load set to launch like a rocket, so I think about my basketball stats to keep from blowing too soon.

We move in sync, our heart rates spiking faster as we climb closer to release. I want her to come again so I can feel her tight inner walls spasm around me. I shift to the left and bring my right hand between our bodies, wedging it in so my thumb can caress her clit. Her reaction is priceless as her eyes spring open and she bows upward into my touch. Searching for release. Calling out for satisfaction.

"Are you close?" That's all I can manage to get out, as my concentration is sequestered to keeping my orgasm at bay.

"Mmm-hmm," she hums, her hands now scraping into my back like painful razorblades. Whether she knows it or not, Ainsley is a little wildcat. And I love that. So I rock into her harder. Hoping to bring her with me. All the while my thumb makes tight circles between her legs.

I can feel her take a deep inhale, holding and clutching it as she tightens around my cock. On the exhale, Ainsley cries out loudly, which I'm certain Lance hears from the living room. Her sounds of pleasure are enough to push me over the edge. She's loud and sexy and it turns me the fuck on.

Sweetness

I pump once more, my cock throbbing, desperate for release that's sure to come any second now. And then I begin to feel the telltale tingle at the base of my spine as I throw my head back in ecstasy. An orgasm the size of a tsunami barrels through me as I shoot my release into her hot, pliant body.

I shudder. Completely spent. A strangled moan escapes my lungs, and I bury my head in the crook of her neck. Breathing in her sweet orange scent mixed with sex. I'm not going to let her move for the next week. She feels too good.

Our bodies are relaxed and sated for the moment, heavy and sticky with sweat and sex. I pull out of her tight heat and roll to the side, holding the base of the condom as I do. I grab some tissues on my bedside table to dispose of the used rubber, tossing it in the trash can across the room. Three-pointer.

I throw my arms up in victory, congratulating myself on my nice shot.

I turn back toward Ainsley who is now grinning at me. Her cheeks are still flushed as she pulls the sheet up to cover her breasts. Bummer for me. I wouldn't mind continuing to play with them 'til I get hard again. Which shouldn't take long.

"You really do eat, sleep, breathe basketball, don't you?" Her voice is soft with a hint of amusement.

"Yeah, pretty much."

"When did you start playing?"

I think back to the first time I held a basketball in my hands. I was probably two, maybe three years old. There's something about the elation I get when I take the ball to the hoop. Exhilaration formed through the control of the ball, my footwork, defending my position in the face of my opponents. And the wild cheers and adoration from those watching me play. It's a heady mix of narcissism and ego stroking. It's also intense and takes a lot of practice.

"When I was really young," I explain, smoothing her hair from her temple and spooning her from the side. "I played on my first team when I was maybe fourth grade. After that, I started attending summer basketball camps and by the time I was in high school, it just became part of who I am."

She nods in understanding.

"That's cool. I don't know what that's like to enjoy something so much that you want to do it every day."

I wink and wiggle my eyebrows suggestively, strumming my thumb under the curve of her sheet-covered breasts.

"I can give you something you'd enjoy doing every day."

Sweetness

She playfully brushes my arm away. "Horndog."

"Hey, get your mind out of the gutter," I chide, gripping the sheet and pulling it down to expose her creamy flesh. My lips hover over her hardened nipples as I glance up through my lashes and smile. "But if you want something to do that will be enjoyable and comes with health benefits...I will gladly be your hobby."

"Health benefits, huh? Do go on."

My cock immediately perks up again as I nibble and lick at her, the sexy sounds of her moans and quiet gasps making me hard as rock. I know it's getting late, and I'm not sure how she feels about staying the night, but I want to fuck her at least one more time before she has to go. My body is in a state of perpetual arousal because of her. I want to lick, taste, and fuck her senseless as many times as I can – for as long as she'll let me.

"Mmm," she murmurs, arching into me as I roll her onto her back and take more of her flesh between my lips. I suck hard in different spots, leaving little red marks along the way. "That feels so good."

I peel back the sheet and her sleek body is now laid out before me, as I skim my hand over her tits, down her flat belly.

Just as I do, her stomach rumbles loudly. If I didn't know it came from her, I'd think it was an earthquake. It was that loud.

"You're hungry," I offer up, stating the obvious. "Shit. I didn't feed you like I promised. Let me go get the pizza. I'll be right back." I stand up and find my pants on the floor, tugging them on as fast as I can. I feel horrible that I didn't even give her a proper date with dinner and drinks. I guess we were starved for other things.

She pushes herself up against my headboard, reaching for her T-shirt to throw on. I quickly pull it from her grasp, watching her wide-eyed expression and question in her eyes.

"No clothes," I order, secretly wondering if I'm an asshole for making my demand. "You're staying naked, because I may give you time to eat, but I'm not letting you leave here tonight until I've tapped that again." I head toward the door. Before I turn the knob, I look back at her over my shoulder and wink.

Ainsley is a wet-dream. Her long, silky hair is mussed from sex, fanning down over her face, her cheeks aglow, and her eyes hazy with passion. She's gorgeous. And in this moment, I realize that I don't want her to leave tonight at all.

"Don't move. I'll be right back."

Sweetness

I make my way quietly down the hallway, hoping to remain undetected. I don't want any questions tonight from the guys. It's well past midnight, but I see the flicker of the TV from the living room as I round the corner. The top of Lance's dark head bobs back and forth against the back of the couch, one leg extended across the cushions, and one foot on the floor. He's holding his phone in his hand and it looks like he's texting. Or maybe Snapchatting. Not sure. Don't care.

All I'm concerned with is getting my girl something to eat and drink. Reaching in to the fridge, I pull out a couple of drinks when I hear Lance's voice coming from across the room.

"So, the hottie from the other night...nice. I was wondering if you were tapping that. She screams loud as fuck."

Something inside me rages with jealousy. Just the fact that he comments on Ainsley's appearance and her climaxing high notes breaks something loose inside me, causing me to curse under my breath. I don't even want him looking in her direction. Yeah, she's smoking hot, with tits and ass for days. But she's mine.

We've never had any rules about hoops hunnies that we've hooked up with. Once we're done, they are free game to have a go at any of the guys. But Ainsley is not one of those girls, and I want Lance to know it.

Whatever my feelings are about Ainsley in the moment, and whatever she ends up being to me, I will not treat her like any of the other girls I've slept with.

"Bro, keep your eyes and hands off her."

My voice is low and stern, with enough malice to prove I mean what I say. Lance swings his head over the couch cushion and grunts.

"Whoa, settle down there, Cowboy. I'm not looking for sloppy seconds. I was just telling it like it is. But seriously – didn't know you went back for seconds. That's new."

"Dude, it's not seconds 'cause you fucking interrupted us the other night when you had to take a leak. But regardless, it's none of your business."

Lance cocks his head to the side and scratches his chin. He shrugs his shoulders in resignation.

"Don't remember much of anything that night. But I'm sorry I inadvertently cock blocked you." He apologizes, looking genuinely sincere. "But wait, if you were with her that night, why the hell are you with her again, Griff? You're never with the same girl twice."

It's understandable why he's asking. In all the time I've lived with Lance, he's never seen me with the same girl more than once, because it's never happened. And it's not because I'm some sort of player – well, not that I'd admit to – but it's only because I've never been interested in making a connection with a girl. I didn't want any relationship. And I certainly didn't want a clingy girlfriend.

Everything with Ainsley is different. For one, she's not into me because I'm a starting basketball player. I had to chase her – and even then she resisted my attempts. I had to wear her down before she'd finally agree to see me. And second, there's more to her than just a sexy body. I know she's smart. Kind. Generous. And she works hard to get what she's after.

"Whatever, man. Her name is Ainsley. And I like her. So lay off."

Before he can say more, I head outside to my car to get the pizza. I return back into the apartment, the pizza box in one hand, drinks in the other and walk back into the bedroom. I love that Ainsley has wisely heeded my warning and remained planted where I left her. Still naked. And absolutely stunning.

She smiles as I hand her the pizza box.

"You like me, huh?"

I clear my throat and mutter. "Shit. You weren't supposed to hear that."

Opening the lid of the box, she grabs a large slice in her hands and brings it to her mouth. Watching her slide it between her lips is an erotic sight to behold. I imagine those same lips wrapped around my dick, and just like that, I'm hard again.

"Why don't you want me to know you like me?" She asks in between bites. A small dollop of pizza sauce clings to the corner of her mouth and I reach to swipe it away with my finger. Bringing it to my lips, I lick it off. Her eyes grow round, and see a flash of lust flicker in her gaze.

I'm on my knees on the bed, my cock now tenting my jeans, as I lean over her. She thinks I'm going to kiss her. I can see it in her expression as she parts her lips just ever so slightly, the pizza slice dangling in her hand at chest level. I hover close to her face, and bend down…and then take a big, delicious bite of her pizza.

I give her an exaggerated groan and she laughs, pulling back the remnants of her pizza in one hand and shoving my face away with the other.

"You jerk," she giggles.

I love the sound of her laugh. It's light and carefree, just how I want her to feel around me. Over the last few weeks she's opened up to me just enough that I know of some of her struggles. So polar opposite of my own. She's been given nothing free in this life, and yet she's optimistic and lighthearted. I, on the other hand, have turned fairly jaded based on the people in my life who've let me down.

We eat our pizza in silence for a few minutes, as I prop myself up next to her, against the headboard. We sit shoulder to shoulder. The movement of her arm when she takes a bite sends vibrations through my body from the contact.

She's finishing her third slice — something I've never seen a girl do before. Normally they tell me they're on some stupid diet and just eat salad. Which I think is ridiculous. I like it when a girl has some meat on her bones. I like to grab hold of something, not sticks.

As I glance down at Ainsley, who is now stretching out beside me, the sheet slips a little to expose the creamy fullness of her tits and my dick starts to take notice again. Break time is over, ladies and gents.

She continues stretching, moving down the bed, sliding past my knees. Her hands go for a joy ride over my ridges of abs, sighing when she gets to the open waistband of my jeans. My eyes stay locked on her as her fingers grip the material and pull it open. I suck in a deep breath, which draws her attention up to my eyes.

"Is this okay?" she asks hesitantly.

As if I'd say no.

I nod, lifting my hips to help aid in her endeavor to rid me of my binding clothes.

"More than okay."

My cock pops out, standing free and proud, as she continues removing the jeans all the way to my ankles where I kick them off.

Ainsley positions herself on her knees at my side, her perfect ass up in the air, which my hand instantly claims in a tight grip. She leans in to press a soft kiss to the tip before her tongue darts out to taste the pre-cum that's already made its appearance.

"Oh fuck, yeah."

When she opens her mouth to take me in, my breath lodges in my lungs. Oh my God, I knew she would feel this good, but it's indescribable the pleasure she's giving me. She licks the underside of my shaft and lingers at the tip, circling it with purpose around the sensitive spot.

I can't help it. My hips jerk in response and she lets out a breathy laugh. Her hand winds its way around the base of my cock and she begins to suck hard. My hand grips her ass like a vice, just before I slide my fingers down her cheeks and between her legs.

She pauses for a moment in surprise and then moans when my finger circles her swollen flesh, finding her wet and hot. My cock hardens exponentially from the vibrations she's casting, as she continues to writhe and whimper in fluid motion. And when I slip two fingers deep inside her opening, it's like Mardi Gras – loud, crazy and purely magical. I growl with satisfaction when she begins to move in earnest, as I plunge in and out in a nice easy tempo.

And then she takes me all the way to the back of her throat.

I can feel the constriction of her tonsils around my crown and I can't help but shout, "Fuck."

My enthusiastic response has her gagging a little, so I suspend my hip movement.

"Sorry – you okay?"

She turns her head up to me and smiles coyly.

I'm so close to coming that one more lick, suck or even breath from her will send me flying over the edge. So I decide to turn the tables around on her. Because if it's anything that I am not, it's selfish.

I move quickly, grasping her hips in both my hands and pulling her up toward the headboard as far as she can go without hitting her head. Then I scoot down toward the end of the bed so my face is nestled right between the warmth of her legs. When she realizes where I'm going with this, she lets out a nervous squeak.

"*Wha-?*"

I don't let her get out another syllable, but plant her over my face and go to town. I feel her thighs quiver and tense around my head, shaking in pleasure. I glance up toward her face, trying valiantly to keep my shit together. With her sweet, wet pussy right in my line of sight, I'm about to shoot off like a cannon all over my chest if I don't stay in control.

"Relax, baby. I want you to ride my face. Whatever feels good. Just do it."

As if she needed my permission, she nods and relaxes into the straddle, and then grabs the headboard for support.

And then she goes to town.

And I fucking love it.

Chapter 15
AINSLEY

Fall in Phoenix.

Still too damn hot.

It's the middle of September, three weeks since the first night I slept with Cade. Three glorious, amazing, incredible weeks of spending every free moment I have with Cade. Which is not enough, but just the right amount to keep me wanting more.

This overwhelming feeling of happiness is like having a drum full of butterflies flittering inside my stomach every waking hour. I'll go for days on Cloud 9, walking around with a stupid, love struck grin on my face. And then a dark, ominous cloud moves in to remind me who I am and that whatever this thing is with Cade won't last. Nothing ever does. Especially not between me and Cade.

I'm not sure the exact moment it became a boyfriend/girlfriend thing between us, but it happened. Definitely not something either one of us expected to happen. We haven't discussed it, but my Spidey-sense tells me Cade's never had or wanted a girlfriend. That's one thing we share in common – because I've never been anyone's girlfriend. It takes time and effort, both of which I don't have. Cade and I are from such opposite worlds; you'd think we'd clash.

But we don't. The weird thing is, even though we are each hella busy – it works. Much to my surprise, and utter enjoyment, Cade is a romantic guy. He texts me first thing every morning, calling me beautiful and sexy. Saying things like he wishes I was there with him. That he wants to hold my naked body next to his. And from there it generally gets X-rated. I've learned the hard way that I have to shield my phone screen, lest someone accidentally get a peek at the naughty nature of my boyfriend.

The other day I was at the kitchen table reading his text while eating breakfast and Anika started reading it over my shoulder.

Cade: *You know what I want to do to you tonight?*

Me: *I'm afraid to ask...but of course I want to know.*

Cade: *See how far your legs can stretch behind your ears.*

Me: *Ha...I'm not that flexible.*

Cade: *We'll see about that. I'll give you a good rub down first.*

Me: *Perv.*

Cade: *And you love it…*

Anika snickered from behind me, as I practically jumped off my chair. I hadn't even heard her come in, I'd been so wrapped up in visualizing Cade and my limberness. I quickly flipped the phone upside down and set it on the table, blushing as brightly as a beacon in a storm.

But those are the type of texts I get from Cade. And they always get me hot and bothered. *He* gets me hot and bothered.

We don't get a ton of time to spend with each other, between jobs, school and his training schedule for his upcoming basketball season. But we do find time when we're both on campus to meet up and grab a bite to eat or chat over coffee. And on the rare occasions when I'm not working in the evening or the weekends, I spend time over at his apartment with him and his friends. Or we go out.

I'm not saying it's been easy, because it hasn't. Especially when it comes to all the jealous hoop hunnies (a term which Cade explained to me that I found horribly disgusting, but accurate). If I had a dollar for every stink-eye glare I get from them when I'm with Cade, then I'd be a very rich girl.

It amazes me how many women will make a play for Cade, even when it's obvious that he's with me. Either I'm completely invisible, or they think I'm replaceable, because they couldn't care less that his attention is on me. These girls will stop at nothing to flirt with him, find a way to give him their number, or fawn over him like he's a demi-god to be worshipped.

I've even noticed that some of his friends have been a little stand offish and cold to me. Not all, but a few. Cade merely suggested that they are probably concerned that he'll lose focus going into season if he has a serious girlfriend. That makes some sense, I guess. Then there's the other reason, which he claims is because they're just jealous because he has the hottest girl on campus.

Yeah, right.

Today I'm in the library with my friend Micaela, or Mica as she goes by, who is my study partner in my program, finishing a project for our Nursing Theories class. I really like Mica. She's a native of Arizona, grew up near Flagstaff and is part Hispanic. Although my skin is quite a bit lighter than hers, and my eyes are blue where hers are molasses brown, we actually could pass for sisters.

We've become close over the last two months, my only female friend outside of my co-workers. Once she warmed up to me (she's extremely shy), she opened up quite a bit about her life, her family and her overbearing Mexican father, who is apparently trying to marry her off to some distant relative. I guess we all have our problems in life and families can be Numero Uno when it comes to life's little dramas.

We've been busy reading and writing for the last hour, when Mica pipes up with a question out of the blue.

"So what's it like dating Mr. Popularity?" Her smile is fragile, but curiously sweet. Mica has met Cade on a few occasions when he's walked me to class or when we hang out in the cafeteria. But she's never said much to him – and doesn't really need to, because Cade is a Chatty Cathy.

I scoff. "Way more complicated than I realized it would be."

Mica tilts her head in curiosity, her shiny dark hair falling over her bronzed shoulder.

"What do you mean? What could be so complicated about going out with a hot basketball stud like Cade Griffin?" And then she frowns, as if she realizes she's said something that was inappropriate or divulged too much. "I mean...he's just really hot."

My laughter bubbles out and over as I watch Mica's face turn beet red.

Dropping my highlighter in the crack of my open book, I settle back into the cushioned chair. We're in a small alcove in the back of the library, two over-stuffed chairs and a small table between us. I think about her curiosity and what it looks like from Mica's perspective, being an innocent observer of my situation.

She and I are a lot alike in our social status. Neither of us are in college to party or be part of the royal society. We're here to improve our lives through academics. And sometimes that comes at a high price.

"Cade is definitely a Hottie McHotterson," I giggle, remembering what he looked like stark naked the other night as we skinny dipped in the pool at his mom's house.

He'd invited me over to meet and have dinner with his mom, but soon after dinner we found ourselves alone when she went over to John's house next door. Both his childhood home and his incredible physique illuminated by pool lights impressed me silly.

"And believe it or not, Cade's super sweet. I didn't expect that from him. I guess I had it in my head that if you met one stuck-up, arrogant jock, you've met them all. But there's more to him than that. Cade's super smart, funny, fun to be around, and is very generous. I'm actually still pinching myself that I'm dating him. It's kind of unreal."

Her mouth opens and closes before she speaks again.

"I see how he looks at you, *chica*. It's part hunger and awe because *eres bonita*."

Thankfully, Spanish was my foreign language elective in high school, so I'm well aware she just called me beautiful, which is really sweet. But even more so, it's that it's nice to know she's also observed the same thing I have with Cade. I was hopeful, but weary about his true feelings. And if she sees it in the way Cade looks at me, then maybe it is for real.

"Thanks, Mica. It just seems weird, though. I wasn't looking for a boyfriend...and *definitely* not a star athlete boyfriend. It hasn't been easy finding time with him. We're both busy. And I get a little paranoid when I can't go with him to these parties, where I know…" I pause, questioning whether I should voice my insecurities that have popped up recently.

The kindness in her eyes tells me I can trust her with my inner most thoughts. "It's just that there's a lot of temptation for a guy like Cade. So many of these girls don't care that he has a girlfriend and will do anything to get with him."

There. I said it. Out loud.

Trust has got to be part of any relationship, as well as open communication. I've wanted to have the "talk" with Cade regarding exclusivity or monogamy on more than one occasion, but it kills me to broach the subject. But if I don't, it will drive me crazy always wondering what he's up to or who's hanging around him when I'm not with him. Which is actually a lot. I only see him a few times a week as it is…and that time will shrink even more when he starts practices, which are in a few weeks.

"Are you worried he'll cheat on you?"

I nod and give her a defeated shrug. "Maybe…no…yes…I don't know. I've only been with one other guy and all I have to go by as examples are my mother's douchewad exes. They all fucked around behind her back."

Mica hums in agreement. "Maybe you should just come clean with him and ask. Clear your head of the question. And ease your mind of worry."

It shouldn't be a difficult thing to ask him, right? But how does one go about it? Is it just a casual statement, something like, "'Hey, by the way…is this dick only for me? Or am I sharing it with anyone else?'"

Awkward.

Mica has a really good point, though. I can't just let it fester inside because it will soon turn into an evil green-eyed monster and I don't want to be that kind of girlfriend.

"You're right. The next time I see him, I'll just ask him. Just to set the record straight." I nod with more self-assurance than I actually feel, but it gives me the confidence I need to address the elephant in the room.

Mica shifts uncomfortably in her chair and her brown eyes go round as saucers. It's then that I realize Cade is behind me. And then I hear his voice, the timber of his baritone, smoky and sweet.

"Ask him what?"

Cade bends down next to my chair and places a kiss on my cheek, while I try to come up with a response, glancing at Mica for help.

"Hey Mica," he smiles at her, his lush green eyes dancing with kindness. "You're looking gorgeous today." He gives a chin nod in her direction before turning to face me.

"And so is my girl. Damn hot."

Cade wraps a hand around the back of my neck and pulls me in. His mouth takes possession of mine, my lips parting to allow his tongue to slide in and ravage me. I hum in appreciation. And I think I hear Mica sigh.

Once he pulls back, I remain transfixed on him. My eyes can't look away. Cade always looks good, but today he's wearing a dark gray suit jacket and pants, a crisp white dress shirt underneath, the collar unbuttoned and no tie. His hair is styled and gelled, so the wavy curls remain in place and his face is free of his usual scruff.

"Hi Cade." I hear Mica say, her voice soft and wispy, but I don't look her way. I know she gets all tongue tied around Cade and his friends. Who wouldn't? Especially if they look this fine all dressed up. His eyes flit between me and Mica, before landing on me again.

"So what's up? What record are you talking about?"

I let out a nervous laugh.

"Nothing," I wave my hand in dismissal, searching Mica's face for help. "We were just discussing our class and need to ask Professor Dalton about our project."

That seems plausible and I think Cade buys it since he doesn't pursue it further. His formal attire, though, has me curious to know why he's all gussied up. Grabbing the lapel of his jacket, I yank him toward me and cock my eyebrow, giving him a wry smile.

"What's up with the fancy duds? You going out on a date with someone?" I catch Mica's flustered gaze. Yeah, probably not the question I should be asking, but close enough. A little passive-aggressive, but it's a start.

Cade grunts and stands up, causing both Mica's and my heads to track his movement. Up. Up. Up. Geez, we both have to crane our necks to keep our eyes on his face.

"We have this stupid press conference and team interviews with the media tonight. Since we're getting closer to Midnight Madness-"

I cut him off. "Midnight Madness? What's that?"

Sweetness

Cade shakes his head and smacks his forehead with his palm in exasperation. When he lifts his hand, his nose is scrunched up in distaste.

"The *one* girl I fall for and she knows nothing about basketball." Mica snickers and bites down on her bottom lip to presumably keep from tittering with laughter. Yeah, I too, noticed his particular choice of words and I can't hold back my grin.

"Midnight Madness is the first official basketball team practice with the coaching staff. It's held every year around the fifteenth of October on campuses across the country. It's actually a pretty big deal and it gets a lot of media attention. It's also open to the public. So if you two want to come, you know, watch me play, I'll make sure you get tickets."

I have to admit, I've never been to a basketball game or even watched one, for that matter. In high school Phys Ed, we had to learn to dribble a ball, and that's about the extent of my knowledge. I know absolutely nothing about the game, except the things Cade has shared with me about offense and defensive plays and the positions of a team. I know he's a shooting guard, but don't remember anyone else's role.

The prospect of watching Cade out on the court, playing hard and showing off his skills, does have some appeal. Mica looks unsure, her doe eyes cast downward, when I speak up for both of us.

"Well, if I'm not working that night, and if Mica wants to tag along with me, I'd love to go. Sounds fun!"

By the way Cade reacts, you'd think I'd just handed Cade a million dollar check from the Publisher's Clearinghouse sweepstakes. His eyes light up with the biggest, dopiest smile across his face and he pumps his fist in the air.

"Yes! That's what I was hoping you'd say." He leans down and kisses me loudly on my forehead, leaving a big old wet mark I wipe off with the back of my hand.

"Cade, hold on…I don't want you to get your hopes up. You know I might have to work. And Mica might be busy that night, too."

Now his smile fades a little and he looks crestfallen like I've just kicked his new litter of puppies. I'm such a shit girlfriend. I always have to rain on his parade with my real-life problems.

"Okay. I understand." And then he smiles broadly again. "But I'll cross my fingers and hope for the best."

That's what I've come to admire about Cade Griffin. He has this positive outlook that never seems to dull or fade. There's been something bothering him, though, recently. There are times I think he wants to tell me something, but whatever it is, he doesn't say. Whatever it is, he does an admirable job of pushing it away and not letting it get him down.

I wish I could say the same thing. I'm normally a glass half-full kind of girl, myself. But lately, it seems there's something going on that I can't quite put my finger on. I can feel it brewing and percolating, like coffee in an old-fashioned coffee pot on the stove. Ever-so-slowly, the temperature rises, the liquid heating within the pot to its boiling point, while the atmosphere around it remains the same, until the hot liquid soon bubbles and roils in its container, spilling over the edge of the smooth surface.

Perhaps I'm being paranoid. You can't blame me. I've only ever seen disaster - when all good things come to an angry, heartbreaking conclusion. Whether it's my mother's elated moods shifting suddenly to sullen or manic. Or her so-called perfect boyfriends revealing their true natures. Or our lives coming unhinged and uprooted for something bigger and better elsewhere.

I've learned to live in fear of attachments, avoiding them at all costs. Believe me, it's not what I want. I do want to build friendships that I can rely upon. And open myself up to a man who can prove to be trustworthy. One who treats me with respect, and love, and courtesy. A man who is honest and has integrity, who doesn't just tell me things I want to hear.

A guy who will ruin me – in a good way – for any future men to come.

So planning ahead to future events with Cade and Mica, even one as innocuous as a team practice, is big for me. It gives me hope where hope has never resided. It's setting an expectation of something worthy to come on the calendar in my heart.

And it scares the shit out of me.

Chapter 16
CADE

I'm a pretty affable guy. It's just my nature. Definitely a characteristic I got from my mother, because my dad is a serious asshole.

But when you're bombarded with cameras in your face, microphones nearly reaching down to your tonsils, and bright lights and flashes blinding your eyes, it takes all your willpower to keep calm and paste on a cheesy grin. Press conferences are the worst. I know that sounds whiny and unappreciative of the notoriety, but a Kardashian, I am not.

I love the game of basketball. I enjoy pushing myself to be better. The buzzer-beater shots that make your soul soar. The claps on the back from your teammates and coaches when you've achieved a triple-double in a game. Or even the solidarity with your team when you've lost a tough game against a stronger opponent. It's the moments on and off the court that build character, strength and mental toughness.

Sitting in front of photographers and sports news crews is one of my least favorite things to do. I loved it at one point – when I first started. It was pretty fucking awesome to see my name, my picture and glowing reviews about my playing skills in the news. Inevitably, though, I started getting asked questions about the draft – would I declare my interest? When would I declare? Would I finish school before getting drafted? Where would I be picked to go?

The problem with those questions is that I've always had to stretch the truth about my decision. Unlike most players from the time they're in grade school, I've never wanted to go pro or play in the NBA. It's just not my life's ambition. My goal, and the last four years of my life, has been dedicated to pursuing an education in the biomedical engineering field. After I graduate with my undergrad, I'll start my Master's program, hopefully landing me a position where I can someday invent a therapeutic medical device to aid in life-sustainment.

That's way more meaningful than basketball.

My friends, and even dad, think I'm out of my mind not to go pro. But listen – only a small majority of players have more than a three-year shelf life. I'd likely make the league minimum, struggle to get court time, potentially deal with injuries, and have to travel an insane amount of the year. I'm sure it would be fun as hell. For a time. Until it isn't.

In the meantime, I'm stuck here – with my team and coaching staff – answering stupid, inane questions about stats, potential chances at a title, and our toughest competitors.

I've just answered a question related to how we, the team, help with the new recruits and incoming freshman, when Ethan Drummond from AGC Sports Network throws out a question that stuns and flattens me. I'm sure it looks like I've just seen a ghost.

"So, Cade…Coach Welby just spoke about integrity and how he requires his players to be role models for the new team members…" Okay, where the hell is this guy going with this?

"In light of your recent arrest, court hearing, and probation, Griff, tell us how can you be looked up to as a respectable leader?"

Oh shit. This is not good.

My mouth dries up and a lump of anxiety bubbles up in my throat as I look down the table with a plea to Coach Welby. The expression on his face is stern, but impenetrable. I have no idea what's going on in his head but I'm sure the shock and fear of the question the reporter just posed is registered all over my face. I blink and swallow as I try to gain my composure.

"Um…" I stutter. I'm seriously at a loss for words.

And then Coach Welby pipes in.

"As you very well know, Mr. Drummond. Kincaid Griffin has been a leader on this team since he started with ASU. His academic successes are currently unmatched, he's been recognized nationally for his athletic skills, honored for his volunteerism, and revered by his past and current team members. He's a leader in every way, on and off the court. Whatever you've read or dug up about his personal life has no merit or relevance to the skills he lends to this team."

Coach Welby's voice is grim and vibrates like an earthquake aftershock through the room. Cameras flash in the back and my eyes dart nervously at all the faces sitting in front of me. Their fingers type furiously at keyboards and keypads, some reporters still using old fashioned pencil and paper. They all observe one thing – Coach's response brooks no argument.

Yet, the reporter continues to push, prying for a juicy response.

"So what you're saying, Coach Welby, is that you condone the stunt Cade Griffin pulled by getting arrested for public intoxication, indecent exposure and an underage DUI?" The entire room lights up in whispers, gasps and a flutter of activity.

Drummond continues, a dog on a bone. Smirking like he's about to receive an award for his investigative reporting.

"Or is it true that you're making an example out of him and you've pulled him from starting the first three games of the season? Do you deny this, Coach?"

Fuck. Fuck. Fuck.

I'm screwed. *We're* screwed.

Me. Coach. The team. My parents.

Everyone is now going to know about this. The idea that this little incident could be swept under the rug and kept secret was a serious miscalculation on our part. My attorney and my father had promised me that the court records, although public, wouldn't fall into the wrong hands or cause widespread interest. Coach kept this between a select few so as to avoid it swirling around and creating a media shit-show.

No such luck. Now it would go national and be a matter of public opinion. Instead of the media focusing on my stats and abilities on the court, my personal life would now overshadow my accomplishments as a player. Over one stupid, minor indiscretion and lapse in judgment.

My dad is going to go ape shit. He already read me the riot act – not once, but twice since the night of my arrest. And the last time I saw him was the day I met with Coach. The day I was informed of my suspension from the first three games.

Most of the team doesn't know about it yet. Coach said to keep it on the down low and that he'd inform the entire team during our first team meeting, which is coming up in a few weeks. But now the cat is out of the proverbial bag and the bomb has been dropped. And it has currently exploded all over my fucking life.

I suddenly feel like my shirt collar is choking me and my chest has been rammed with a wrecking ball. I'm having trouble breathing, my lungs are filled with lead. I can feel the wide-eyed stares of my teammates. I hear some snickers of disapproval from the audience.

Looking over to my left, I notice Lance has his head down and is picking at an invisible spot on his dress pants. The fucker doesn't even look up.

And Carver. His shoulders rise and fall with each breath and his mouth is formed in a tight line, forehead etched with lines of anger and concern. For all the crazy-ass stunts this guy has pulled over the years, and the trouble he's gotten me into, Carver is a decent guy. A true friend who I know has my back no matter what. As the team captain, it's painfully obvious he's disappointed this came out this way and he wants to help me fight my battle. Unfortunately, there's nothing he can do or say that won't implicate me further.

There's no way out of this. I have to face the music. Take it like a man.

My attention goes back to Coach Welby, who is now about to lose his shit, based on the severe twitch in his eyes, and have it out with this weasel of a reporter.

"On the court, Kincaid Griffin is a warrior," Coach compliments me, turning his head to look me directly in the eyes. "He led this team last season with an average of 20.6 points per game. I love coaching him and I'm thankful I have the opportunity to continue coaching him during his last season with the Sun Devils. I've watched him over the last three seasons develop into a great basketball player, athlete and even better man. His enthusiasm and drive are unmatched, and he's a great mentor for his younger teammates. As with all my players, Griff has grown up by making mistakes. But like all of us, including myself, it's how you handle those mistakes that will be remembered. I'm proud of Griff's character and his ability to accept responsibility for his actions. And I'm thrilled that he'll continue to play out his senior year at ASU."

I'm a little awestruck at Coach's kind words. While I'm not his top player, I'm an integral part of the team and I've never been in this kind of trouble before now. Yeah, my stats are good. Solid. But unremarkable next to some other players on the team or in the division. I'm thankful I have a good relationship with Coach.

"Coach Welby, you didn't answer my question. Is Kincaid Griffin suspended from playing this season?"

Coach's reply is curt and quick. "No. Next question."

Technically, he answered the question truthfully. I haven't been suspended for the entire season. I still get to practice with my team, but I just won't get court time during our first three pre-season games. Which of course sucks but it's not the end of the world.

By looking at the downtrodden faces of my teammates, I know they're pissed at me right now. Worried that it could hurt our record. But the first three games are pre-season, and don't have much weight against our season standings. I'm determined to come back stronger, better, and more focused than ever before.

Mark my words. Nothing will be a distraction.

****

The press conference ended ten minutes ago and the team now sits in the large screening room in the athletic facility that we use for pre-game prep and discussions. I'm flanked by Van on one side and Christian Lancaster, our center, who towers over everyone at six-foot-eleven, on the other. Carver and Lance sit across from me in our oval-shaped conference style seating, all the guys still in our dress suits. There's a low murmur of hushed whispers, but otherwise it's quiet. Waiting for the boom to come down.

And then Coach and the assistant coaches walk in, shutting the door closed behind them with an ominous click. Coach W stands at the front, near the whiteboard, and his gaze travels across the room. His eyes land on me for a second and then move on.

"Gentleman, you all did great out there. I know talking to the press falls pretty low on your list of favorite things – but you all spoke with the perfect balance of enthusiasm, attitude and humility." We all chuckle a little at that, because some of the guys are pretty arrogant when they tout their abilities and achievements.

Coach clears his throat. "Now, in light of what you all just heard about Griffin...I'm sorry if that was a surprise for many of you. I specifically asked that Griff keep it under wraps. Technically, what occurred this past summer was a personal matter and did not affect the team in any way. However, now that it's come to light, I'm going to use this as a teaching moment for all of you. I expect – no, I *demand* – that you all follow the law, and the rules of this program, pre, post and during the season. None of you pussies are above it. I will not tolerate reckless behavior and law breaking. Now…Griff is paying for his mistakes through the court ordered probation and I've also suspended him from the first three games of the season."

The room is filled with groans and mumbled curses.

Yeah, I feel like a fuck-up. I hate letting my team down.

"Cade, you got anything you want to say?"

My jaw drops open and my head jerks up, feeling the penetrating stares of the guys in the room, all looking at me. Some with disdain. Others with sympathy. And my brothers who know me the best with support and encouragement.

I take a deep breath and collect my thoughts, straightening my shoulders back against the uncomfortable chair.

"Thanks Coach," I begin, my voice a little rocky. "I made a stupid decision recently. I was busted for a DUI and underage drinking. I'm lucky because the situation could have been far worse and the punishment harsher than it was. I'm paying my dues, serving community service and owning up to my mistake."

My eyes scan the room, taking into account all the guys who have been by my side over the last several years on the team. We don't always get along, or agree on things, especially when it comes to basketball, but we all respect each other. And I don't want them to lose the respect they have for me. That would be the worst punishment of all. Because it's what I value the most.

"I'm sorry, guys, that my behavior and mistakes have impacted this team. You're all my brothers. You don't deserve to have to carry the burden of my mistake."

I hang my head in shame for a brief moment. When I look back up, I find Coach at the front of the room. "I appreciate all the support I've received from Coach W. He didn't have to stand by me, but he did. And I can't thank him enough for being there for me. I will work hard to make sure none of this shit affects the team or our upcoming season, because I know we're gonna have a kick-ass year. And mark my words – we *will* get to the championship. So who's with me?"

My voice grows louder and my words more emphatic as I neared the end of my speech. And when I finish, there's a brief moment of silence before a loud burst of cheers flood the room like a dam opening up and the water crushing through the barriers. It fills me excitement, hope and an incredible sense of belonging. And a little bit of sadness, as I know this will all be over soon. Once I graduate and my college career comes to an end, the comradery and brotherhood in this room right now will be a distant memory. But one that I'll cherish for the rest of my life.

The team begins to disperse after the Coach concludes our meeting, and a few guys come up and give me their support. Pats on the back, bro hugs, and laughter go a long way in making things right. But I still feel a sense of remorse and shame. Like I've tarnished what could be the beginning of a great new year. It's my worst fear that this will haunt me the remaining six months of my final season.

Van stands up and moves toward me. When he's directly in front of me, his hair falling around his shoulders, he reaches out for my hand and gives me his usual bro handshake. I accept it with gratitude.

"Dude, I'm sorry about your situation. That really sucks."

I nod my head in agreement.

"Yeah, thanks man. It is what it is. I'm moving forward and trying to put it behind me."

"Good to hear. Let me know if there's anything I can do for you, okay? You're a big part of this team and I won't let others talk smack about you." He turns and grabs his gym bag from the floor by the chair he just vacated.

"You bet. Thanks, bro. Thanks for having my back."

Van's hair slips around his face, covering a portion of his ears. He usually wears it in a manbun with a headband when he's playing, or underneath a beanie, so it's weird to see it hanging loose. I guess chicks dig the look, but I don't get it. Seems like a lot of hassle to me. I like my cropped do. No fuss, no muss. And Ainsley doesn't seem to mind it, either.

In fact, she likes to grab on to the short hairs when I'm between her legs, either pushing my head harder to her or yanking me up after I've made her come with my mouth.

The thought of going down on Ainsley has me sporting wood. I mentally tell my dick to quiet the fuck down, but he knows what he wants. And that's Ainsley. Aside from our brief chat in the library earlier, it's been days since I've been with her. Which sucks. Our schedules always seem to get in the way. She hasn't even had time yet to introduce me to her mom or her sister. I'm not sure if she's just leery of the introduction or if there's something she's trying to hide.

My mother loves Ainsley already. Called me the day after I brought her over for dinner and told me what a lovely, bright girl I'd chosen. And I'm looking forward to when she meets my sisters over the holidays. I know they'll love her, too. And just like that, my mood has brightened exponentially as I think about the upcoming holidays with Ainsley, even though it's not yet October.

Carver still gives me shit about settling down with Ainsley. He just can't wrap his head around being with one girl all the time. He's the biggest man-ho I know, and has no less than three girls a week. It amazes me that he continues to find new chicks to hook-up with. Although he's a great friend, I'd never let him anywhere near my sisters. He treats girls like they're disposable. Even knowing his reputation, girls still look at him with starry eyes and the hope that they'll be the one to change his tune.

Fat chance, ladies.

The room has cleared out and I stand alone toward the back, with the exception of Coach Welby and our head trainer, Scotty. They finish up their chat as Scotty heads out the door, and Coach centers his attention on me.

His voice fills the room, laced with sympathy and disappointment. "Well, Griff. It went as good as could be expected." He begins, signaling for me to join him at the front of the room. "I knew we wouldn't be able to keep it away from the press for too long, but at least it's out there in the open now so we can move forward and focus on getting you ready for the season."

I come to a stop in front of him, my head inclined slightly because Coach is even taller than me. He'd played college ball back in his day and is a minimum six-foot-eight. My eyes are cast downward until I find the grip of his huge hand on my shoulder.

"You did great today, Griff. I'm proud of you. And honestly, I've seen guys with a lot less character screw up far worse than you and come out of it without even a scratch."

Coach is referring to Tashawn Bryce, a former player when I was a red-shirted freshman. He was arrested and charged, but subsequently cleared, of rape charges when he was a senior. It was an ugly situation, where the school and the authorities were at odds with the public. The entire fiasco brought down a firestorm of bans across the entire athletic programs and put in stricter penalties for student athletes who were accused of criminal activities.

I remember at the time that the public outcry was harsh. Fans boycotted the games. They posted scathing remarks on social media sites, all shouting for reform and how the system was corrupt because the accused always got off scott-free due to their athletic status. And maybe that is true. Justice is blind.

A part of me is pissed that my case went in front of the judge and didn't get dropped when Tashawn's charges were ten times bigger than mine. The evidence against him was damning, and yet he still got away with only a slap on the wrist. It stands to reason that it was because he was a big name and a huge prospect for the NBA. He was actually drafted first round by the Cavs.

Sadly, last year, more charges were filed against him. This time, it was caught on video and he was prosecuted for felony rape and kidnapping charges. Jesus. How does that even happen? It makes me sick to my stomach that he could get away with a crime while he was a student and then perpetrate a similar act again. The victims in all this – the women in these cases. There was not justice immediately, but a zebra doesn't change his stripes. He was convicted in the end.

But since that incident, the school has a zero tolerance policy. And that's why Coach had to suspend me for the first three games. I understand it and don't fault him for doing what is right. I am the fuck-up in this situation. And I was determined to clean up my image. To be a better team mate. Be a good citizen. And turn things around for my future.

"Thanks Coach," I say, determined to remain humble and prove that I'm worthy of his admiration. "I know I made you and the team look bad out there, and I'm really sorry. That's not what I want to remembered for. I'll work my ass off this year to make sure I leave in good standing."

He nods. "I know you will, kid. I have faith in you."

The words he says, full of confidence and pride, have me choking back tears. My own father has never even told me this. Never declared his love or adoration toward me, or any of his children, I'm sure.

I'd tried so hard as a kid to please my dad. To be the son my dad wanted me to be. But I could never live up to his expectations. My dad was an asshole who just wanted a trophy wife and family. The only time he'd say anything remotely complimentary about me was in front of others who he wanted to impress. He never once paid me a compliment in private.

I have mad respect for Coach Welby. He is a fantastic coach. A great man who cares about his men.

I want to grow up to be like him. Because I'll be damned if I'll be anything like my dad.

Starting with how I treat the women in my life.

The problem is, I haven't mentioned anything about my fuck-up to Ainsley yet. I've been too scared she'd look at me differently, so I haven't brought it up. I've got to go find her and tell her the story before she finds out about this from anyone else.

I just hope it isn't too late.

Chapter 17
AINSLEY

If it's one thing I've learned over the course of my life, especially as an outcome of being raised by a mother with chemical dependency and a mental illness, it's that whenever things are going really well in life, you can damn well be sure that something is bound to happen to burst your bubble.

Call me cynical, or pessimistic, or whatever you want, but that's the way it goes. And the same holds true now. The last month with Cade has been an amazing journey and I can't help but thank my lucky stars that we met and I gave him a chance. Yet I've had this growing concern that I've harbored, feeling that something is off with Cade. Like there is something he wasn't telling me. And I've been walking around on eggshells, waiting for the other shoe to drop.

And today's that day.

"Hey, Ains. Your boyfriend's on TV. Wow, he looks *really* good. So hot." Kimmi exclaims with a girly giggle, wiggling her eyebrows as she turns up the volume on the small television we have in the kitchen breakroom.

I swat her shoulder as I walk by because she's so irritatingly sweet. Aside from Mica, she's the only female friend I've shared my feelings about Cade with. My sister and mom know I'm dating someone, but I've not given too much detail, sidestepping any introductions. Maybe it's my lack of faith that things between Cade and me will last, or maybe I don't want to jinx my relationship. I fear that once he meets my mom, he'll question why he's even with me.

It's been so busy over the last few days and I've been burning the candle at both ends, leaving no time for Cade. I know he's frustrated, and it's eating at him, and I wish it didn't have to be like this, but work, school, and Anika come first. It makes me sad, and I long for a life where I could be a normal girl.

Although I saw him briefly yesterday before he went to his team press conference, we didn't get any alone time together.

And let me tell you, that alone time is pretty damn impossible not to want.

Just the thought of what Cade does to me in the bedroom makes my lady parts tingle. In fact, I have to squeeze my legs together to get rid of the ache that he manages to cause even when he's not around.

Sweetness

Sex with Cade is unbelievable and makes me want him all the time. In the past, sex was like checking off boxes in order to feel like a real woman. But I never enjoyed the act as much as I do with him. He's a fantastic lover. With his ripped abs, strong chest, and taut ass, he's the perfect male specimen. I could spend hours running my fingers over the toned planes of his body, touching every part of his magnificent physique, created by years of strength training and bench presses.

Unfortunately, I'm resentful now that I know what I'm missing. Like the other night, when I only had a few hours to spend with Cade, naked and sweaty, before I had to resign myself to heading home. There's no curfew assigned – my mom never really cared enough as long as I was there for Anika. It's a battle between being responsible and being with Cade. And I hate that I have to choose.

He'd been spooning me in his arms the other night on his bed, after a hungry and furious bout of sex, our bodies contentedly wrapped up in one other. Cade was trying his best to get me to stay the night with him – tugging at my sensibilities. Using our closeness to get me to cave.

"Please don't go, baby," he had pleaded, his fingers gently sweeping up and down my back, sending shivers of pleasure along the way. "I just want to wake up with your naked body in my arms. Is that so wrong? And I promise, baby, in the morning, I'll make it so good for you...I swear."

He nipped my ear as he whispered the sensual words, his tongue teasing around the maze of my ear's outer shell, as his hand traced my overly sensitive nipple in a circular motion.

"Mmm. I believe you."

Turning to face him, I had grabbed his ass in confirmation, pulling him into me so that our bodies were aligned tightly to one another. Although we'd just made love ten minutes earlier, I could feel his cock lengthening between my legs, loving the fact that he could get hard again so soon. That I got him hard.

I had been torn between wanting him again and having to go home. There is a big part of me that fears he will realize he doesn't need me. If I can't be there to satisfy his needs, then someone else could. That worry plagues me all the time now. I'm not the typical girlfriend that can be with him whenever he wants me. I have obligations that interfere with our love life. So in moments like that, I desperately needed him to know just how good it felt being inside *me*. To realize this was special so he wouldn't go looking for it elsewhere.

I've also grown bolder the more and more sex we have together. I am a faster learner, and maybe a bit of an overachiever, as I became more familiar with what he likes and how he likes it. He made it easy for me to let go. Which means I am really loud in bed. He teases me about it constantly, as does his not-so-subtle roommates who now affectionately called me "'the screamer'". I was embarrassed at first, but Cade told me he loved it and it drove him wild when I made a lot of noise in bed. So what can I do?

That night, Cade had flipped me on my back as he hovered over me, his broad shoulders blocking out everything above me. He had been my entire focal point – there was nothing better to look at in this world. Kissing Cade was better than ice cream, or fireworks. His lips felt perfect melded with mine. Hot, wet and hungry. As his mouth took possession of mine, my lips automatically parted to grant him full access. As he sucked on my tongue, I felt his hand encircle my breast, squeezing and plumping it between his fingers, his thumb flicking the tip of my nipple.

My hips arched off the bed when his mouth left mine and his lips latched on to the hardened peak, pulling it between his teeth and sucking hard. As he shifted his mouth to the other breast, the short, bristly hair on the top of his head tickled underneath my chin, causing me to giggle.

It stopped him in his tracks as he jerked his head up to gape at me in surprise.

"What's so funny?"

I laughed again. "Your hair is tickling me," I snorted, flicking my hand through his hair. "But don't let that stop you. You may continue." I waved my wrist at his face, ordering him with my demand.

His eyes lit up in concert with the lazy grin painted across his face. He had been just too damn gorgeous. I let my gaze fall from his eyes to his biceps, which are taut and displayed beautifully as he held himself above me.

The tip of his cock slid between my wet legs and had me sucking in a loud breath in surprise. My eyes immediately darted up to find his burning with intensity. I couldn't make out what he was thinking, but if the teeth biting into his bottom lip was any indication, it was something pretty sexy and hot.

"Ains," he whispered, pressing down against me so I felt at once both safe and anxious with his posturing. "Do you trust me?"

I had nearly laughed out loud, because no, I'd never really trusted anyone in my life. Not my irresponsible mom. Not the authorities, who on more than one occasion turned a blind eye to our plight and living situation. And certainly not men. The only men I had been exposed to in my childhood were drifters, cons and habitual users. No good losers who I wouldn't have trusted farther than I could've thrown them.

But I considered his question. In the time I've known Cade, and come to learn how sweet and honest he is, the answer was unequivocally a yes. I do trust him. He is who he says he is. No pretense. No hidden agendas. He is open and honest with me about everything. So my response was clear, quick and without hesitation.

"Of course I trust you."

Cade returned to kissing my neck, leaving a path of little bites along the soft flesh, his warm breath spanning across my overly sensitive skin. It was this type of intimacy that made me crazy for him. Needy and wanton.

"I used the last condom earlier," he had murmured, heightening my awareness of his steely dick between my thighs. "I don't have any more with me. I haven't had time to pick up another box."

He accentuated this with a glide of his length across my wet entrance. We groaned in unison. Equal parts lust and dismay.

"I want to fuck you again..."

My body responded with a resounding Yes, as I tilted my hips up to gain friction.

"Can I? Can we..."

My eyes popped open as my brain finally clues in to what he's asking. What he wanted.

My fingers had clenched into the back of his neck. "You mean, no protection?"

He hesitated slightly, pausing to consider his next words.

"You're on the Pill...and I'm clean. And fuck, I want to feel you, be inside you without anything between us..." More kisses, on the other side of my neck before he kissed me fully on the mouth. I opened up for him, my brain and body being pulled under from his tenderness and sweet seduction. "It's never felt like this for me, Ains."

Nothing between us. The pinnacle of intimacy and trust. That sounded so good. His admission, a secret confession in the dark, had sent shivers of anticipation down my spine.

And just like that, I gave in. There was no going back. I was in so deep with Cade that this was just the next logical step.

I did trust him. I knew he wouldn't hurt me. And I wanted to feel all of him, too. I wanted everything with him.

My voice was barely audible as I answered him with the only possible response. "Okay."

Cade's surprised reaction had been almost comical. "Oh fuck…are you serious? Oh shit…" His voice trailed off as he closed his eyes and aligned himself with my entrance.

I giggled briefly until I felt the hard, but silky smooth cockhead pushing at my center, ready to submerge into my tight heat.

The moment had been suspended in time, in slow motion as we both looked down at the juncture between our bodies and watched in awe as he disappeared inside of me, inch by glorious inch.

My body instinctively bucked up against him, my pelvis pushing against his to gain friction. When he stilled above me, I frowned, digging my nails into his taut ass cheeks to spur him into action.

"What's wrong? Why'd you stop?"

Cade's head fell forward, his eyes closed tight in agony.

"I need to slow down, otherwise I'll come. I'm too close already...I didn't know how incredible you'd feel. It's too much."

That was true for both of us, but I loved hearing the desperation in his voice. His hard, hot length was lodged so deep inside of me I could feel it to my toes. But I needed him to move. That was the point of this whole exercise. And my body needed that coveted release more than it needed to breathe.

"Don't stop, Cade. Please...."

The long, exaggerated groan ripped through his chest, as he complied with my request. And damn, when that boy started to move again, it was with wild abandon. It was with purpose. As if he were driven to perfect the art of love making.

It took no more than four erratic strokes and he was already grunting out his release.

"I'm sorry...oh fuck, I'm gonna come..." I had watched in awe as his head tipped back, strong chin pointed upward, jaw clenched tight as the orgasm washed over his beautiful face.

My own orgasm, which didn't normally make an appearance without some form of manual stimulation, came barreling out of nowhere like a freight train. Just as he flooded my body with his climax, the tingles formed in my lower abdomen, spreading like the warmth he released inside me. I cried out – loudly – blinded momentarily by white spots of ecstasy behind my eyelids.

Cade's body relaxed on top of me, a hot blanket of muscle covering my now lax and sated existence. The heat emanated from his entire being and cocooned me in peaceful easiness. I was literally blissed out and so happy I felt high.

As he pulled out of me, I felt the remnants of his orgasm run down the side of my thighs. It was a weird sensation - kind of gross and sticky, but at the same time a reminder of the closeness we just shared. The closest you can ever be to another human being. I immediately missed him, as I grabbed his wrist to stop him from getting out of the bed.

"Don't worry, I'll be right back. I'm just going to get something to clean us up." He placed a sweet kiss on my forehead as I reluctantly let him go. I watched his gloriously toned ass and powerful legs move out of reach and into the bathroom, where he flicked on the light.

Closing my eyes, I replayed the beauty of the moment and thought about how lucky I was to have opened myself up to

Cade. It was a scary proposition, one that I feared would lead to potential hurt and rejection.

But he proved me wrong and exceeded all my expectations. I'd even been considering finally introducing him to Anika and my mother. Nothing was finalized yet, but I knew sooner or later I'd need to make that decision, allowing one part of my life to join with the other.

My eyes sprang open as I felt the soft glide of a tissue against the inside of my leg and my cheeks burned with a sudden flash of shyness. Once he'd taken care of me and threw away the evidence of our lovemaking, he snuggled in beside me, his heavy arm wrapping around my waist and pulling me close.

"That was incredible," he had said, as his breaths became steady and slow. The low rumble of his voice filled me with a languid peace, like a lullaby made to put me to sleep. "Thank you."

I fell asleep that night with a smile on my face and awoke that next morning to find myself stretched out next to a softly snoring Cade, who apparently sleeps on his stomach. I hadn't expected to fall asleep, nor stay the entire night.

As I got up and ready to leave, I placed a parting kiss on his cheek, as he mumbled out a goodbye before turning over and falling asleep again. But I remember as I walked out his front door that morning how great it felt to be in a relationship. I let down my guard with Cade, like I'd never been able to do before. I trusted him with my entire being.

Until I heard the commentary from the news reporter on TV this morning.

"So, Jim, that's a pretty astounding revelation about ASU's shooting guard, senior Cade Griffin, who was arrested for a DUI and underage consumption…"

What. The. Hell?

I blink my eyes in confusion as a video from the press conference yesterday flashes across the screen. This must be some kind of mistake. There is absolutely no way they have it right. The news reporter obviously has the wrong name.

"That's right, Carl," the reporter continues. "The news was leaked yesterday by AGC Sports News that Griffin was arrested last month and sentenced to probation by the Maricopa County Court for his lewd and reckless behavior, along with an underage DUI. In my opinion, the repercussions were too lenient and Cade Griffin got off too easy. A recent study proved that college athletes who are charged with criminal behavior get away with these crimes seventy percent of the time, due to their status and privilege. Either the charges are dropped or not prosecuted. It's a travesty that these kids receive special treatment in the eyes of the law…"

I can't listen to this any longer. I turn away and cover my ears, bending my head in despair.

"Ainsley, are you okay? What's the matter?"

Kimmi's voice of concern has me blinking back the angry tears that have formed, unbeknownst to me, in the corners of my eyes.

While I'm stunned speechless, and am in a state of denial, there must be some truth to this story. Why would the media make up such a sordid story about Cade being arrested and suspended from the team?

And if there is truth to this story, even an ounce of it, then why the hell hasn't Cade mentioned anything to me? That question, and the possible answer to it, has me in a tailspin. All I can think about is that we've just spent the better part of a month getting to know each other – sharing thing about our lives. I thought this meant something to him. I thought I meant something to him.

The only logical conclusion means that I'm not important enough to Cade for him to want to confide in me. Seriously – this bit of news isn't some small, insignificant detail in his life. This is huge. It affects everything in his life – his family, his time, his reputation, his team standing. His future.

Kimmi clears her throat and turns off the TV. Her voice is soft, full of pity. "I don't understand, Ainsley. Did Cade never tell you any of this?"

I cover my face with my hands and shake my head.

"Oh sweetie…I'm so sorry." She wraps her arms around my shoulders.

Her strong hold gives me little comfort. No matter what the reality and outcome of this thing with Cade is, the fact remains the same. My boyfriend chose not to share this with me. He kept me in the dark – like a fool. And now the world knows, right along with me.

"No. He never mentioned anything."

There's a few beats of pause as it looks like Kimmi is weighing in how to respond. I'm sure she's just as uncomfortable as I am.

"I'm sure he meant to…but maybe he was embarrassed. Shamed. I don't know."

I laugh out loud. "Seriously? The Cade Griffin I know doesn't get embarrassed."

Kimmi rubs one of her delicate fingers across her eyebrow, a nervous habit I've seen her do when she's stressed. "It's possible, considering he what was caught, um, doing. And I'm sure it hasn't been easy, since the courts tried to make an example out of him, and granted him a year probation and community service."

Community service? Probation? Is that why he'd been coming to visit Simon all this time? Because it was court mandated?

God, I am such a freaking fool. It was never out of the goodness of Cade's heart. He was ordered to do it.

I am as livid and angry as a rattle snake that my very own boyfriend pulled the wool over my eyes, keeping me in the dark over his sudden interest in his grandfather. He has been lying to me.

My brain quickly calculates the timeline of our initial meeting. He started pursuing me *days* after he was arrested and sentenced. Cade literally flirted with me the first time I met him at the café and then he doggedly pursued me days after being caught getting a blowjob in his car.

The contents of my stomach roil back and forth, the nausea burning its way up my throat. I swallow down the bile ready to make its escape, as I fumble toward the bathroom door in the back of the kitchen.

Kimmi calls out my name, but the ringing in my ears is too loud and the thoughts of betrayal take up too much space in my head.

I barely reach the toilet before losing it.

And the little voice in the back of my head plays on a loop, reminding me of all the reasons why I never should have put trust in a guy like Cade.

Because I just got played by a player.

Chapter 18
CADE

Ainsley isn't returning my calls. I've been trying for the last two days and each time it goes directly to voicemail.

I've also tried texting her with no response, either. I'm on the verge of stalking her, but decide I'll just wait until today during my usual Thursday visit with gramps. That way, I can talk to her face-to-face.

It's fairly obvious she's seen the condemning news story on me. It's everywhere right now. The hottest story out there. Everyone has an opinion about what happened, how it was handled, and what a douche I was. The news outlets have done everything to make it sound more titillating and scandalous then it really was. One of the newspapers even tracked down Callie (yes, that was her name) and gotten a full account from her point of view on what went down that night. As in, her account of going down on me.

Christ, I hope she earned some money for that, because it made her sound like a whore anyway. Everyone is painting me as a fucking loser. Some sleazy, jerk athlete who treats women like dirt. In hindsight, maybe I did. Getting a girl, who is barely legal, to suck me off in the front seat of my car in a parking lot is kind of a douche thing to do.

Believe me. I get that. And I've owned up to my behavior. I've worked hard to change my lifestyle. To be a better man.

Ainsley has made me see that change was possible. Being with her has changed me. I'm not the same guy I was two months ago.

Ainsley, with her kind heart, positive outlook on life and all around sweetness, has touched something inside me that was buried for years. In fact, since my parent's divorce, my philosophy on love and relationships has been tarnished.

Maybe this new 2.0 version of me is simply me growing the fuck up. Whatever it is, it's made me realize that I have fallen for Ainsley. And I am in desperate need to explain to her why I didn't tell her the truth about what happened to me.

I'm nervous as I step into the front entryway of my grandfather's nursing home. I've been practicing what I'm going to say and how I'll bring it up with Ainsley when I see her. It's the only thing I've been thinking about the last few days.

Moving into the kitchen, I glance around and see a woman standing at the kitchen, hovering over one of the house occupants as she cuts a sandwich for him. She turns her head to the side and smiles. I've never met her, but I assume she's the owner because she's not wearing the scrubs uniform.

"Hi there. You must be Cade, Simon's grandson." She wipes off her hands on a rag and walks toward me, offering me her hand in greeting. I shake it and smile, returning her greeting. "I'm Gail Marshall. It's great to meet you."

"Hi Gail. Yes, I'm Cade. Um, is my grandfather around?" I look around the room to locate him. He's usually at the kitchen table when I arrive, ready for either one of our games or to eat lunch. But he's not there today.

Her smile falters slightly, the wrinkles around her eyes become more prominent as she glances away. I don't know her, but I can tell instantly that something's going on and my instincts aren't wrong.

"I'm so sorry no one contacted you, Cade. Simon was taken to the hospital last night. He has a pretty bad upper respiratory infection and he didn't want it turning into pneumonia. So as a precautionary measure, we had him admitted. Since you aren't on his emergency contact list, we didn't call you. Your mother has been notified."

Anger strangles me like a noose. Why the hell didn't my mom call me? She knows I've been spending time with gramps and that I'd want to know what's going on. I barely get out a response to Gail as I pull out my phone and tap out a frustrated message.

Me: *When were you going to tell me about gramps?*

Mom: *I'm sorry Cade. I didn't want to worry you.*

Me: *Well, too late. What hospital is he at?*

Mom: *Regence.*

My contempt at the moment is high. I spin on my heel and start toward the door before realizing that I haven't seen Ainsley yet, either.

I look over my shoulder back at Gail as I grasp the front door handle.

"Is Ainsley working today?"

Gail quietly nods in understanding. I'm sure it's written all over my face. My need. My absolute and utter pain over the probability of losing her.

"Ainsley is at the hospital with your grandfather."

****

There have been only a handful of times I've visited anyone in the hospital. My sister Kady had surgery on her torn meniscus when she was thirteen after injuring it in a soccer game. And another time when my cousin, Deena, had a baby and my mom made me tag along. Talk about the most boring hour of my then fifteen-year-old life.

Yet, neither of those times had me worried or concerned for someone's life. The anxiety I feel right now over seeing my grandfather lying listless in a hospital bed, looking white as a ghost, has me choking on my worry.

Standing in the doorway of the room I was directed to, my gaze shifts from my grandfather's body over to the beautiful form of Ainsley sitting next to his bed. She's hunched over his bed, her back to the door, holding his hand and talking to him softly.

"Mr. Forsberg, you know you're too stubborn to let this infection get you down. Plus, you promised me you'd be my date to watch Cade play in his upcoming basketball game. I need your help because I don't know anything about basketball, so you have to be my very own walking Wikipedia. That's an encyclopedia for my generation." She laughs quietly at her attempt at humor, as her hand gently strums across his.

It's probably wrong to stand here, unannounced, and listen to her speak to him, but I can't gather the strength yet to make my presence known. Once I do that, I know the reaction I'll get from her. If it's one thing I've learned about Ainsley, it's that in her world, there is only black and white, right and wrong. Good and bad. There is no in between for her. Without question, because I've kept my situation from her, she's going to see me as a goddamn lying son-of-a-bitch.

I'm just about to take that monumental step inside the door when her voice fills the room again.

"I really liked him, Simon. He's been so good to me. He reminds me an awful lot of you. I bet you were just like him when you were younger. It's probably how you got your wife to go out with you in the first place. All that charm and that pretty boy smile." She laughs. I grin from ear-to-ear.

I may still have a chance, after all.

"But he lied to me. He didn't tell me the truth about something really important. It really broke my heart that he couldn't trust me enough to share it. I'll admit, I am a tiny bit jealous over what he did with that girl…but I know it happened before me. He's a popular guy. I get it. But I was so hurt finding out the way I did. To find out that I wasn't as special to him as I thought I was…" Her voice wanders off. "I thought we had a good thing going…"

I hang my head and clear my throat. Lifting it back up, I see Ainsley swing her head over her shoulder to find me standing in the doorway.

"We did," I say, taking a few steps forward. Slowly, like I'm approaching a wounded and lost animal, worried I might scare her off. She stares at me with contempt. I don't blame her.

"We do have a good thing, Ainsley. And I can't tell you how sorry I am that I didn't tell you. I wanted to…but I just hoped it would go away. I didn't want to face telling you because I was so ashamed of my behavior. You had such high expectations, but you liked me. I didn't want to lose you. You deserve someone so much better than me, so I tried to convince myself that if you didn't know about it, then it didn't happen."

My knees hit the ground next to her chair, my head almost level with hers. Reaching out, I place my hand on top of hers, which is still resting on Gramp's hand. She snaps it away.

She looks mortified that I'm there. "How long have you been here?"

"Long enough."

Ainsley lets out a dramatic sigh and begins to stand up when I place my hands on her shoulders, gently pushing her back down until her butt hits the chair again.

"Please," I implore her, hoping to have this time to get things out in the open. "Let me explain."

She shakes her head emphatically, closing her eyes and turning her head away from me.

I try again. "*Please.*"

Maybe the combination of desperation and sincerity in my voice does it, because her shoulders droop in a look of defeat and she slowly turns back to face me. Her sad eyes fix on my face.

Not wanting to lose a second of the time I have with her, I begin.

"I fucked up. I knew better, but I was stupid and easily influenced that night. When I was busted, I took responsibility for my actions and never disagreed with the repercussions. I was lucky they didn't take my license away from me. The probation restrictions are fairly light, but I'm still cautious. I don't want to mess up again. That's why I didn't drive you

Sierra Hill

home the night of my party. I'd never endanger myself or anyone else by being that stupid."

"Why didn't you come clean with me? I thought…well, I thought we were…"

I interrupt. "We are. I care about you so much, Ainsley, more than I ever thought possible. The only people who knew about what happened that night were my parents, my coach, Carver and Lance. That's it. I couldn't risk your judgment or you ending things with me, so I didn't tell you."

Ainsley's expression is blank. "So you didn't trust me, then."

It's as if a lead balloon has expanded in my chest and as I inhale, is ready to burst.

I let out a deep sigh. "It's not that, Ains. It's just that you have such high standards." She gives me a dubious look. "Look how long it took you to finally go out with me…I didn't want to ruin it by admitting I really am an idiot."

She scoffs and rolls her eyes.

"Listen, I know this isn't coming out right. The point is, I'm deeply regretful that I kept this from you and I'm so sorry. But I don't regret the time I've spent with you. This semester has been the best I've ever had, even considering the trouble I got myself into early on. I've never felt this way about anyone before. You are special to me and I'm so sorry for not opening up to you about it." I swallow, the lump getting stuck in my throat before I say what I have to say next.

"I understand why you hate me. I deserve your anger. I get it. But I need you. And, I love you, Ainsley. Please forgive me."

Three little words. I didn't know they existed until now. I knew my feelings were serious about Ainsley, but hadn't put two-and-two together yet. Although, since the night we made love without a condom, I knew, deep down, it wasn't just sex. We have a connection. A bond. Something that goes so deep I can barely live without it.

Based on Ainsley's expression, perhaps this wasn't the right time to divulge my true feelings. But if it's the last time I ever get to talk with her, I'm not giving up without a fight.

Ainsley looks like she's about to bolt. Her wide-eyed incredulous stare bores through me before she turns her head to look down at my grandfather, who hasn't moved a bit. I hadn't even considered that he may be able to hear all of this, but I don't really care. My honesty is liberating.

"You love me? Are you freaking serious right now?"

Oh boy, the venom in her tone is pretty clear. She's going in with the upper cut. "You've just kept this huge secret from me — *for months* - and that's how you show you're in love with me? And what about the reason you've been visiting your grandfather? That was all court mandated? Does *he* even know that?"

Well fuck me up a river. I hadn't thought about how gramps would feel when he found out that my visits weren't of my own volition.

I shake my head, lowering my eyes away from her condemning glare.

"No," I admit. "I don't think he knew, unless my mom told him. But that doesn't mean I didn't enjoy my time with him. My gramps is a great guy and he's taught me a lot. We weren't close up until recently. Before my parents divorced, we didn't spend much time with gramps because my father didn't like him. He didn't get invited over for holidays or anything, so I didn't see him much. But now that things have changed, I do want to spend time with him. Court ordered or not."

"Well, good for you, Cade Griffin. So glad you've finally grown a heart. You should be given a pat on the back and an award for best grandson. How charitable of you." Her words are icy cold, harsh and stinging.

Ainsley stands again to go, but this time I don't protest. She's dressed in bright blue scrubs today, and her eyes, although hard, are the deepest blue. Midnight almost. She bends down to grab the handle on her purse and slings it over her shoulder. Moving over my grandfather's form, she places a soft kiss on his cheek and whispers something in his ear. His face remains impassive and unresponsive.

As she turns and steps around me, I notice a wet teardrop on the end of her thick, ink lashes. Everything in me wants to jump up and hug her. To plead her to stay. To tell me she loves me too and she'll forgive me.

But I know she'd refuse. Instead, I stand and watch her walk out the door. Taking my heart with her.

Just as she hits the bright florescent hallway, Ainsley turns back to me with a sad smile across her mouth.

"I'd appreciate it if you moved your *required* visitations to a day I'm not on duty. I think that would be best for all of us. Good-bye, Cade."

"Ainsley, wait…" I choke out, but she stops me with her hand in the air.

"I mean it, Cade. Please don't make this harder than it already is, okay? Just leave me alone."

And with that she walks away, leaving my heart trampled on and lifeless on the germ-infested hospital floor.

Chapter 19
AINSLEY

Keeping myself busy and distracted over the last few weeks has been easier than I thought it would be. There's was only one problem. Cade is everywhere.

Not necessarily in person, but avoiding any mention of Cade around campus or in conversations with Simon, has been more than a little troublesome.

Everywhere I go there are reminders of Cade. Anywhere I turn on campus, there's something posted about the upcoming Midnight Madness event. Posters of the team, including Cade's ridiculously gorgeous mug, hung all over the walls and walkways of the campus. It's incredibly annoying. Why couldn't he be just a normal ex?

Mica has been a true friend for me during this entire breakup. She's listened calmly to my angered outbursts and gripes, nodding her head in solidarity and friendship. We've just spent the last two hours in the library working on our thesis for our mid-term papers that are due soon. As this is my first fall season in Phoenix, I'm still getting used to wearing shorts, T-shirts and sandals in autumn. It's counter-intuitive to the natural seasonal order of things.

We're packing up our books and getting ready to head home when Mica brings up the subject I've been avoiding since I ended things with Cade.

"Have you decided whether you're going to bring Mr. Forsberg to the Midnight Madness practice this Friday?"

Whether it's been self-preservation or just stubbornness on my part, I've not mentioned that topic with Mica since the invitation well over two weeks ago. Mica's dropped hints here and there, because I think she finds the prospect kind of exciting. Just like me, she doesn't get out much due to her family and work obligations. While our lives are very different, we do share a lot of the same familial commonalities. Her heart has been set on getting out and living a little, this event being a perfect opportunity to do that.

And I know without a doubt that Simon wants to go more than anything. Although he hasn't mentioned anything about my relationship with Cade, he has not so subtly been dropping hints about this Friday's practice and how excited he is to watch his grandson play. Nothing like a little passive-aggressive guilt-trip to put the pressure on. Thanks, Simon.

Since his stint in the hospital, the infection in his lungs taking him out of commission, he's been slowly recovering back at Ethel's. His rehabilitation is pretty admirable for a man his age. He's been testy and a little surly, which isn't unusual for someone in his condition. The only thing that seems to brighten his mood is talk about watching Cade play ball.

Dammit, he knows how to get his way.

It's not uncommon, as an aspect of my job at Ethel's, that I am asked to escort our patients outside the home – to doctor appointments, movies, social events, etc. If they were willing and able, I'm normally happy to help them get there. Unfortunately, in this instance, it pains me that I have to play chauffer for this particular event.

Truth be told, while I'm still mad at Cade for not confiding in me and trusting me with the truth, it upset me more that he pulled the wool over Simon's eyes. Cade's weekly visits clearly made Simon happy, so I'm sure learning that Cade's visits were a part of his probation detracted a little from that excitement. Or maybe it didn't, because Simon still made sure to share all the details with me about what he and Cade did during their recent visits. Possibly to make me jealous.

Lifting the heavy bag over my shoulder as we walk together across the quad, I glance over at Mica wearing her oversized sunglasses and consider her question. She's so tiny and cute, she could totally pass for Ariana Grande's doppelgänger.

"I don't think I have much choice in the matter," I huff, stopping for a second so I can pull my hair up into a bun and out of my face. "I'm working with Glenna on Friday and she doesn't drive at night, so I'm stuck driving the van for Simon."

Mica nods her head and considers. "Do you still want me to come along? I don't have to watch the *hermanos* on Friday night because my mother will be home. I don't have anything better to do. And there is no way I'll let Alberto find out I have no plans."

She cringes, as if creeped out by the mere thought, and I let out a laugh. She's told me about this distant cousin of hers, through marriage, that her father has been trying to set her up with for the past year. I guess Alberto is quite a bit older, in his early thirties, owns the auto body shop where her father and brother work, and smokes cigars that make her gag from the smell. I feel bad for Mica and her family situation. As the oldest child in her family of six, she's expected to do what she's told. She's shared with me that she had to fight her father tooth and nail to go to college. Even though she earned a full-ride, her father would have rather she just be a 'good little Mexican daughter and marry and produce grandchildren'.

Thank God Mica found her voice and stood up for what she wanted. Her intelligence and dedication will make her a great nurse. I can't wait to see her at work during our clinical internships.

Stepping into her, I wrap my arms around her small frame in a friendly hug. "I'd love for you to come with me! You'll really like Mr. Forsberg. He's so sweet. And you can keep me company during the boring game. I mean, really…it's not even an actual basketball game. It's just practice."

I try to feign disinterest, but she sees through me with her watchful brown eyes that appear too big for her face.

"Do you think we'll get to meet some of the players?" She asks in a shy, angelic voice, her maple-syrup eyes gleaming in the sunshine.

Tilting my head, I examine her expression. Hmm. Interesting. I think she might be crushing on someone.

"Mica," I say, curious now. "Is there a particular player you want to meet?"

She shuffles her feet, kicking at a non-existent obstruction on the walkway.

"Um, no…not really."

"Mica?" I prod.

She sighs, her shoulders lifting and falling in resignation.

"Fine. Okay…but you can't ever repeat this. Or tell him. You can't say a word. You have to promise me." She pleads, looking mortified at the prospect of being outed. I nod my head in agreement, solemnly swearing to never say a word.

She pauses for a moment, biting her lip as she considers what she's about to let slip.

"It's Lance."

Lance?

"Really?" I exclaim loudly, absolutely floored by her admission, as she anxiously glances around us to ensure no one is in earshot. "You mean Lance Britton? As in Cade's roommate?"

I'm kind of astounded by her confession. She's only met him once before, to my knowledge, when Cade and Lance stopped by the coffee shop one day while Mica and I were studying. They were on their way to the gym. Lance was his usual goofy self. At the time, I was too enamored with Cade to notice anything between them, but now that I think back, Mica was pretty giddy. And gigglier than I'd ever seen her before.

"Wow."

Mica slaps me on the shoulder with her open palm, but it's barely a tap. She couldn't kill a mosquito with her tiny bare hands.

"Yes, *that* Lance. I think he's kind of cute. And funny. And *tall*." She sighs dreamily.

I roll my eyes. "Well, duh. Everyone seems tall to you, Tinkerbell."

I jab her back with my finger just as I hear my name being called across the courtyard. It's startling that someone would recognize me on campus. That doesn't happen often. Try never.

Speak of the devil.

"Ainsley, wait up!" Comes the booming voice of the man himself.

My gaze moves between the incoming basketball player only twenty feet from us and Mica's wide-eyed surprise. She looks like she might just hurl.

"Hey. Thanks for waiting." Lance stops in front of his and catches his breath, smiling down at us, but his attention lands squarely on Mica.

Mica shifts nervously between both feet, her eyes landing everywhere else but Lance. She sucks in her lower lip, her teeth practically biting a hole clean through. I try to hide my amusement over her pained expression.

"Hi Lance. What's going on?"

Regardless of whether Cade and I are together, I have no beef with his friends. And Lance is a nice guy. We've hung out a number of times when I was over at Cade's, and I even helped him once on an assignment for biology he was having trouble with. I haven't seen him since my last sleep over at their apartment. The thought sends a phantom-like pain through my heart.

Lance shakes his head, as if clearing a fog caused by Mica's presence. It's pretty cute. Lance seems to be a little taken by her, too. Such a nice development.

"Oh, yeah. So, the thing is…" He trails off, clearing his throat, his voice froggy. "Well, shit, Ainsley. I shouldn't be saying this, and he'd kick my ass if he knew I was telling you this, but Griff's really fucked up. I don't know what happened between you two, but he's a mess right now. Me and the guys are getting kind of worried. We've all got a lot riding on this year and if he goes into practice looking the way he does right now, Coach isn't gonna start him after his suspension is lifted."

Lance shoves his hands in the front pockets of his shorts, looming over me like a freaked out Sasquatch.

Admittedly, I'm a bit surprised that Lance is divulging this to me. It's no longer my business. Cade and I are done. He's his own man and can act anyway he likes.

I stare up at Lance with more confidence than I possess. "I'm sorry to hear that, Lance, but I'm not sure what you want me to do about that. It's not my problem. Or my fault." He's the one who screwed up, dammit. The blame shouldn't be pinned on me for his bad behavior.

I can feel my temper start to rise, the blood heating underneath my skin. The sweat beads slinking down my back with the silent accusation he's made. Like I'm the Yoko Ono of the basketball team, bringing Cade down. I'm not the reason for his screw up. It was his decision not to come clean with me and I can't continue in a relationship based on dishonesty.

"Ainsley." He pleads, looking like I've just kicked his puppy. "I know it's not your fault. And Griff deserves whatever lashing you gave him. But all I'm asking from you is to give him a chance to explain. To let him apologize, or whatever. At least give him that. Based on what I've heard, you haven't returned any of his calls. He needs closure."

Mica nods. "I agree. You should give him a chance to explain."

I give her a death glare and shove her foot with my toe. "Traitor. Thanks a lot for taking my side."

"I am on your side. But you can't just shut him out of your life like that. You need to talk it out, *amiga*, like adults do." She has the good sense to look contrite.

Well, she has me there. My initial reaction was to close down so I couldn't get hurt any worse. My head told me to give him that concession, allow him to explain. My heart said not to get suckered again. They were probably right, I should find closure and allow him to set the record straight. If anything, it would at least end things on a less sour note. Then I could walk away with my head held high. Even if my heart was dragging in the dirt.

"Fine," I concede, begrudgingly. "I'll talk to him. But that's it. He's on his own from there."

You'd think I'd just announced they won the lotto. Mica let out a loud whoop of joy and Lance picked me up by the waist and swung me around like a lunatic as I flailed in his arms.

"Thank God. I thought I might have to resort to kidnapping to get you to see him. So can you stop over tonight? We don't have a lot of time to get his ass straightened out."

I nod at him in agreement, much to my chagrin. This isn't how I planned on spending my only night off this week. But when you're pressured by your best friend and a very large, loveable giant, you don't have many other options.

Lance sets me back down and then looks me straight in the eye. "That's great. But I need to warn you…"

Oh great, here we go. Nothing is ever as easy as it seems. Especially for me.

"Cade's been drinking…heavily. Hasn't been sober in days. So…he may not be in good shape."

My heart sinks with a sadness for what my sweet man has been going through. Shit, I've tried to keep those feelings tamped down. Stay firm. Don't be allowed to get sucked back in.

"Thanks, Lance. You're a good friend."

Lance lifts his shoulders in a casual shrug and smiles.

"I know he'd do the same for me. I'll see you ladies later. And hey, Mica…" He stops, spins around, giving her a carnal perusal that has even my face heating up.

"Hope to see you again, soon."

He literally bounds down the sidewalk like a giant Tigger. I chuckle at his animated goofiness as I shift my gaze to Mica. Her eyes are transfixed on Lance's retreating form, mouth agape in awe and wonder.

"Ahem."

Her head pops up to look at me, suddenly remembering that I'm still present. A brilliant smile blazes across her face. Mica's just nineteen, so sometimes I forget that she isn't as desensitized to the world as I am. The joyous expression she wears tells me she thinks life is coming up roses.

"*Dios mio*. Did that really just happen?"

I laugh. "Yep, that really just happened. And I think your man crush may just have a little crush on you, too."

"Whatever," Mica waves me off. "Estas loca, chica. You're crazy if you think he likes me. I mean look at him. He's a bona fide basketball god. And I'm…" She gestures down her petite body.

"Exactly…he looked at you all right. And let me tell you. He likes what he sees. That boy is enamored."

We finalize our plans to meet up at the practice on Friday and say our goodbyes, but not before I promise to call her tomorrow to tell her how things go with Cade tonight.

****

I decide to go home for dinner tonight before making my unannounced visit to see Cade. I haven't had a real conversation with Anika for a few days and I feel the need to see what's going on in her life. She's been a lot more reserved and distant as of late. I guess that's par for the course with teenagers, but it fills me with dread.

After I've showered and changed, I walk out of my bedroom and notice the light on underneath my mom's door. It's actually been a while since I've caught up with her, too. She's been dating someone again, although I haven't met him. But Ani said he seems "normal", whatever that entails. Apparently, he's been making my mom smile, according to Ani. So that can't be all that bad. For now.

I hesitate at her door for just a second and then I knock.

"Come in."

I rarely go into my mom's bedroom unless I've done the laundry and have to put her clothes away, so when I step in, the first thing I notice is the floor. It's littered with clothes and empty hangers. My gaze shifts then to an open suitcase out on her bed - half full.

"Going on a trip?" I ask hesitantly, the dread weighing on me like a thick cloak.

She lifts her head and blinks at me, smiling sweetly, but the smile not quite reaching her eyes. It's a telltale sign. I feel the tension rising in the air, like a like a ticking time bomb about to detonate.

My mother is a very beautiful woman. She's still youthful at forty-one, although the last few years have been unkind to her physique. She's lost a lot of weight, claiming it's from being on her feet all the time at the salon and forgetting to eat. I'm not so sure about that, but I'm not about to comment. It wouldn't change anything even if I did.

Things are a lot better now than they were a few years ago, so I try not to dwell on that time in our lives, when we were living out of a car and my mom was in rehab. Mom had spiraled out of control and it was one fateful night that I found her passed out unconscious in a pool of her own vomit, convulsing through her OD. I took her into the ER and that's when they diagnosed her with her condition. Bipolar. Mental illness. Alcoholic. Drug addict.

A social worker spoke with me about it, educating me on the facts about her illness and learning that many people with mental illness will try to self-medicate themselves using drugs and alcohol. She explained that once my mom was properly medicated, things would even out. My mom also agreed to voluntarily check herself in to a rehab program run by the state and get the help she needed. I was eighteen at the time, old enough to act as the legal guardian for Anika, so they couldn't place us in foster care.

I did what I had to do to make it through those harrowing six months. We crashed at some friends' houses for as long as we could. Stayed in a women and children's shelter through the Y for a few months, and then just found it easier to crash in the old beat-up wagon my mother owned. Not ideal, but I wanted Anika to remain in school and with me. I worked during the day, saving up where I could to spend on cheap hotel rooms once a week. Where we could take showers and sleep soundly through the night.

I did all of that in the hope that my mother would get better. That once she worked through her issues, evened her brain chemistry out, she'd come back full force and be the mother that I needed her to be - for me and for Anika.

And now as I look at my mother, her long dark hair swept back over a shoulder, the same blue eyes I have staring back at me, I want to scream at her. Gauge those eyes out. Because I know what's coming next.

"Hey, baby. How are you? I've missed you." She moves around the bed and steps toward me, intent on giving me a hug, which I sidestep to avoid. I watch as her shoulders slump in despair.

"When were you going to tell me you were leaving?" I practically spit, the anger encroaching the space between us. Her face acknowledges the truth. "Oh, I see…you weren't going to tell me. You were just going to leave us here…leave Ani on her own again."

Oh God, Anika.

My sweet, darling girl. So innocent, yet battered from the life she's been given. Fuck, I'm so mad right now I want to hit something. *Don't you know how much this hurts? She needs a mother. She needs you.*

This time, I'm determined to keep myself together. I won't shed a tear over her absence. I'll pick myself up by my bootstraps, as I always do, and find a way to make the best of it. I won't let the hatred and anger make me bitter. Disenfranchised. What good would that do?

"Ainsley, sweetie…it's not like that. I swear." She reaches for my hand but I snap it away from her grip. "Brad asked me to come with him to South Dakota. He's going to be working there for a while and he said there's lots of jobs up there for me, too."

"You have a job here, the last I heard."

"I quit."

Not surprised. But hurt that she's so willing to drop everything for a man she barely knows to chase after him to some godforsaken wasteland. And no, I haven't been to South Dakota, but it sounds horrible. Cold. Desolate. Isolated. Just like me.

A sob wrenches from my chest and before I can stop myself, my body is racked with immobilizing despair. Not for me, but for my sister.

"Please mom…don't do this. Don't leave Anika when she needs you the most. Because I can't do it alone. I can't…"

My mom is quick and her arms are thrown around me tight before I even have a chance to wiggle away. Although I want to hate her, I can't. I know she's done the best she can for us, even in the midst of dealing with her demons that possess her mind.

"I've already talked to Anika and she's coming with me."

My stomach bottoms out and an instant tidal wave of nausea hits me. The urge to puke is threatening me, but I swallow it down because I need to keep myself together. My mind races through objections as to why Anika needs to stay here. Stay with me. But it will be of no use. Once my mother makes up her mind about something, there's no swaying her decision.

This throws me for a loop. On one hand, I know I can't raise Anika alone right now. I'd have to quit school to be with her. There's no other way.

On the other hand, losing Anika – letting my mom take my sister with her is a sure fire disaster.

"Mom," my voice comes out as a squeak. "Ani's life is here. She's doing well in school. She has friends here. She's on a volleyball team. Don't take her away from all that." I want to say *for a stupid guy that'll dump you in a few months*, but I don't. Keeping a level head in this situation is what I need.

Mom shakes her head emphatically. She's made up her mind. It's done.

"I want her there with me. Like you said, she needs me."

"What I meant…"

"I know you love her," she acknowledges, her hand resting on my shoulder, which is tense and knotted. "And if things don't work out, we'll come back sooner."

Screaming at her will do nothing, but at least it would release my pent up hostility.

My body sways a little and I reach behind me to find the edge of the bed, where I sit down in a stupor.

"How long do you think?"

Mom's face scrunches up in consideration over the question.

"I don't know. Maybe three, four months."

My hands grip the bed spread in my fist.

"You're making a mistake. This isn't good for her to leave. I want you to know that I think you're wrong."

She gives a sigh of resignation. Of finality.

"I know. And I'm sorry."

Not as sorry as I am. I can't stand to be in the same room with her any longer, so I stand and slowly shuffle to the door and into my bedroom, passing Anika's open door as I do. She's not home right now, but I know it will be tough saying our goodbyes.

I can already feel the loneliness take up residence in my heart. She's all I have. My little sister is the only one I've always counted on to be there with me, no matter what.

Getting myself dressed and ready to head over to Cade's, it dawns on me that now, more than ever, I need someone to lean on. Cade broke my heart and my trust in a way that no one else has before, except my unstable mother. Yet, I need him. He's the only one who can help me get through this. The problem is, in order to let him be there for me, I must forgive him. Because then, and only then, will we have a chance to become friends again.

And I need a friend right now more than ever.

Sweetness

Chapter 20
CADE

I'm wasted.

Piss ass drunk and feeling hella sorry for myself.

I've been like this for days. Maybe longer. I can't remember.

All I know is that I feel lost and alone, even when I'm constantly surrounded by friends and acquaintances.

And that's a pretty amazing accomplishment considering that, at the moment, I have a hoop ho practically sitting on my lap.

I'm actually pretty pissed that Lance and Carver - the dickweasels - decided to throw a party tonight. In honor of our last weekend of freedom before all hell breaks loose with the start of our final college basketball season. Once the doors open next week with the first official practice, it's buh-bye free time until March. Well, if we make it into the NCAA championships, that is.

I need to get my head out of my ass if that's gonna happen. I know it.

Sweetness

Lance and Carver are worried about me fucking things up this year. I get it. They should be worried. All the motivation and drive to turn this into my greatest year ever has up and vanished with the loss of Ainsley. Carver even called me a vagina the other day over my stupid antics. Oh wait, no, he said, and I quote, *"you're acting like my grandmother's dried up twat."* Yeah, I don't want to think about why he knew how dry his grandmother's vagina was. Ew. Just ew.

"Yo, Griff. Get your ass over here and let's rip these guys to shreds." I barely register the demand from Lance, who is standing over at our makeshift beer pong table. I swivel my head behind me at Christian and Gabe, who are on the opposite end of the table from him.

I wonder if it's worth it for me to move from where I sit. I've got a beer in one hand and an arm around this chick – Sabrina, or something – who lets out a small noise of protest that I'd even remotely consider leaving.

She's been eying me all night, asking me every few minutes if I need anything or just trying to engage me in conversation. I've tried to tell her she's wasting her time because I'm not in the mood for anything right now. Not basketball. Not school. And certainly not a hoops hunny.

All I care about is Ainsley.

321

Damn. I actually avoided thinking about her over the last hour until she just popped in my head again. Or maybe that's the booze helping my brain to disengage. It's been a long time since I've been this trashed. Not even on my twenty-first…ah fuck, there we go again. Ainsley. She was the reason I wasn't over-the-top sloshed at my birthday party. But tonight I just wanted to shut all my thoughts off from the last two weeks. And Sailor Jerry is doing an admirable job at that.

The wave of media attention that's pummeled me since the day of the press conference was annoying as fuck, and equally as daunting. It's as if I've gone on a safari wearing a fresh meat vest and the lions (aka reporters), are descending upon me with the intention of tearing me apart limb by fucking limb.

The team's media publicist, Jacqueline, did what she could to shield me from the spotlight, but the pappz hit me out of nowhere, regardless of time of day or where I am. One night, as I was leaving campus, I stopped by the 7-Eleven to pick up some water and power bars. As I came back outside, this guy comes running up to my car shoving a video recorder in my face. I nearly pissed my pants out of fright, he freaked me out so bad. I swear, he came out of fucking nowhere.

Everyone and their mother wants to know about all the gritty details of my run in with the law and if I feel like I got off too easy. Public opinion over my case is all over the board – mainly due to all the recent press about privileged white athletes getting away with murder, so-to-speak, when other non-white players busted for similar criminal acts are getting the book thrown at them.

Look, I screwed up, but it wasn't criminal. It didn't hurt anyone. And it wasn't rape. Every time I hear about one of these rape cases my heart breaks for the victim. Why the hell do these things still happen? I mean, I'm a guy – I love women and I love sex. Sex is great and fucking awesome, but taking advantage of a girl, when she is not into it, is completely outside my understanding.

Guys need to take a step back and respect what their partner is doing. It's one thing to think with your dick. I've obviously done that quite a lot in my past. But if she says no, or stops things from moving on to the main event, then the show's over folks. End of the fourth quarter. That's the buzzer. You don't make a flagrant foul just to get some action.

While I'm raging over this issue in my head, I hear Lance once again yell over the noise.

"Griff! Come on…while we're young, dude."

My body protests having to leave the couch, but I need to take a piss anyway. As I shift in my seat, Sabrina leans into me, the swell of her half-exposed tits pressing in against my arm. Warm and soft and pliant. (Not gonna lie, my dick perks up in interest even if I don't.)

She's practically on top of me and I quell the urge to shove her cheap perfumed body away from me, but I can't muster the strength.

"Griff…come back quick." She whispers into my ear with a purr, soft and persuasive.

If we were sitting here two months earlier, I would ditch the idea of beer pong and lift her in my arms, drag her back to my room to get it on. But not now. Not when the mere idea of touching another girl after Ainsley makes me want to cringe with disgust.

My head tilts to the side as I look her over. She's not bad – pretty long blonde hair falling in soft curls around her apple-round cheeks, bright blue eyes hopeful for what might come.

But they're not the blue eyes I want to look into.

I don't want to be a dick, but I do need to correct her assumptions about what is going to happen. In other words, it's not going to happen. I cup my hands around her cheeks, giving her what I hope is a charming smile, and try to let her down easy.

"You're a great girl, Sabrina. But I'm not the guy for you tonight. Sorry." I place a quick kiss on her cheek, just as my eyes lock with a very recognizable pair of sapphire blue eyes. The one's I've missed for weeks. And right now they are staring at me with a butt load of hurt, pain, and question – all three that I unintentionally put there.

Fuuuuck.

My body jerks away from Sabrina so fast it nearly gives me a case of whiplash. I drop my hands like her face is a burning inferno, a confused expression appearing across Sabrina's face, which I don't acknowledge it. I don't have time.

Ainsley loses her balance and stumbles backward, her body bouncing like a pinball between people on either side of her. My feet hit the floor and I sway ever so slightly. My drunken state is not conducive to running after the girl I love. The world spins a little, as I'm forced to close my eyes for a second to gain my balance. When I open them again, she's disappeared. But I can see the front door open and shut, and know she's made her escape outside.

The guys are yelling for me again, but I dismiss them with a wave of my hand, as I run after her.

It's like a maze trying to make my way outside, spinning around two girls who stand near the door, red solo cups in hand. I mumble an apology as I've accidentally bump one of the girls' arms, so her hand goes flying, beer spilling over the other girl's mini-dress. She gives me a "watch it, fucktard". Guess I'll be paying for that later.

My mind races as I head out the door, swiftly glancing to the right and left trying to lock down Ainsley's whereabouts. It's dark outside, only a few overhead street lights illuminating the parking lot of our complex. I know she didn't drive, since she doesn't have a car, so it's unlikely she's heading into the lot. I immediately start walking toward the main street. Fuck, she took the bus again. Damnit. I hate when she has to use public transportation at night. It's unsavory and unsafe.

My legs start to sprint as I see the shadow of a shape about twenty yards in front of me.

"Ainsley!" I bellow, hoping not to wake up any neighbors. We've already received one citation and warning earlier this school year for our loud, ruckus behavior.

I don't expect her to stop and am stunned when she does, her back still facing me. Taking the opportunity that luck has provided me, I hightail it over to her standing form. She doesn't move an inch. Doesn't turn around. Doesn't speak. I approach her with caution.

I softly call her name again, now only a few feet away. It's only a whisper – or more like a drunk whisper. Her name is said in the form of a prayer. With gentle reverence. With hope. I'm about to drop to my knees and wail in both joy and relief.

"Ainsley. Oh my God, you're here. Don't leave. *Please.*"

There's silence now; surrounding us – establishing the distance recently created by our break-up. Inching closer until I'm close enough to reach my hand out to touch her shoulder, I hear a sharp intake of breath. A silent sob. Wait, it is. She's crying.

It's faint, but I know the sound. I've heard it enough in the dark when I lived at home and my mom would cry. It broke my heart then and it's tearing me apart now.

Without thinking, I reach for her, placing my hands upon her shoulders, turning her to face me. She doesn't resist, her eyes are closed tightly, either to block me out or to steel herself against the tide of emotion.

"Fuck, baby. I'm sorry. What you just saw in there, nothing was happening, I swear. Nothing was going to happen. Please believe me."

Ainsley sniffs and shakes her head, the tears now streaming down her face. The idea that I could make this strong, confident woman cry guts me. Slays me like a fucking knife. Right in the heart.

"Please, come sit down with me," I whisper, ushering her over to a bench in the small park on the apartment property. There's a street lamp overhead and it sheds a soft glow across her achingly sad face. I've caused this and I want to eliminate it. Remove it from her beautiful soul. I don't blame her for being upset over what she saw between me and Sabrina. It probably looked damning from that angle.

My hand trembles as I reach for hers, which she placed in her lap. The first touch of her warm, soft skin has my chest filling with an emotion I've never felt before. It's like my heart is the big, vast empty swimming pool, like the ones in the California drought in the seventies – the ones I'd seen in a documentary I watched once on the *Lords of Dogtown*. They used these empty pools as their skate parks and playgrounds during that drought year.

My heart has been a dried up pool during my absence from Ainsley. It was just an empty space, nothing to fill it with. It's amazing, though, that the minute she's back in my arms, it's like the heavens have opened up, flooding my soul with happiness.

"I'm so sorry, Ains. That wasn't at all what it looked like. I wasn't with that girl. I swear."

She lets out a noise that's something between a snort and a maniacal laugh. "That's so cliché. The whole '*We were on a break*' excuse...." Ainsley uses air quotes, shaking her head with a sad smile, before returning her gaze to me.

I can't let this go. Can't let her think that Sabrina and I were going to do anything. I may be drunk, but I was not going to sleep with her. That's not what I want anymore. I haven't wanted another girl since the moment I met Ainsley.

"Seriously, Ains. I was just trying to break the news gently to Sabrina that I wasn't into her. She'd been hitting on me all night. I just wanted to be left alone with my rum." I think I slurred the last few words, my tongue already feeling the hair of the dog. God, tomorrow morning is not going to be fun.

She takes a moment to look me over, evaluating the validity of my statement. I feel like I'm on the witness stand telling the world that '*I did not have sexual relations with that girl.*'

"Cade, I understand. Even if you were with her tonight before I got here, I have no reason to be angry or jealous. I was the one who ended things. I'm the reason we're not together. Well, or at least…"

I grab her hands, maybe not as gently as I should, but I'm emphatic that she understands me and what I need to say.

"No, you're wrong. I'm the reason you made the choice to break up, and I'm so fucking sorry. I never wanted to hurt you. I was just so scared to tell you the truth because I thought you'd leave me. And by keeping it from you, it happened anyway. You mean the world to me and the last person I'd ever want to hurt. I've missed you so goddamn much, Ainsley, it's killing me. I can't let you go. I don't want anyone else in the world. You're it for me, Ainsley. No one else matters…it's you who has my heart, baby…and I don't want it back." I give her a tentative smile. "But I do want you back…and I want to be more like you."

Ainsley lets out a little laugh. "More like me? In what way?"

Stroking a thumb over her knuckles, I tilt my chin up and smirk. "You're a good person, Ainsley. You treat people with kindness. Even when things have been hard for you, you have this quality – an inner light – that makes people love you. Everyone who meets you, loves you."

"Oh my God. You make me sound like Mother Theresa or something. And I'm hardly a saint."

"Maybe not…but you're an angel."

This makes her laugh, which I fucking love. It hits me then that she's sitting here with me. Not that I'm not absolutely grateful that she is, but I don't even know why she showed up tonight. I hope it's that she wants to give us another try. That she wants to forgive me for my stupidity and give me another chance. God, I pray that's why she's here. Or maybe she's going to break my heart all over again and tell me once and for all that we're through.

"Ainsley," I start, then falter. I'm not sure I really want to know, now. Hearing her say goodbye again would send me in a tailspin. Fuck, I don't know if I could take that.

"Yeah?"

"You're here."

She raises her eyebrows, giving me a smirk that suggests I've just made a dumbass comment.

"You're a little slow on the uptake tonight, Griff. But yeah, I'm here." She tentatively swipes underneath her nose.

My hands have a mind of their own and can't stop from reaching over to touch her cheek. My thumb strokes the soft skin just under her jaw and she automatically leans into it with a sigh. This seems like a good sign.

"I'm glad you're here. You've made me so happy just seeing you tonight. But is there a particular reason you are here?"

My fingers slide through her hair, sighing at the silky texture of it, as it cascades down and over her shoulders. I might have a slight case of whisky dick because of the copious amounts of rum I've ingested tonight, but damn if my cock doesn't jump against my zipper at expression across her face. The tears have dried and she lets out a sweet sigh of contentment as I continue threading my fingers through her strands.

"I was invited." She states, without further elaboration.

She was? By who? Only Lance and Carver knew about the party before tonight.

The question must be written across my face, or I said it out loud, because she answers it immediately.

"Lance invited me. I saw him earlier today in the quad. He mentioned that I should come over tonight to talk to you. That maybe I should consider forgiving you."

Huh. I didn't think Lance even gave a shit about my break up with Ainsley. It's not like we've talked about it a lot, 'cause we're guys. But it's not a secret that I've had my head up my ass the last few weeks and have been pretty down in the dumps over losing her. Perhaps he was getting tired of my constant moping and drinking – which a guy does when he thinks he's lost his girl.

And I did believe I'd truly lost her. When a girl doesn't return your calls, your texts and avoids you at all cost, that's generally a pretty good indicator that she thinks you're a piece of shit, and no chance in hell you're going to get back with her.

Lance is my hero. I want to run back to the house and give him a bro-sized bear hug for doing me this solid behind my back. First things, first though. Before I go thank Lance, however, I want to kiss Ainsley. I want to linger in her sweet fragrance. To taste the salt from her tear-stained cheeks. To sip at her puffy, swollen lips and make them mine once again. She is mine.

I stop myself before I lean in and reacquaint my mouth with hers. We still need to talk.

"Take a walk with me, Ains. I want to talk."

I present her my outstretched hand and pull her up to her feet. Most of the booze in my system dissipated with the adrenaline rush of seeing Ainsley again, but my stance is still a bit wobbly, so I lean into her for support. It feels good to be touching her again.

Ainsley drops her head toward the ground, her long hair falling over her shoulders, as she kicks a loose rock on the sidewalk. We walk in the direction of a small park down the street, the sounds of the party slowly growing more distant.

I'm surprised when Ainsley speaks first, her sassy playfulness exactly what we need in this moment. Her positive attitude always amazes me. Most people, if given the hand she was dealt, would be sour-assed motherfuckers with a penchant for mayhem and self-destruction. Yet Ainsley has a way of turning lemons into lemonade when faced with adversity.

"I don't suppose you've watched the news lately?" She giggles. I fucking love that sound. And I love that she can make light of the situation, starting off this long-overdue conversation with some levity.

I nudge her shoulder with mine as we continue to stroll, hand-in-hand, down the sidewalk.

"Oh, you mean have I heard all the salacious gossip about that hot, ASU basketball player? And the trouble he got himself into?" I slap my hand over my mouth in feigned shock and then make a *tsking* noise. "I may have heard a thing or two."

I turn to look at her, and as expected, her lips quirk up into a knowing grin and she rolls her eyes.

"Seriously, though. That was a colossal fuck-up, Cade. I can't say I'm not a little disappointed in you. What if you would have driven that night? You could have gotten in an accident and hurt yourself. Or worse, been killed or hurt someone else. I thought you were smarter than that."

Without warning, I come to a complete stop and the momentum snaps her back like a human rubber band.

I want to come clean and make my apology count. While it's true, that night I was definitely not thinking with anything but my dick, that's not who I am any longer. Nor who I want to be. Ainsley's influence over me has made me realize that.

"Ains…listen to me. I made a huge mess of things. I thought I was invincible and couldn't be touched. It was a stupid move, but you have to know me by now. I would have never driven in my inebriated condition that night. I was behind the wheel, yes, with the key in the ignition, but I wasn't going to drive and I never planned on it. I'd never put anyone in jeopardy like that. You have to believe me."

Taking a moment to consider my sincerity, Ainsley tilts her head and bites down on her luscious lip. What I wouldn't give to suck on that lip right now.

"I know." She says in a small voice.

Relief is fast, flooding me with a powerful urge to wrap her in my arms and never let her go. And just as fast as it pours through me, it's gone with her next question.

"But why didn't you ever come clean with me before now? I guess that's the part that hurts the most and what made me break things off with you. I don't know that I can trust you now. What the hell am I supposed to do with that?"

Ah fuck. That's what I was worried about. Ainsley doesn't trust easily to begin with. I'd made such good headway with her up to that point, and *snap*. Just like that, it's gone.

Cupping her jaw, my thumbs caress the soft skin along her jawline. Her mouth puckers and her brows narrow with a pained grimace.

"If I could have a do over, everything would be different." I feel my shoulders deflate, my forehead pressing gently against hers. "I'd change everything about that night. I would've stayed home and studied, and not given in to peer pressure to go out. I would've resisted the urge for a quick hook up. And I certainly wouldn't have gone out to my car with that girl."

My breath comes out in short bursts, as if I've just done sprints up and down the court during warm ups. Something in my chest pinches tight, squeezing my heart with an angry fist.

"But you know what, Ainsley?"

"What?"

I place a chaste kiss on her forehead. "If none of that ever happened, I may have never met you. I wouldn't have been at the coffee shop the morning of my court date. And I wouldn't have run into you again when I was leaving the meeting with my coach the next day. And I wouldn't have been required to go visit my gramps. Fate intervened and turned my mistake into the best thing that could have ever happened to me. I'm now closer than ever to my grandfather. I've met and fallen for the most perfect girl in the world, who I hope will forgive me and give me another chance."

Ainsley's hands wrap around my neck and she smiles. Goddamn, that smile is brighter than a thousand suns and warms me more than the arid Arizona heat.

"I do forgive you, Griff. I'm yours if you still want me."

I scoff like it's the silliest thing I've ever heard and press my lips squarely against hers, taking possession of what I've missed for weeks now.

"I've never stopped wanting you, Ainsley. You're all I've ever wanted."

Chapter 21
AINSLEY

Things have definitely changed since my mom and Anika moved to South Dakota two weeks ago. After they moved, I asked Mica if she wanted to move in with me temporarily. She'd been living with one of her aunties in a seedy part of Phoenix, so she was more than happy to get out from under their wings and into a nicer place. I also posted a roommate wanted ad out on the ASU student boards. The likelihood of my mom coming back is less than one percent. But if Anika did return at some point, well, she would just live in the master bedroom with me.

I've made sure to call Ani every night and text her daily to make sure everything is okay. She seems quiet and reserved, resigned to the fact that she's on the move again. I feel hopeless and useless to do anything but lend my ear.

The positive side of having Mica sharing the apartment with me is that she's a clean freak. She cleans for a living, so our apartment is always spotless. And to be honest, she is quiet as a mouse. Most of the time, unless she's out in the living area or kitchen when I am home, I don't even know she's there.

The same thing probably can't be said about me, because when I'm home in the evenings, Cade is usually with me. And let's just say even using loud music to drown out the noise we make together in the bedroom still doesn't do the trick.

Like now, for instance.

Cade's sexual appetite cannot be assuaged. This boy – *man* – is insatiable. Last night when he came over was the first time in days that we'd seen each other. Things got heated and hot within two seconds of him shutting my bedroom door. We'd fucked like bunnies twice last night and fell asleep in each other's arms.

I've been lying awake now for the last ten minutes, the sun just starting to make an appearance through my east facing window. My lids slowly open as I stare at the ceiling above me, the wall of heat from Cade's naked body pressed tightly against mine. He has his boxers on, but the expanse of his broad, gloriously naked chest gives me lots of dirty ideas. My eyes divert from the boring popcorn ceiling to his very entertaining torso, as they roam over his ridiculously cut abs, which are rising and falling along to the rhythm of his light snoring.

I slide my hand tentatively down along the peaks and valleys of his stomach and sigh. He's kind of a freak of nature. Golden tan, marble-smooth, and bigger than a freaking...

It's then I notice the monster has been awakened. And yes, I do call his penis a monster. Because he is a big boy, with big body parts that make my vajajay shout in joy. I swallow thickly, my eyes drinking in the sight below. Urging me to touch and fondle. My mouth even starts to water.

I stare in awe as his cock grows even bigger, poking out through the opening in his cotton boxers. It's almost become a staring contest between his dick and me. But I have the advantage, because while it has the 'come hither' vibe, I'm the one in control. I'm the one who has the pair of hands, the fingers…the mouth…that can do whatever I damn well please with him. As if he knows what I'm thinking, he begins to twitch.

Mind-reading hard-ons. Who knew?

Without looking up at the face of my sleeping giant, I scoot down so my toes hang off the end of the bed and my body sidles up against his legs. The soft hairs on his legs tickle the tips of my breasts and I have to bite my lip to keep from giggling out loud. I make an effort to be stealthy, but I'm practically frothing at the mouth to uncover my treasure.

I still when Cade's throat rumbles with a loud snore. My body jerks in surprise as I wait to see if he wakes up. He doesn't. So I continue to act all 'Agent Provocateur' allowing my fingertips to score the length of his thigh, beginning at the kneecap and moving up to the edge of his underwear. I wait, wondering if my morning adventure will wake him, smiling when he doesn't even move a muscle.

Well, one of his muscles moves. Technically, I think it's an organ, with muscles.

Either way, it's in really good shape.

My hand continues to move, tracing the outline of his sac through his shorts, cupping it with a gentle squeeze, before moving on to the main attraction. This man and his enormous erection could be the death of me. He makes me want him in every single way. Cade, who started out to be the biggest jerk I'd ever met, has become my friend, my lover, and my confidant. Cade has shown me what it's like to be cared for. To be respected. To feel cherished. And dare I say it, to be loved.

He's only told me that he loves me that one time – at the hospital when we were there with Simon, but hasn't said it again. Yet I know, with every fiber of my being, that he does. And I love him with the same level of certainty.

Raising my head, I shift my body upright, careful not to jostle the bed too much, so my mouth can reach its intended objective. At the first brush of my tongue against the smooth tip of his cock, Cade unconsciously groans in his sleep. I smile, moving up on my heels to get better leverage. I lower my head and slide my tongue around the sweet underside of his shaft. The taste of musk and man overwhelms me and I'm instantly turned on.

Working to finagle his cock out of the confines of his boxers proves to be difficult, so I give up and just pull him out the opening. I wrap my hands around the base and grasp him hard. Cade gives a hungry moan and his hips instinctively jerk off the bed. My eyes fly to his. They are half-lidded with sleep and lust, gazing down at me with fascination. His lips part as if he's about to say something.

Then he plops his head back down on the pillow and mumbles.

"I thought I was dreaming," his breath rushes from his lungs. "Fuck, baby. Don't stop."

And with that sentiment, I get to work.

Blowjobs have never been my favorite thing to do. In the past, they were mainly done as learning experiences, but were always given half-heartedly. As a medical professional, I tend to get wrapped up in the clinical aspect of the act. There are just some things you just shouldn't consider when you're down 'there'.

However, all thoughts of hygiene fly out the window as I take Cade in. His wide, smooth crown slides into the warmth of my mouth and I begin to suck. I've become an expert on how he likes me to handle him. Sucking the tip, using my tongue in that sweet spot, and then running the length of his shaft with the flat of my tongue before sucking him all the way back to my throat always does the trick. And then I do it all over again in the same manner.

It gets him so worked up that he typically only takes a few minutes before he's shouting out my name. And oh my God, I love that sound.

It's part torture. Part torment. But one hundred percent pure, consuming lust. And it sends me into lethal territory, producing such an overwhelming high that I feel like my body will combust. Not a bad way to go, if you ask me.

My eyes remain closed as I begin to work Cade with my mouth, enjoying the low, deep groans he emits when my tongue hits a certain spot.

"Just like that," he pants, his hands finding the top of my head, gently exerting pressure and control as he cups my head.

"Mmm." I give him my moan of agreement, the sound vibrating across his cock. I squeeze his shaft and I hear a roar of approval, his thighs tensing beneath me.

There's a slight sting at my hairline, as Cade slides a strong hand through my hair, shifting it out of my face and yanking it tight in his grip. And then he's coming. I look up at his lust-filled face, contorted into a beautiful grimace, his hips halting their movement as he lets out a long, satisfied curse.

"*Fuuuck.*"

When he finally goes still, I extract him from my mouth with a smile, taking a swipe at the edge of my lips with my fingers. I use this moment to admire him, as a feeling of utter contentment floods through me. He's all mine.

At least I think he's all mine. We really haven't had the 'talk' since we've gotten back together. I certainly don't spend every waking moment with him – *hardly* – so I have to trust him and I assume we are exclusive. But maybe I'm just fooling myself. There's always some female presence when he's out and about around campus, or at parties. He's never given me any reason to doubt him – even the night I showed up at his party to find him wasted with a skank practically on his lap.

We haven't discussed our relationship status since we got back together, and aside from his grandfather and his mother just the one time, I haven't met any of his family. Then again, I've never introduced him to mine. But there's not a chance of that now since they're gone.

A pair of strong arms lifts me up and out of my thoughts, sliding me up the bed so I'm lying on my side facing him.

Cade's fingers stroke my cheek. "Hey baby, what's going on? I can practically see your worried thoughts."

His lips give me a gentle peck on my mouth. "And there is no reason…" *Kiss.* "For you to be worried…" *Kiss.* "Because that was the best morning blowjob I've ever gotten…" *Kiss, kiss, kiss.*

I shake my head, one of my hands landing on his solid chest, giving him a playful shove. "One of the best, huh? Just exactly how many morning BJ's have you had to compare it to, Number 23?"

I always use that nickname when I'm joshing with him. His lips quirk slightly and his cheeks burn bright red. *Busted.*

And then he blows me away. "There may have been a few, but not been anyone who mattered. None given to me by someone I'm in love with. That I *love*."

Well, when he puts it that way…all my insecurity and jealousy vanish. *Poof.* Like a cloud of marijuana smoke from Lance's stash. Did I mention his roommate is a pothead?

I feel a rush of…I don't know what. My stomach shimmies, as if a thousand butterflies just took flight inside my belly. In my chest. Flitting and flapping in waves, floating up into the sky. Bringing me with them.

Part of me is hesitant to accept his love. Resistant. What the hell do I know about love, anyway? I've never really seen it in any form until now. Or even felt it.

Before I can get too deep in thought, Cade's hands land of my hips and he's slipping them under my ass, flipping me over on my back.

"What are you doing?"

"I can't have the girl I love worrying about anything," he states so matter-of-factly, as he lifts his eyes to me while he scoots down the bed. "That just won't do."

He begins to place kisses down my stomach, and I shiver under the exquisite feel of his overnight beard growth scraping against my tender skin. But my hand reaches down to cup his cheek to stop him before he goes any further. I might be crazy, but we have to talk. And if I wait until after he makes me lose my mind, I'll never get up the nerve.

"Cade," I whisper. "Come back up here."

The look of confusion is almost comical, as if he can't believe I'm stopping him from giving me what I know he was about to give me. Yeah, it does seem kind of loony, come to think of it. But if I don't get things off my chest, I won't be able to enjoy myself.

Cade doesn't move at first. "What is it, baby?"

He tries to distract me by placing an open-mouthed kiss between my legs, his fingers playing with the edge of my panties. And believe me – it is oh-so-distracting. My body is in total agreement that he should keep going with that. But my brain, and thoughts, are in complete opposition. I wiggle out from under him and scoot out of his mouth's reach. With a heavy sigh, he capitulates and throws himself up the bed with a thump. The weight of his massively constructed body sends me airborne for a brief moment and I try to stifle a giggle.

Once we're both comfortably situated, our bodies still affixed skin to skin, his hand leisurely strumming up and down my side, I decide to lay it all out there.

"Am I the only one, Cade?" I let that question detonate between us.

For a second, I think I've put him into an utter panic. His eyes grow wild, something akin to shock visibly exploding in his deep moss greens.

His mouth opens and closes, as if trying to find the words. I'm not quite sure what to make of it. But before I can put any more thought into it, he closes the distance between us, his hand cupping my face, kissing me firmly. Intensely. With purpose. Brooking no argument.

As he pulls away, I open my eyes to see a hint of gold gleaming in his irises.

"Ainsley, are you asking me if we're monogamous?"

I nod my head. "Yeah."

He lets out a bite of laughter and I grit my teeth in anxious agony. This whole topic is very uncomfortable, and now I'm kicking myself for bringing it up.

Cade sighs, propping himself up on his elbow and staring intently at me.

"There are very few things I love more than basketball, ya know? Of course I love my mom, and my sisters, and my grandfather...and maybe pizza and beer. But that's as far as the list went..." I raise my eyebrows.

"Until I met you, Ainsley, basketball was my highest priority. School and family were a distant second. But no one, not even my friends, held as much as my attention as the game...and never any girl before you."

His hand continues to gently, and sweetly, stroke the skin along the curve of my waist, leaving a heated trail of longing.

"I never thought about my future much. All I knew was that I didn't want to play in the NBA or European leagues. And I knew that I wanted to one day be part of creating some life-saving medical device. Honestly, outside of that, I never considered how empty my future possibilities would be until I fell in love with you. Maybe I'm rushing things when I tell you this, and I don't mean to freak you out...but I know, with one hundred percent certainty, that I want you in my future life. What I hope you get from all of this is that there is no one else but you, Ainsley. And the way I see it, baby...you're stuck with me."

Cade leans down and places a soft kiss against my exposed shoulder.

I'm a little bewildered by what I've just heard. I'm not even quite sure what he means by it all. My life has always been centered on the here and now, dealing with the difficulties of my day-to-day life, just trying to get through each day to make it on to the next. I've never been prompted to give voice to what my future might be like.

When you're raised by a mom with manic episodes of mental illness and chemical dependency problems, you get used to avoiding hopefulness. And that's what dreaming of the future will do to you. It'll set you up for the crushing probability that none of what you actually want or dream of will come to fruition.

The corners of his mouth tug up in that knowing smile of his. "So, to be clear, Ainsley. In case you didn't understand my rambled speech, yes, we are exclusive. There's been no one else since the day I met you. I've not looked at another woman and I have no inclination or desire to. You're it for me."

My brain is muzzy, still trying to process what he's just told me. I smile and slip my hand around the back of his neck to get him closer as I lean in to whisper in his ear. The scruff on his face tickles my lips and I can't help but run my tongue along the edge of his jaw.

"Good to know, Number 23. And just so you know, I'm all yours to do whatever you want with."

Cade promptly goes back to working up an appetite. Breakfast will have to wait.

Chapter 22
CADE

The first official practice – also known as Midnight Madness – is in a few short hours from now. The moment we've all been waiting for since the disappointing end to last season. The beginning of my final college basketball season.

The great thing about our team this year is that with the exception of a few red shirt Freshman that were added, and the three graduated seniors from last year, we are nearly the identical team. Which means we are ready to capitalize on our cohesiveness and prove our greatness to our opponents.

The only problem: Jeremy Munson, one of our junior forwards, just tested positive for anabolic steroids. We are required to undergo a mandatory annual medical evaluation. Under the NCAA drug testing policy, as well as the school's athlete's code of conduct, an initial positive test of any steroid, peptide hormone or a diuretic will result in suspension of eligibility to compete in intercollegiate play for one calendar year. So basically, he just fucked his entire junior year season. And he messed up his scholarship, as well as our team's balance.

Fucking Jeremy.

I'm not all that close to him, since he's ridden the bench for the last two years. If I had to guess, I'd put money on the fact that he started taking the steroids to beef up and increase his chances of starting. And now the dickweed just screwed everyone over.

As a college student athlete, we have our special set of challenges at school. We are held to a higher standard than other students, although some would argue we are given more leniency with consequences to our actions. Touché. Maybe some are.

If we want to play, we have to take things seriously. That requires studying hard to remain eligible to play; conducting ourselves with the highest level of integrity and sportsmanship - both on and off the court. We have to be mindful of sexual relationships – ensuring consent and being careful to avoid getting trapped by a girl looking for a future payday. As well as ensuring the girl we're with is respected and not mistreated.

Regardless of all those expectations, there's always a fuckwit who abuses their status and takes advantage of vulnerable women. I mean, what the fuck, dude? Like that Vanderbilt football player who was convicted of sexual assault of his own fucking girlfriend when he allowed her unconscious body to be used and gang raped. All while he taped it and handed out condoms?

Seriously messed up shit.

I'm sorry, but you've got to be sick in the fucking head to ever think that's okay. Sadly, I've seen it all too often at the frat parties I've attended. Even as I think back to my own conduct the night I was arrested, I realize I should've been more careful with that girl. She was drunk, or at least tipsy, when we went out to my car. Although we didn't have sex that night, had it gone any further, who knows what she could've claimed happened?

It's a scary prospect, and gives me discomfort to think about it now. I have to give it to my dad, he did provide me some good advice when I entered puberty. He told me to always manage myself above the fray. Be smart. Don't act like a fool. And never disrespect a woman.

I didn't really understand it at the time. Hindsight always being twenty-twenty, I now see why he was so disappointed over my conduct that night. I didn't listen to him. His guidance went in one ear and right out the other.

Had it happened to either of my two younger sisters, I would have gone ape shit and flown into older brother protective mode. It makes me a hypocrite when I discourage any of my buddies from even looking at my sisters. I've made it very clear that I will kick any guy's ass, even my friends, who fuck with either of my sisters.

Even as we speak, it's like swatting bees away from the hive with my sister Kylah. She's home for fall break and I invited her to come meet Ainsley and attend my practice. Both roommates, including Van who came over for pre-practice dinner, have been staring slack jawed at Ky for the last two hours. I'm about to throttle them.

They've been eyeballing her like she's fresh meat, wearing a pair of short-denim shorts, and a T-shirt that is stretched tight across her chest where it reads Talk Nerdy to Me. Her medium-length bob is pulled back into a ponytail, her wispy bangs hovering just to the top rim of her glasses. Yeah, she's a geeky, gawky girl…but is still beautiful with assets that a lot of guys enjoy looking at. And right now, they're all looking at her.

Motherfuckers. I glare at them all.

"So, Kylah, what are you studying out there at that fancy school you're at?" Lance asks, but not before shoving a piece of garlic bread into his pie hole. The guy has no manners.

I glance over at Ky, who is daintily picking at her spaghetti, a faint blush rising across her already rosy cheeks. Did I mention that Ky is the shy one of the twins? I swear, the girl gets embarrassed any time the spotlight is on her. It's kind of cute, though.

"Oh…um…" Ky practically chokes on the words. "Molecular biology."

A collective sound of impressed acknowledgements surrounds the table. I pop my head up from my plate and see Carver half listening, his focus on his phone in his lap. Lance is noshing on food, chewing with his mouth open as he shakes his head, and Van…well, his expression baffles me. If I didn't know better, and know he has a long-time girlfriend, I'd think he was interested in my sister. But thank God he does have a girlfriend, because otherwise I'd have to kick his ass.

I asked Kylah over for dinner tonight because my mom and John are away on a cruise, and I didn't want Ky to be sitting home alone with nothing to do. She'd probably be sitting home alone right now reading a book or watching a Game of Thrones episode. When I asked her about seeing her old high school friends, she just shrugged and said "maybe". The girl has no social life.

"How'd your big speech go last week?" I ask, knowing she had to take a public speaking elective and it just about killed her to get up in front of people. "What was your topic again?"

Ky nibbles on her lip, her face splotchy and cheeks pink. As she lifts her head to look at me, her moss-green eyes grow wide. With the exception of Kady, who got my dad's blue eyes, we share the same eyes as my mom.

"Well, I wanted to do a speech on a topic I was comfortable with, so I pitched the idea to my professor about organic chemistry and how there's been a serious decline of honey bee population in the U.S. over the last few years. It's affected by changing climates and global warming and it poses a real threat to agriculture." She takes a breath and lets out an exasperated sigh. I chuckle.

Yep, that's my nerdy scientific sister.

"Wow, okay. Well...that sounds *interesting*." Not really, but I can't tell her that. She seems really excited about the topic.

"Exactly!" she exclaims, like we're in solidarity over the issue. "But my communications professor said I needed to take a topic that I'm *not* familiar with. Which is absolutely ridiculous."

Van pipes in. "So what did you select?"

It's as if Ky had no idea there were other's at the table because her head whips around to give Van a wide-eyed stare.

She gulps, blushes and then grins, giving a shy tilt of her head toward the floor.

"My roommate, Sienna, suggested I give a speech on dating in the technology-driven world and how the impacts of social media are affecting relationships."

My fork drops out of my hand, hitting the table with a loud clatter. Ky swings her head over my direction, her eyebrows raise in surprise.

"So you spoke in front of an audience about how to hook up?"

My little outburst garners the attention of Lance and Carver again, whose heads pop up with interest.

"Hells yeah," Carver hoots. "Do tell. I'm always looking for new methods of meeting the ladies."

I swat at him, pushing at his shoulder.

"Like you need any sort of help." Lance's got that right.

Carver is the king of hook-ups. Girls flock to him in droves. The guy has this player charm that somehow allows him to sweep in, get in a girl's panties, and sweep right back out before the girl barely registers what the hell just happened. In fact, I'd bet he's been chatting with at least three chicks on his phone in the last ten minutes alone.

My eyes dart back to Ky, who I see has the sense to roll her eyes and shake her head at Carver's response.

"No, you idiot. My thesis was on the way it *negatively* affects our generation's ability to find love in this short-term, quick hook-up society, because all the internet sites only cater to finding sex."

Lance snorts. "What's wrong with that?"

What a douche. I punch him in the right bicep – *hard*.

He pulls back and rubs the spot where I slugged him. "Ouch – dude. Why you be hatin'?"

Kylah scoffs as if she can't believe the audacity of his ignorance.

"Men."

Van doesn't agree with her assessment.

"Hey, that's not a fair point. It's not just men on those sites, you know. Unless it's a gay site, there has to be interest from the opposite sex. Otherwise, the sites would be of no use. So, in essence, there's some implied duality in this situation, where women are just as culpable for causing the decline in relationship infractions."

Whoa. *Go, Van, Go.*

Kylah considers this for a moment and then concedes with a nod of her head.

"True. And that's kind of why my speech failed."

"Oh no. I'm sorry to hear that." Van is showing an awful lot of interest in this conversation. I'm not sure I like it.

Kylah shrugs and looks down at the fork in her hand.

"Yeah, it was pretty pathetic. I was so nervous about having to speak up in front of the class, that in my preparation for the speech, I completely spaced considering both sides of the coin. So when I was challenged, I got flustered and couldn't speak to that point. It was a dumb thing to do."

My sister has always been this way. She has a tendency to get down on herself and lacks self-esteem. It's like Kady sucked it all up from her in the womb.

I reach over to wrap my arm around her shoulders, tugging her in for a hug.

"Ky. Don't do that. It was just one lousy speech. We all have our moments. Even Carver here...Mr. Perfect..."

Carver's head jerks up, his eyes glaring at me. "What the fuck, man? What'd I do to you, fuckwad?"

"Oh yeah...remember basketball camp our junior year in high school? When you stole the ball from me and dribbled down the court like a cocky hotshot, just about to slam dunk the ball, and you tripped over your own feet? Hilarious!"

Everyone at the table laughs over the absurdity of Carver, the epitome of cool, making a fool of himself. Carver scowls and flips me the bird, mumbling a "*Motherfucker*" and goes back to looking at his phone.

"Yeah, Kylah. Don't be so hard on yourself. Speaking in front of a room full of strangers is the worst thing ever." Van states with conviction.

"You guys do it all the time at press conferences. And you make it look easy."

I shrug my shoulders. "It doesn't mean we like it. Sometimes the questions are bullshit and they try to trip you up. It gives reporters a hard on to score us down a notch. Bastards."

Kylah shifts in her seat, a regretful expression overtaking her face. "Like they did with you, Cade?"

I grumble. "Jesus, Ky. You saw that? That is not the shining moment in my career that I want to be remembered for."

Van jumps in, saving me from utter humiliation in front of my baby sister. "Yo, Griff. It was a fucking ambush. That asshole…" He suddenly stops, glances over at Kylah and blanches. "Sorry, Ky."

She giggles and waves him off.

"Anyway, we all screw up sometimes. Some of us more than others. It's how you carry yourself out of the mess that speaks to your character. Right, Griff?"

Van's got me there. He's sticking up for me, giving me the opportunity to save face in front of Kylah. Good man. But I still don't like the furtive glances he's giving her out of the corner of his eye whenever she isn't looking.

There's one thing I won't tolerate, no matter how good the friend. It's one of my friends hitting on my little sister. Kylah's as innocent as they come. Unmarred and virginal. There's no doubt in my mind she's still a virgin.

Just then it hits me. Shit…she's been away in college almost a whole semester now. I wonder…has she? Nah…no way. Not possible. But I make a mental note to text Kady later to see if she knows anything. She and Ky share everything.

A knock on the door stops any further thoughts on this topic. I practically jump out of my chair and rush to the door. I've been waiting for Ainsley to arrive with my gramps. She had to finish with the dinner schedule at the home before she and gramps could leave. They're early, which makes me happy.

Swinging the door open, ready to grab her in my arms, I find the one person I'm least expecting to find standing in front of me.

"Dad."

"Son." He says with a quick nod as he presses forward into the hallway. I'm confused. I didn't invite him over, and definitely don't want him here. But from the sound of the happy squeals coming from my sister behind me, it's safe to assume Kylah did invite him. It's for that reason I'm not about to turn him away.

"Daddy!" Kylah shouts, running toward him with open arms. He gathers her in his embrace and places a quick kiss on top of her head. His eyes are closed and his expression is warm and loving. I guess we share that one common trait. We love the twins to pieces.

"Sweetie, I'm so happy to see you. Come on, let's go sit down so you can tell me all about school and how everything's going."

I notice a twinge of something pass through Kylah's eyes, but it quickly disappears as she pastes on a happy smile and turns to walk away, her arm grasped in the crook of my dad's elbow. I have no time to worry about what was in her expression when the door opens again. This time it's exactly who I am expecting.

"Hey there, handsome." Her voice is utter joy to my ears.

I give her a welcoming smile, picking her up by her waist and spinning her around. "Hey yourself, beautiful."

Because we have an audience, I restrain myself from mauling her right there. She feels so ridiculously perfect in my arms I don't want to let her go. She squirms and wiggles out of my grasp so I can't do anything but drop her back to her feet.

I turn toward my grandfather and give him a hug.

"Hey, Gramps. I'm so glad you could come tonight. I know it's getting way past your bedtime, old man. Hopefully you can take a nap in the stands." I joke, tapping him on back.

He snorts, giving me a mocking punch.

He waggles a gnarled finger at me, eyebrows raised. "You're not too old that I can't still bend you over my knee and smack the sass right out of you, young man."

I'm about to retort when my dad clears his throat and walks forward toward us, holding out his hand to my grandfather. I forgot how awkward things were between my dad and gramps. Not knowing the entire story between my parents and my gramps, I'm at least familiar with the fact that my dad had practically forbidden us from visiting gramps when my parents were together. Apparently they've been in opposition since well before I was born.

"Simon," my dad says quietly and respectfully.

"Hello, Allen. Good to see you. How've you been?"

My dad, ever the professional, gives his canned response. "Good, good. Work always keeping me busy."

I can't stop myself when I release a loud snorting sound. Both of them look my way, but I ignore them and move to Ainsley, leaving them to their awkward reunion.

"Hey, baby. Come meet my little sister." I direct Ainsley over to the couch where Kylah is sitting, looking both shy and excited. She's never met any girl I've been with, but she knows everything about Ainsley, since I've been talking nonstop about her for months. She's aware of how we met, what happened between us and that we're back together again.

Ky gets to her feet and is about to shake hands when Ainsley smiles broadly and pulls her into a hug.

"Kylah, it's so good to finally meet you. I've heard so much about you. Your brother is so proud of you and what you're doing. You're more beautiful than your pictures. I'm so happy you get a chance to visit. It must be hard to be away from home for such long periods of time."

I watch with assessing eyes as Ky steps back a few inches and out of Ainsley's embrace. The smile on her face seems genuine, but doesn't quite meet her eyes.

"Hi Ainsley. I'm so happy to meet you, too. And yes, it's good to be home for a little while. I have been kind of homesick." Her smile fades and her bright eyes lose a little of their light. I wonder what that's all about, but now is not the time to delve into the subject. I'm sure she'll tell me at some point.

The guys at the table are cleaning the dinner dishes and they all yell out a 'hello' to Ainsley.

"Hi guys!" She waves and smiles before grabbing my hand and squeezing. "Geez, Cade. You mentioned that Kylah was smart, but you didn't tell me how absolutely gorgeous she is."

Ky does exactly what I expect her to do when she hears Ainsley's compliment. She blushes and drops her chin, shifting on her feet with embarrassment. Just then, a low voice speaks up from behind her.

"My girl is both beautiful and brilliant."

My dad places an arm around Kylah's shoulder giving her a proud squeeze. It's then that I realize I haven't introduced my dad to Ainsley. I honestly never thought I'd have to. At least not so soon. My dad has no idea I'm involved with someone. At least, if he does, he didn't hear it from me.

He clears his throat and offers his hand in greeting. "Hello. I'm Allen, Cade and Kylah's father. And you are?"

"Ainsley Locker," she says with confidence, shaking his hand. "I'm, uh…" She looks to me for direction.

"Ainsley's my girlfriend, Dad. You've actually met her once before." I threw that zinger in just to catch him off guard.

My dad gives me a confused look, and I kind of enjoy putting him on the spot like this. I know he wouldn't remember her from the café, since that morning was a blur and he'd been so pissed at me. But getting in this little dig makes me feel like I have the upper hand for some reason. Immature, I know.

Ainsley swivels her head to me, her eyes full of question.

"Yeah, the morning of my court appearance. She was our waitress at the café after the hearing."

My dad's head nods, like he remembers her. What bullshit.

"Ah, of course. I thought you looked familiar. Well, it's a pleasure to meet you again, Ainsley. So do you go to school with Cade?" I know where he's going with his question. He wants to know if she is *just* a waitress. Like it would a crime if that's all she did as a profession.

My grandfather joins us by sitting down, as Ainsley moves to his side to help him lower himself to the couch.

"Actually, Allen…Ainsley is my nurse." He smiles up at Ainsley with an expression of gratitude and appreciation. "She's one of the most kind and gentle nurses I've ever had. She's patient and treats me like a human being, not an old person. This girl is nothing but sweetness and light."

From behind me I hear Lance mumble, "*I bet she gives good sponge baths, too.*" I turn around and glare at him hard. He knows better than to say things like that about my girl. Thankfully, when he sees me staring at him, he has the sense to look remorseful.

"Flattery will get you everywhere, Simon." She responds, patting his hand. Then she looks up at my dad. "I'm actually a CNA right now, not a full-fledged nurse. But I'm in the nursing program at ASU."

It must all click together then for my dad, because he adds, "My goodness, I'm impressed. You're a nursing student, work at a café and the nursing home? How in the world do you have time for all of that?"

My chest swells with pride to epic proportions. I tug at her hand and pull her up to her feet, wrapping my arm around her waist.

"She's amazing, that's how." I kiss her cheek as she grins. "And I'm a lucky guy she finds time for me in her life, too."

Ainsley clucks her tongue and gives me a mocking side grin. "You are pretty damn lucky, aren't you?" She elbows me in the ribs when I tickle her side.

Carver comes into the living room with his duffle bag flung over his shoulder. "Hey, I hate to break up this little meet and greet, but we need to get over to the arena to warm up." The other guys come up behind him.

I let go of Ainsley and turn to head back to my room to grab my stuff. Before I do, I look at my dad.

"Are you coming to the practice, dad?" I'm not sure if Kylah invited him or not. But I guess I could ask if he wants to come see the first practice. It's the only one open to the public and he's always come watch me in previous years.

Allen Griffin rarely looks anything but confident. He has to exude self-confidence for the type of profession he's in. But right now, he looks anything but certain. I'm kind of floored.

"I'd really like to, if you don't mind. But I understand…"

Ainsley, sensing the awkwardness of the situation, pipes in.

"I think it would be great if you joined us. You, Simon and Kylah can give me some pointers about what's going on, because I have no idea. I've never actually watched basketball before." She gives an apologetic smirk.

My dad lets out what sounds like a deep sigh of gratitude. He nods his head in acceptance, which Kylah does the same, but with more enthusiasm.

"I'm with you, Ainsley," she says, owning up to her lack of interest in basketball. "We'll stick together, okay?"

And with that, I know the night is off to a great start.

Chapter 23
AINSLEY

The excitement in the stands is palpable. A living, breathing animal that shifts through the arena, moving with energy, as fans clamor for a view of their team's first season appearance. Scanning the stadium, it's a sea of maroon and gold.

Taking it all in fills me with a raw thrill that courses through my body, sending little currents of electricity that I can feel in all my extremities. Excitement and nerves spread through my system as I wait to see Number 23 out on the court tonight. *My* Number 23.

After the guys left the apartment for the arena earlier, I sat around chatting and getting to know Allen and Kylah. I noticed some tension between the two men during our conversation, but most of the focus was put on hearing how things were going with Kylah's studies and activities.

Kylah is definitely Cade's sibling because of the strong resemblance. They have the same eyes and smile, although Cade's smiles are constant, where Kylah's seem reserved. It takes more for her to offer one up. But when she does, it absolutely lights up her face. She's just a sweetheart. I liked her instantly. In some ways, she reminds me of Anika, and that thought gives me a pang of sorrow.

I tried calling Ani earlier in the day, just to see how everything's been going, but didn't hear anything back. Which is highly unusual. Since she left for South Dakota, she's in constant contact with me. Whenever I've talked to her on the phone, she sounds sad, but tries to hide it. She doesn't want me to know how hard it is for her to be away.

She admitted that she's angry with my mom for dragging her away. I don't blame her one bit. I'm still livid. My mom could've left Anika behind with me, where she was adjusting just fine in her new school and with her new friends. But instead, she had to be selfish – like always – and insisted on bringing Ani with her. Uprooting her life for another errant decision.

While I've learned a lot about her mental illness and the impulsiveness of her decisions, what I don't understand is why she believes there's always something bigger, better and brighter somewhere else. It's like her disease has her seeing the grass appearing greener everywhere else but where her feet are planted.

Tonight, though, I try to keep those thoughts and concerns at bay and just enjoy the moment, and all the excitement surrounding me.

Mica joined us late, and she and Kylah sit to my right, talking and laughing about something that I didn't catch. And Mr. Griffin and Simon are on the opposite end, both sitting a bit too formally next to one another. Then the lights in the arena dim and the music begins pumping, the entire crowd jumps to their feet and goes bananas.

I reach to the left and help Simon stand up by putting my one hand on the crook of his arm and the other behind his back. Once he's steadied, I find him smiling the biggest, cheeriest smile I've seen on him in a long time.

The sound of the crowd is deafening, with bull horns and shouts of excited fans going off all around us. I can barely hear anything, the decibels of sound exceeding what's probably healthy. I feel my blood pumping, my heart racing in anticipation of the team storming out onto the court. And just then, I see them running out of the tunnel.

The team mascot, Sparky, the devil with a trident, is dancing around, high-fiving each player as they make their appearance. It's then that I see Cade, his white warm-up track suit fitting his fine body perfectly, Number 23 embroidered on the back for all to see.

I hear Kylah scream, "There he is!" We're all clapping and cheering and my sense of pride is overwhelming. Along with my possessiveness. There's a row of girls behind us that have been chit-chatting all night, giggling as college girls do. More than once, I heard Griff's name come up in their conversation. Talking about how hot he is. And how they heard he's an animal in bed. It took everything I had to restrain myself from turning behind me and telling them, "*You ain't lying, sista.*"

But I didn't. And now I focus on him as he whips off his tear-away pants, stretching his arms overhead and bending in a deep arc to the right and left. It's enough to make all the females in the whole building swoon and faint. I don't blame those girls at all for loving what they see out there. His body is show stopping – he's ripped in all the right places. Especially his biceps. Holy heavens, when he wears his basketball jersey, and grabs the ball before passing it off, they bulge and flex in concert with the motion and I want to lick him all over. It's hot enough to melt the hinges off of the gates of Hell.

And that's not a bad analogy considering the devil with a pitchfork is even fanning himself right now as he/she watches Cade in action.

Practice begins and the players are all out on court going through shooting and passing drills, a little three-on-three action at one end of the court, and some callisthenic activity in between. I watch everything as it happens, leaning over a few times to ask Simon and Mr. Griffin questions. We're about an hour in and things come to an abrupt stop as the players take a time out to regroup, grab some Gatorade and take a break.

I turn to say something to Mica when I hear an audible gasp from the girl behind me. I'm about to swivel my head to find out what her deal is, when I hear a very distinct and low voice.

"Hey sweetness. What do you think so far?"

My eyes are greeted to the sight of a gloriously sweaty and breathless Cade, who leans over the seat to give me a kiss on my cheek. The audience behind me erupts into a collective sigh. And how pathetic is it that I'm eating it up? *Yep, take note, girls. He's mine.*

"Meh…I've seen greater excitement at your grandfather's Tuesday night Bingo games."

Simon laughs and they all know I'm kidding. Cade grips his pecs and gives a mocking huff, as if I've wounded him deeply.

"You slay me, Ainsley. You're so mean."

The girls take that opportunity to lean over and interrupt.

"Excuse me, Griff. Can we get your autograph and picture?" One of them asks while the other three giggle in concert. Geez. Are we in Junior High?

Cade looks up at them as if he's just now realized he has an audience. So like him, completely oblivious to his gawking fans. Wiping his sweaty palms on his shorts, he takes the pen handed to him and torn ticket they offer him. As he's signing his name, he speaks to me without looking up.

"I know you need to get gramps back home in a little while. But can I call you later?"

I raise my eyebrow, because I know what he's really asking me for is a booty call.

He hands the autographed memorabilia back to the girl and leans in so they can take a selfie. Ah, my loveable player. How can I say no to this guy?

"Sure. You can call me. I'll be around."

Tomorrow I don't work at the café, so I can sleep in. I'd asked Kimmi in advance for the day off since I knew I'd be out late tonight. As if on cue, Simon yawns and I realize it's after one a.m. already. Time flies when you're having a good time watching your man do his thing.

Cade waves goodbye to everyone and gives me a kiss on the head before he heads back out onto the court. I watch his ass move in the polyester shorts and sigh right along with the other girls. Yeah, things are good and I'm a lucky girl for once in my life.

****

I'm lying on my stomach on my bed, trying unsuccessfully to read through my anatomy text book, as my eyelids practically droop in their heavily weighted sleepiness. I've been home now for thirty minutes, after dropping off Simon at the home and returning with Mica to our apartment. I'm thankful she has a car, even though she calls it her piece of shit. She bought it off her brother, who is a mechanic and fixed it up so it runs without any problems.

My phone buzzes with an incoming text and I expect it to be Cade telling me he's on his way over.

But it's from Anika.

Anika: Help me. Please.

WTF?

I scramble up to my knees and dial her number immediately. But it goes directly to voicemail. So I text her back.

Me: I'm trying to call you. What's going on? You're scaring me.

There's a pause. And then I see her working on her response.

Anika: Please don't get mad…I'm at a McDonald's outside of Grand Junction.

I rack my brain. Isn't Grand Junction in Colorado? But she's supposed to be in Pierre, South Dakota. My hands shake as I try to dial her again. This time it rings a few times and she answers.

"Hello?"

"Ani!" I say with a sigh of relief. But it's only momentary, as the terror of the answer to the next question reaches my brain.

"Why are you in Grand Junction? Where's mom?"

I hear her sniffling. And then a sob escapes her and it tears through me like a hot knife slicing through bread.

"*Sh*-she…he beat her up last night. We hitched rides and we're stranded here. I don't know where she went. She said she'd be right back but that was two hours ago."

Oh no. Oh please Lord, no.

I knew this would happen. I fucking knew it. Not that she would get beat up, which honestly right now, I feel like she deserves. But I did expect things wouldn't work out with that guy. Sooner, rather than later, she'd find something more enticing and would leave again.

Okay. I need to think. I have to figure this out because Ani's depending on me. She is all alone and scared. And who knows what kind of seedy element is lurking around the McDonald's at one-thirty in the morning.

"It's okay, baby. I'm here. I'll help you." I look down at my trembling hands and I fist them tightly. I'm so angry with my mom right now I could strangle her. That's if I ever see her again.

I mentally calculate the distance between Mesa and Grand Junction. I've never been there, so I have no idea if they have an airport or where Anika is in comparison. The only thing I can think of is calling the police and at least having her safe for the night.

"Ani. Is the McDonald's open? Are you inside right now?"

"No, I wasn't getting any reception in there. I'm standing outside right now. But yes, it's open. I think they're going to kick me out. I've been sitting there for hours." She sobs and it breaks my heart even more.

"They won't kick you out. I want you to go back in there and ask for the manager. I'm going to hang on the line. I'm going to talk to them, okay?"

She does what I ask and after a few minutes a husky-voiced woman gets on the line.

"Yeah, this is Darlene. What can I do for you?"

I fill in Darlene on what's going on and explain the situation. Thankfully, I find out that she's a grandmother of a teenage girl and is more than willing to let Anika stay in the back office for the night or until the police arrive. I'm scared to death about contacting the police, but Darlene says that she has a friend on the force and Anika would be in good hands.

Once we have things arranged and I feel good about her safe-keeping for the night, I get back on the line with Anika and fill her in.

"Ani, I'm going to be there as soon as I can. I'll drive through the night…"

"But…" Anika tries to interject, and I know what she's going to say. I have no car.

"Yeah, I know. I'll see if I can borrow Mica's car. Or maybe Cade can lend me his. But don't worry. Just keep your phone handy and don't leave that room, you hear me?"

Her sobs quiet down and I think she's resolved in the fact that I won't abandon her. Unlike someone else in her life. Goddammit, Mother.

We say goodbye and I rush around my room packing everything I will need for the next two days. Just as I'm zipping up my bag, I hear Cade knock softly at the front door. I swing it open, and the smile that's on his face immediately disappears when he sees my troubled look.

"What's the matter, baby?" He steps in and is about to embrace me when I stop him with my arms on his chest.

"I need your car...it's an emergency." I'm nearing a breakdown. I can feel it bubbling up from my stomach, as my legs shake and tremble. "It's Anika. My mom...she left her!"

I'm in hysterics now, sobbing and wailing as he takes hold of my shoulders and gently backs me up into the living room and out of the open doorway.

"Baby, calm down. It's okay. I'm here. We'll figure this out."

"N-no...I need to go *now*." I wail. Fat tears streak down my face. I've never felt this out of control and helpless. Frustrated and lost. Yet just at the sight of Cade, his reassuring voice and words of affirmation, helps me stay focused. He's my rock. My support. My everything.

"She's stuck at a McDonald's in Grand Junction."

"Colorado?" He asks, his voice jumping an octave.

"Y-yes. I need to go get her. Please."

He grasps hold of my wrists and pulls me to him. He's warm and solid. I feel like a collapsing bridge being held up only by the support of a steel girder.

"We'll go together."

Chapter 24
CADE

We drive through the night, hopped up on coffee and adrenaline.

It's close to nine a.m. and we still have two more hours to go before we reach Grand Junction. My eyes are dry from lack of sleep, but my focus is sharp. I give a sidelong glance over to Ainsley, who's slumped in the passenger seat. Her shoeless feet are propped up underneath her and she leans her head against the window. She's had her eyes closed for a while now, but I know she's not sleeping, even though she's exhausted from the emotional turmoil.

Before I'd gotten to Ainsley's apartment, I'd been riding high and pumped up from all the energy consumed last night at practice. It's an experience like none other and hard to describe to anyone who has never played in front of thousands of fans. It was only a practice, with lots and lots of tedious drills, but it was special. My heart was full knowing that my family was there watching me play, along with Ainsley. I tried not to let it go to my head and act like an idiot hotshot out on the court, but I took a few shots that I knew they'd be impressed with. It was worth the nasty glare I got from Coach when I did. He's always telling me to *'lose the attitude, kid'*. Even if he says it with a knowing smile.

After showering and getting changed in the locker room, I had booked out of there so fast I barely registered any of the guys asking me to go out to celebrate. I had no time for any of that because I was intent on getting over to Ainsley's as fast as I could so we could celebrate in our own private way.

Finding her in that state of shock that I did when I arrived nearly brought me to my knees. If I ever find her mother, I may not be able to hold back from decking her. I realize that's not the best approach, and hitting girls and all that…but goddamn, I was furious.

Ainsley had lost all composure. She was mumbling incoherently between sobs, barely making any sense. My fear spiked to unprecedented levels and my fight instinct took over almost immediately. I would do anything for this girl – whether it be rushing through a towering inferno or driving all night to find my girl's sister. There is nothing I wouldn't do for her.

I've got to take a piss from all the coffee I've been drinking, so I pull off I-70 in a truck stop area in Thompson Springs. Ainsley nearly shoots out of her seat, her body straining against the seat belt that's protesting her movements, her eyes darting to take in the scene.

"Are we there? Is Anika here?" Her voice squeaks with panicked concern, her disorientation evident. Maybe she had been asleep.

This is so hard on her and it breaks my heart to see her so worried.

"Baby, it's okay. I just have to take a leak and grab something to eat." I point to the Cracker Barrel building we're parked in front of. I'm starved since I haven't eaten anything of sustenance since last night before practice. I'd planned on fucking Ainsley first thing after the event and then eating...but neither of those two things happened like I'd hoped.

Ainsley slips back into her seat and sighs groggily. I unbuckle my belt and reach over to pull her face to mine. Her eyes tell me everything. Weariness. Gratitude. Fear. Love. I kiss her once, mainly because I need to feel her lips on mine. But also to reassure her that everything will be fine.

"I'm going in. Do you want to stay out here or do you need to use the restroom, too?"

She nods her head and we both get out of the car. It takes us about five minutes, I use some extra time to splash some cold water on my face to try and wake myself up. I'd never advise anyone to drive all night long after practicing hard out on the court. The dark circles clinging underneath my eyes are good indicators that it's not advisable.

We order up at the counter for take-out and are told it will be about fifteen minutes. We probably could've stopped at a fast food drive-thru, but there's nothing better than the biscuits and gravy from Cracker Barrel. They're my favorite.

The front shop is filled with pointless (in my opinion) knick-knacks and junk, but Ainsley seems enthralled with all the gifts. I find her standing in front of a display full of country home décor items, her fingers lightly touching a hanging windsock. She's quiet and lost in thought until I move behind her and wrap my arms around her waist, pulling her into my chest. Her body releases the tension and she stifles a sniffle.

It's busy and noisy in the restaurant this time of morning, the waiting area packed with people, so I have to lean in to hear what she says.

"I promised her she'd never be homeless again. She would never be abandoned and alone. I failed her." Ainsley drops her head in grief and despair.

"Shh." I try to quiet her, mulling over in my head what she just said. A thousand questions pop in my head. "What do you mean homeless again?"

Although people mill about and there's constant motion around us, we remain in our own little bubble. I dare not move, instinctively clutching her closer to me, for fear that there's a real possibility that she'll bolt. I can already tell from the tension rippling through her body that what she's about to tell me will be an anvil dropping on my head. Heavy and painful.

Ainsley maneuvers herself in my arms so she's facing me. Her normally sparkling sapphire eyes are now the color of a storm at sea. She raises her lashes, followed by her chin as she confronts me with the answer I'm dreading hearing.

"My mom is bipolar and an addict. Alcohol. Pills. You name it. She didn't get a firm diagnosis until two years ago. That was the worst night of my life."

I squeeze her shoulders and direct her outside to the front porch where they have all the big old rocking chairs. She sits down and I scoot in as close as I can.

My hand finds her knee which I knead lightly, reassuringly. I want her to know it's okay. I'm there for her. But her eyes have a far off distant look, like she's seeing something horrible happen in front of her but she can't stop looking.

"I'm so sorry, baby. That's awful."

She shrugs. "Yeah. It is what it is. I had to take her to the emergency room when I found her passed out. I had no idea what she'd done to herself. Empty pill bottles were lying next to her on the floor. I didn't want Anika to see it, but I couldn't prevent it. She still has nightmares about it.

"I hated my mother in that moment. Whether she lived or died, I hated her for being so selfish that she'd put her daughters through something that excruciatingly painful. Can you imagine? Seeing your mother lying on the floor in a pool of her own vomit? Uncertain if she's alive or dead?"

I'm not sure if that's rhetorical. So I just shake my head.

"We learned of her condition after she detoxed. And then she decided to enter into a state-run rehab program. She was in there for six months. It was a good thing, though. It helped her a lot. But it sucked for me and Ani. I was eighteen, but still in high school. I could only work part-time. We had nowhere to live. Nowhere to go. No family. Nothing."

"Fuck. I'm sorry." I sound like a broken record.

"The only thing to our name was an old Mercury station wagon. We lived in that fucking piece of shit for two months. Every night I sang my crying sister to sleep and promised her...I goddamn promised her, Cade, that we'd never go back to that again. She'd never be alone. My mother would get better and never do that to her again. I am a fucking LIAR!"

The porch has filled up with people waiting for their tables and I notice out of the corner of my eye a woman and her husband look our way before they get up from their rockers and move to the other side. As they pass us the woman gives us a dirty look and a disgruntled harrumph. I want to tell her to go fuck herself, but what good would it do? It might only upset Ainsley more, which I'm trying to prevent.

"Ainsley." I whisper, my thumb stroking the top of her hand. The hand that works so hard to support herself and her family. I'll never know the depths of the love she has for her sister. Or how difficult it must be for her to endure that type of life. I'm overcome with guilt for the way I've allowed myself to get caught up in what I feel my father has 'owed' me after leaving our family. The material possessions I take for granted. The college tuition that was just handed over to me.

I am nothing next to this strong, capable and mature woman. Her life has meaning. She makes a difference in the lives around her. And she doesn't even realize it.

"Baby, you did everything you could for your sister. I know it wasn't your choice to live in a car, but you made sure she was taken care of. I'm sure the alternative could have been a whole lot worse. You were just a kid yourself. God, I can't even imagine what I would've done at that age if I'd have been responsible for the twins. I couldn't even do my own laundry."

She eyeballs me through her long, tear-coated lashes and lets out a small laugh.

"You can't even do your own laundry now." She deadpans. That's my girl.

I give her legs a slight push in the opposite direction, as they swing away from me and then back again. She leans down, placing her elbows on her knees and cradles her head in her hands. It hurts me to see her in so much unnecessary pain.

"I'm just so angry. And bitter. I know my mom has a disease, but goddamn her all to hell. She has the means of controlling it, but doesn't. She chooses freedom over her daughter. And Ani is the one to suffer. I can't imagine what she's feeling right now. I hate my mother." She seethes.

We sit in silence for a bit, contemplating the situation and the next steps, until the pager in my hand buzzes indicating our order is ready to go. As I drive out of the parking lot onto the access road toward the highway, Ainsley quietly but resolutely speaks.

"I swear. One way or another, even if it's the last thing I do, I will make sure that Ani never has to live with my mother again. Mark my words. My mother will never get her back."

If it's one thing I've learned these last few months with Ainsley, it's that whenever she sets her mind to something, she makes it happen. I have no doubt she will make this happen, regardless of the obstacles. And I'll be by her side the entire way.

Chapter 25
AINSLEY

When Anika was younger, maybe five or six years old, she liked to play hide-n-seek, almost obsessively. I was a pre-teen at the time, and would become so mad at her when she'd interrupt me from my reading. I could always be found with a tattered copy of my Babysitter Club books in hand.

I remember one time, we were living in this run-down, old house-turned multi-family dwelling, that held lots of good hiding spots for a little kid to get into. The place was a converted old Victorian-style home, with fading shingles and creaking wood floors.

It had been a hot summer day and Anika was antsy for some interaction. I, on the other hand, just wanted to be left alone. My mother was off somewhere – God only knew where. I'd been left alone again to watch my little sister, who had been bugging me incessantly all afternoon to play with her. And I kept telling her to knock it off and to go find something else to do.

It had grown late in the day, the stifling heat seeping into the small apartment, creating a hot sticky restlessness. It had grown quiet in our tiny apartment - too quiet for a room that should hold a small child.

My panic level rose as I called out her name, searching everywhere within the confines of our sweltering little apartment but coming up empty. Where the hell was she?

I began to call out her name – louder and louder, my voice ragged with fear.

"Ani!" I yelled, in both anger and fright. It was like she'd completed vanished. Disappeared.

By this point I had searched every square inch of our apartment – in every spot I knew she usually hid away. But I came up empty. She was nowhere inside. It was then I noticed the front door cracked open.

I burst out into the hallway, dim and dingy, the only light filtering in was from a small dormer window at the end of the long hallway. The doors to the other flats were shut, the occupants either at work or festering in the oppressive heat of their rooms.

"Anika! Where are you?"

There was an old staircase that went down to the main entryway where the main floor apartments and the mailboxes were. There wasn't much down there, but I looked anyhow. No sign of her.

Running outside, I called her name, frantically inspecting every spot in the yard. Down the street there were kids playing in a neighbor's yard. They were older boys and I saw no sign of a little dark-haired girl. I called out again, pausing to listen for her sweet voice. It was then that I heard the little giggle of my six-year-old baby sister.

I should have been overjoyed that I found her, uninjured and safe. Instead, the anger unleashed inside of me. How could she have done this? Didn't she know how irresponsible it was to leave our house without an adult (or me) present?

"Anika Michelle Locker! Get your ass out here right this minute!" I fumed, spinning around in a circle still trying to locate her whereabouts.

It was then that I heard her tiny little laugh again. It was coming from up above. Tilting my head up toward the sky, I saw a glimpse of her red T-shirt. She was sitting up on the ledge of the second story window. She'd somehow managed to fit through the opening of the dormer window and out onto the ledge.

"Wook at me, Ainswy!" she chirped, her little lisp evident from excitement. "I'm wike a baby bird in my nest. Weddy to fwy!"

Until this very moment, as I step inside the emergency group home where Anika was placed last night by the local authorities, I had forgotten about how small and innocent she'd looked that day. Her big, round eyes looking down at me in wonder. With so much hope. Enthusiasm for life. Imagination.

But now, as Anika hesitantly walks toward me, a weary expression embedded in her sad face, I realize she's lost all of that joy she once had that day on the roof. Her eyes now convey her knowledge of betrayal. All the innocence lost. All the hope gone.

I open my arms and she comes running into me, grasping me tight and burying her head in my chest. I can feel the wetness of her tears soaking through my shirt.

I rub the back of her head. "Shh...I'm here now, Ani. I won't let you go. I've got you, baby."

We stay like that for a few moments as Cade talks to the social worker in the office down the hall. I know that we'll need to go through a mass of paperwork, along with a meeting with the social worker, before we can take her home with us, but all of that is just insignificant details. My sister is safe once again and I will never let her go. Whatever it takes, I will get custody so that my mother can never put her through this kind of hell again.

****

Two days later, Anika and I sit at our kitchen table, eating breakfast together. I've taken a few days off of work to get her situated back at home. Since I hadn't yet rented out the third bedroom, she's back in her old bedroom. In need of both privacy and normalcy.

We haven't talked too much about the Grand Junction incident, but I've certainly tried to coax it out of her. She's been unusually quiet and reserved since returning home. My hopes and prayers are that it is simply the shock of being abandoned and nothing that happened while she was living with my mother and Brad.

"He's a really nice guy, Ains." She says through a bite of her Cheerios.

My head flies up from the table where I'm reading one of my assignments. "Who is?"

I get an eye roll. Which is a universal sign from a teenager letting you know you're an idiot.

"Cade, dummy. It's kind of obvious he's totally in love with you."

She goes back to her Cheerios and I turn my head away so she can't see my expression. Since we've gotten back, I've been avoiding Cade. Both on purpose and due to the circumstances. He knows I'm busy with Ani, and he's been focused on basketball.

He'd held me all night long the night we returned from the road trip, as I cried and wept in his arms. Cade gave me a safety and security I'd never had before. It scared the living daylights out of me. With everything that had happened in my life, and the sheer magnitude of raising a teenager on my own, I didn't know what that would do to our relationship.

He had so many great things ahead of him his last year of college. Events, parties, travel for away games, championship games. And all I had ahead of me was a future full of financial and legal responsible for my younger sister. That is a lot of baggage for a hot, young star-athlete to want to take on in a relationship. I don't want to drag him down or become a burden. Sooner-or-later, he will come to resent me. It is that simple.

He has to realize that I will never be one of those Friday-night fun, Barbie cheerleader girlfriends who'd be able to drop everything to watch him play ball, wearing his jersey and cheering from the sidelines. And when he and his teammates hold their after-parties, I can't be the girl partaking in the drunken festivities alongside him.

No. I'd be the one who was home every night making sure my fifteen-year-old sister finished her homework and was ready for her school the next day. Accountable for making sure she had food on the table, clothes on her back, and the emotional support she needed. A now motherless and fatherless girl.

Yes, Cade is an amazing guy. I honestly question how lucky I am to be involved with such a good guy. He's been my rock through this entire ordeal. Yet I'm not too naïve to realize that my new fulltime responsibilities will create a wedge between us. It's inevitable. Something has to be done about it now, before things get any more complicated between us. Before I can no longer live without him.

I smile at Anika, and try my best nonchalant response. "Yeah. Cade is pretty great. But we're not serious."

She drops the spoon in her bowl with a clatter, her eyebrows furrowed with a frown.

"You're kidding me, right? That guy is in deep, Ains. Puhleez…He drove like eighteen hours with you the other day, across two state lines. If that's not serious, I don't know what is."

I scoff. "What do you know about serious? You're fifteen." I try to give it a teasing edge, but there's some truth there.

"I know enough." She says quietly under her breath.

Shit, yeah. I know she's witnessed the wrong type of love and the abusive kind that my mother has been on the receiving end of. She's seen plenty of the ugly kind of love.

Reaching over the table, I grab her hand in mine.

"I know you do, Ani. But I want you to know something else. Guys are going to come and go in your life. And I hope they will all be good, honest, trustworthy men who will prove to you that they are worthy of your love. But in the end, you need to realize there are only two people you can ever truly rely on in this world. I'm one of them, and I will never leave you. I will always be here for you."

I glide my hand down the backside of her head, her silky strands billowing under my touch.

"The other person is yourself. You are strong and able. And you don't need a man in your life to do the things you can do yourself. You got that?"

She nods her head. "I got it."

I resume my reading as we sit quietly for a few more minutes until she breaks the silence with her question.

"Do you love him, Ains?"

I close my eyes before I speak. Because I can't lie about that. I do love him. So much that it breaks my heart knowing I need to end things with him. So much that I'd rather do the selfish thing and allow it to continue, rather than do the right thing and let him go.

"Yeah. I do."

Chapter 26
CADE

The last week has been a tornado of activity. I'd expected things to get crazy once the season started, but I had no idea how insane it would really be. Between school and daily practices, I come home exhausted, barely able to keep my eyes open long enough to eat, shower, change and study.

And it has only caused the distance I've felt between me and Ainsley to grow wider. Ever since we returned from Colorado, things have been different. Her normally chipper and enthusiastic demeanor has turned flat and solemn. We haven't talked on the phone at all this week. I hadn't seen her in our usual meet-up spots on campus. In fact, I haven't seen her show up for her classes at all.

It worries me that she is retreating. Again. I know she is dealing with a lot right now and how upset she is over what happened in Grand Junction. I want to give her space, but the bigger part of me wants to take her in my arms and never let her go. Just like the night we got back, when I held her in my arms as her body was racked with sobs. It broke my fucking heart that she was placed in this horrible predicament.

When I learned about her mom's issues and the time she and Anika were homeless? Holy hell, I wanted to beat someone. It never occurred to me that kids had to live on their own without family support. It's ignorant on my part, because I don't live in some bubble or ignore the homeless on the streets, but I've never known anyone who'd been homeless. My naiveté was obvious in my assumptions that homelessness is always by choice.

Giving Ainsley the space she needs has been hard. My instinct was to smother her with love and shower her with constant affection, but she isn't that type of girl. She needs to know she can do this on her own, and I applaud her for her courage. So I took a step back and have been waiting for her to reach out to me. The problem is, I'm not very patient. It's nearly a week and I've heard nothing from her, leaving me no other option but to stalk her at work.

She's normally on shift at Bristol's Café on Friday mornings. The team had an early workout and practice this morning – Coach being mindful that his players want to enjoy their Friday evenings, so he schedules us bright and early. I'm freshly showered, making my way past the Wells Fargo Arena, and the Nadine and Ed Carson Student Athlete Center, turning on Mill Avenue and walking toward Sixth Street.

As I near the front of the café, with its large paned window overlooking the street, a man sitting on the edge of the sidewalk breaks the quiet around me, posing a question out of nowhere.

"Do you know that the Sun is one of two-hundred billion stars in the Milky Way galaxy?"

I'm startled by the odd interruption and stop in front of the guy and his dog. He's an older gentleman, probably in his late fifties, but could be younger. The sun's exposure has taken a toll on his appearance. His greasy hair is slicked back from his face, hidden underneath a tattered baseball cap that's definitely seen better times. The mangy looking dog lays unimpressed next to his owner, head down between his dirty paws. Even the dog looks miserable. Poor pup.

Engaging in conversation with a vagrant is not something I'm generally comfortable with. Not that I'm worried for my safety, because I could definitely take him in a fight if I had to, but because I don't have a lot of experience with it. Many homeless are less than stable and suffer from chronic and untreated mental illnesses. I learned that from Psych 101. The thought reminds me of what Ainsley shared about her mother and I'm sad wondering if she will end up like this man.

Deciding that I can spare a few minutes, I crouch down on bended knees and give the guy my full attention.

"Nah, man. I didn't know that."

He seems a bit surprised himself that I've joined in on the conversation. Maybe I was wrong and he really wasn't speaking to me, but to himself. Oh well, no backing down now.

The man adjusts his scrawny frame so he's now sitting fully erect, instead of slouched over like he was, and he looks me squarely in the eye.

"I know who you are." He points an accusatory finger at me. "You're him."

Um, not sure what to say to that. So I decide to just go with it.

"Yep, I am."

"You're the one lurking around my sweetness. And I don't like it."

Okay, now I'm confused. This guy's definitely off his rocker.

"Your sweetness? I'm not sure what you mean."

His hand trembles as he points toward the direction of the café.

The sound he emits is a cross between reverence and sorrow. "My sweetness. The sweetest girl in the world."

My head automatically follows the line of his finger and I look over my shoulder to find Ainsley standing at a table inside facing the window. Her eyes are cast down and then she lifts her head, our eyes meeting for the first time in a week.

The sight of her and her beauty has me off balance, my body swaying a bit in my crouched position. Catching myself, I smile, because I'm so happy to see her. But the light in her smile doesn't seem to be there. Her face is shrouded in an emotion I'm not comfortable dissecting.

Now I know the man is talking about Ainsley. And my guard goes up, my body stiffening just like it does when I go up to block a shot. My job is to protect the basket. In this case, it's to protect the girl I love.

"You know Ainsley?"

The dark spheres of his eyes lock with mine and he tilts his chin up defiantly.

"In vain have I struggled. It will not do. My feelings will not be repressed. You must allow me to tell you how ardently I admire and love you." He says with dramatic flair and a crazy-ass stare. I wrinkle my face in confusion and start to stand up again because I have no idea what he's just said. He takes pity on me.

"Jane Austen, Pride and Prejudice. A classic."

Like that explains anything. This guy is really out there. One moment he's talking astronomy and the next, romantic classics. I've had just about enough and I'm about to turn away when I hear her angelic voice.

"Everything all right out here, gentlemen?" I glance at Ainsley and then back to the guy and back to Ainsley again. "Crockett, I brought you a muffin for breakfast. From yesterday's blueberry batch, your favorite." She hands a wrapped muffin to the guy (what kind of a name is Crockett?) and I notice the dog's ears perks up, too.

Crockett grabs it from her hand and grumbles a low "Thank you."

"Cade, what are you doing here?" It's not an accusation, but is said in a manner that makes me wonder if she doesn't want to see me.

"I was done with practice and thought I'd swing by. I haven't seen you for a few days. I miss you." I go in to give her a hug and she pulls back to avoid the contact. Her eyes dart from side to side, as if she's concerned by who is watching us.

With a tug on my T-shirt, she implores me to follow her. "Let's go around back to talk, okay?"

By this point, I sense there's something going on and I've missed the boat. The feeling is like standing in the ocean, knee deep in water, watching the incoming wave from a distance, just waiting for its impact, realizing that in any moment I'm going to be flattened.

Fuck, I'm screwed. This is it.

I've never been in a serious relationship before, but I know about breakups. I've heard enough horror stories from my buddies to know that it hurts worse than a kick in the nuts. So I dig in and prepare. Put up my defenses. I will not allow this to happen. I'm not going down easy. I'll foul out before I let her take a shot.

"What's going on, Ains?"

Ainsley stands stiff against the brick of the building, which has to be emitting an intense level of heat right now. She crosses her arms -to shield herself, somehow? – and takes a big breath.

"Cade -"

"No." I say. The sound echoes and reverberates off the brick and her head snaps up like she's been slapped.

"No?   No, what?"

"No to whatever you're going to say."

I move in, crowding her space until I'm inches from her and my hands land on the structure behind her. It's a dominant move to cage her in. Maybe I want her to feel intimidated, I don't know. All I know for certain is that I will not accept whatever she's going to say to me.

Ainsley's places her hand in the center of my chest – maybe to push me away – but I capture it with one of my own. I take in the shape of her beautiful mouth. Her perfect, pink lips tremble.

"I can't be with you anymore, Cade. It's not fair to either of us. I have too much going on to make this work. I don't have the time. You need something more than I can give you."

I'm angry. "That's bullshit, Ains. When have I ever asked you for anything more? I love you. You're everything I need. Everything I want. Don't you understand that?"

Ainsley forcefully pulls her hand from mine and elbows her way out of my grip. I let her have her space. For now.

"You don't get it, Cade. We are too different. Look at my life right now! It's a mess. And you're...*you*," she says with a wave of her hand. "You're the Golden Boy with endless possibilities. Do you know how it feels when people look at me when we're together? It's all there in their condescending glares. I'm not good enough for you. You're their star – their idol – and I'm a speck of dirt – a girl from the other side of the tracks. I can't have the weight of my life dragging you down your last year of school."

I'm stunned. Momentarily speechless. I've never considered in any way, shape, or form that she was less than me. Or even had an inkling that she could possibly degrade herself like that. She's always exuded confidence and pride. She let things roll off her shoulder. But now she throws this at me like it makes any difference to who we are together. My love is bigger than her oppositions. It shouldn't matter what other people think.

The silence between us grows bigger. Heavier. From the door in the alleyway I can hear the sounds from the kitchen. Pots and pans banging. The low hum of a dishwasher. The voices of the line-cooks and kitchen staff. The loud *thump, thump, thump* of my breaking heart.

"Ainsley…none of that matters. Nobody else matters. Only you. I love you. And you're not weighing me down…you're lifting me up. With you, I can do anything. You're the air I breathe."

I can't read the expression on her face. And that worries me. She sucks in her bottom lip, worrying it with her teeth.

And then the world drops out on me.

"Cade, we're over. This won't work. I'm sorry, but I don't love you."

Chapter 27
AINSLEY

I've never lied in my life.

But I knew the only thing that I could say that would possibly make a stubborn, six-foot-five wall of man let me go was to tell him that I didn't love him.

Which is a bold-faced lie.

Of course I love him. If I didn't, I wouldn't go to this great length to protect him from my crazy, chaotic life. I don't want, or need, a white knight to feel like he has to fix me or support me out of some misplaced sense of duty. Even if he truly does love me, I don't want him to ever feel like I'm holding him back from enjoying his life.

Cade is a rising star. Regardless of whether he declares his interest in the NBA draft or not, he has so many great opportunities on the horizon. His future is within reach. He's a smart guy who will graduate with honors in May, and between now and then, he deserves to enjoy the limelight and all the fun that comes along with being a college athlete.

There is simply no other way around this.

"You're a horrible liar, Ainsley. Don't act like the martyr here."

I almost smile because he's right about that. I bite my lip harder to keep from agreeing with him. Instead, I tilt my head up and glare at him with defiance.

"You're a great guy, Cade. I'll admit, I enjoyed my time with you. But I just can't do it anymore. And come on, it's not like you won't find someone else to replace me within five minutes flat. Just like last time." I snap my finger to emphasize the point.

That little truth hurts more than I want to admit. The girls swarm even when I'm standing right next to him. Once word gets out he's single again – all those hoops hunnies will be crawling over him like ants at a picnic.

His face contorts in anger and his voice rises in frustration. "Goddammit, Ainsley. How many times do I have to say this? What do I have to do to prove it to you that I've never been unfaithful since the moment we got together? I wouldn't do that. I don't want any of those hoop ho's. It's you I love and *you* I want."

Nail, meet coffin. I'm about to close the lid tight and bury this thing once and for all.

"It doesn't matter. I just can't live that way. It'll eat me up inside. And you'll come to regret me. To be perfectly honest…I still don't trust what you say."

There. He knows how much trust is an issue for me. And while it isn't actually the way I feel, and I have forgiven him for what happened before between us, I can still use it as a weapon to defeat him. To win this war that should never have to be fought, but is the only way to end this once and for all.

Just as I thought, the words cut him deep and he hangs his head in defeat.

"I'm not going to argue with you, Ainsley. And I'm sure as fuck not going to beg. So if this is what you want…"

No, it's not what I want. But it's what you need.

"Yes," I say instead.

"Fine. Have it your way." He looks at me with sad, soulful eyes, more blue right now than I've ever seen them. "I still think you're lying and I don't understand why. But I'm sorry you feel that way."

He leans in and kisses me on the cheek one last time as I watch him turn and go.

Cade doesn't look back.

****

The minute Kimmi sees my face when I walk back through the kitchen, she immediately throws her arms around me. All my walls crumble. I ugly cry for over twenty minutes until the tears dry up long enough for me to grab my things and go home.

Two days later, I'm still wallowing in self-pity and heartbreak. I've been sprawled out on top of my bed quilt for the last hour, blubbering into my pillow. Trying to be quiet so no one will hear me. Unfortunately, Mica has the ears of a hawk. Or is that eyes? Either way, she's extremely intuitive, making no buts about knocking on my door and inviting herself in.

"Lance asked me out," she deadpans and then groans, taking a seat on my bed.

Rolling over to my side, I sloppily wipe away the snot running down my nose on the used Kleenex and push myself up onto my elbow.

"And this is a bad thing? I thought you liked Mr. Hotshot Basketball Player."

With the exception of all the drama in my life recently, it's been awesome having Mica with us. She's turned out to be a great friend and confidant. I want her to be happy, and I know with a hundred percent confidence that she really likes Lance.

"Yeah, well, I turned him down."

I spring up the rest of the way and grab her shoulders for affect.

"You what? Are you kidding me? That's just plain cray-cray."

"What's the point? I'd be in the same, if not worse, situation as you and Cade." She points out, as if I understand how we are so similar in that respect. But I don't have a clue what she's talking about.

"That makes no sense. Our situations are completely different. And you've been crushing on him for months! Why won't you even give it a try?"

Mica turns to face me, wrapping her legs cross-styled and leans forward, chin in her hand.

"Well, let's see. First there is the height challenge. We'd look ridiculous together."

"That's easy…wear heels! Plus, look at all the celebrity couples that handle that problem without complaint. What's-her-face from the Nashville TV show and her super, duper tall boxer fiancé. And oh, country singer Jesse James Decker and her hottie hubs Eric. Oh, and Stephan Curry and his wife. See? Problem solved." I'm feeling pretty proud of myself for coming up with all these names off the top of my head to prove my point.

Mica takes a moment to consider this, rubbing her chin and nodding.

"Fine, but then there's my family obligations. And the fact that my dad and brothers would shit bricks if they find out I'm dating a gringo, who is not Catholic, by the way. They'd never let that happen."

"You're not living under his roof anymore and you are a full-grown woman. You should be able to date whomever you want."

Mica scoffs, like I'm an idiot.

"I wouldn't want to put that kind of burden on Lance. It's not fair to him to suffer the wrath or consequences of *mi familia.* He seems like a good, fun-loving guy, and he doesn't need that serious weight on his shoulders."

I gently shove at Mica's shoulders so she falls backward on the bed before bouncing back up again.

"Oh my God! You're not honestly going to let that stop you, are you? He can totally handle any and all that comes with dating you if he likes you enough. Don't sell yourself short just because you think you know what's best for him."

Mica's raised eyebrows, tilted head, and wrinkled forehead indicates she's just proved a point she was trying to make. Oh shit. That point wasn't about her and Lance. It was about my stupid problem with Cade.

A sly smile curves across her face telling me she knows she's got me by the balls on this one. *Face palm.*

"You're a bitch and I don't like you anymore." I say in jest.

"No, you love me. Just admit it. And for that matter, why don't you just admit that you made a mistake by telling Cade to vamoose."

"I will do no such thing."

"Chica." She gently pries my fingers loose from my ankles, which I've been holding on to tight enough to leave a mark. She clasps my hands in hers. If someone walked in, they'd think we were having a séance.

"You've been crying over him for days. Which proves to me that you still love him. So why aren't you with him?"

Mica knows all about the break-up discussion the other day and the reasons I told him to leave. She is my rock and sounding board this weekend, listening without interruption as I wailed and squeaked over the painful reasons I had to let him go. Yet, she goes and shoves those very same reasons in my face, but this time replacing me and Cade with her and Lance, and I fail to see the problem. The obstacles I listed can all be overcome if I want to. Love conquers all, isn't that what they say?

I sniff back my tears. "Because, it's the right thing to do."

"From the looks of it, it's not the right thing for you. And when I saw Cade today…"

My eyebrows shoot up in question. "You saw Cade? Where?"

She has the decency to blush. "Lance invited me over this morning and made me breakfast. Or tried to, at least. He's a horrible cook."

We both laugh and she continues. "Cade loves you so much, Ainsley. And I think it's really unfair that you've made this unilateral decision because you think it's in his best interest. He's a grown man. He can make up his own mind. And you can't control destiny."

Destiny.

That one word has my tummy fluttering thinking back on how we connected. Not once. Not twice. But three times we ran into each other by happenstance. Two impossibly opposite individuals with completely different upbringings and circumstances. Yet, we meshed. It's like what Cade said TV sports announcers call a perfect shot. "*Nothing but net, baby.*"

All this time, Cade was right. I am acting like a martyr. I've always put others' needs before mine in order to survive. That's who I am – a caregiver. My thoughts are consumed with the comfort of others. How can I make them feel better? What can I do to help them? What's best for their well-being?

Maybe it's high time I consider my own needs for once. When I'm with Cade, I'm happy. He gives me the strength and support I need – and is my solace. I'm not like my mother, who relies on jerks who use her, leave her and hurt her. Cade only wants to be loved in return.

Instead of returning the love, I've pushed him away, unaccepting of the love he's so freely given.

I jump off the bed and search the floor for my flip-flops. Finding them, I slide my feet in them and then look around for my purse. Just as I'm about to ask Mica if I can borrow her car, I see her keys in her outstretched palm.

"Gracias, amiga." I smile and place a kiss on the top of her head.

"You're welcome. Now go get that boy and tell him how you feel, because double-dates will be pretty awkward if you don't."

A bubble of laughter hitches up my throat and I head out the door in search of the man I love.

Chapter 28
CADE

"Fuck you, Edwards. You're a motherfucking douche. You ambushed me on purpose, fucker!"

Carver and Lance have been playing Call of Duty all morning, yelling at each other and being fucking numb nuts together. Nothing unusual there for a Sunday morning. Things started off semi-quiet earlier, the only noise coming from Mica in the kitchen with Lance. That guy is going well above his normal means of wooing to get that girl.

It reminds me of the effort I put in with Ainsley.

Fat lot of good that did me. Fuck. Now my mood is tanking even more.

I'd woken up with a raging hangover and a headache that's crushing me blind. And all I want is to go back to bed and find Ainsley waiting there for me so I can wrap her up in my arms and make my problems disappear.

But her absence *is* the problem. And it can't be solved when she is the only answer to the equation.

Ainsley feels that the only way to fix her problem (which is all in her head, if you ask me), is by eliminating the X and Y from the equation entirely. But logically, if you want to solve the algebraic equation, you have to solve for Y. And the answer lies with both of us — together - we are the linear equation.

I find my way into the kitchen to grab some coffee and some aspirin when a soft knock sounds at the front door.

"You guys expecting anyone?" I yell from behind the couch and they both shake their heads and continue their loud-ass playing.

I glance down at my attire and shrug my shoulders. If someone dares to make an unannounced visit on a Sunday morning before noon, they'd better expect to find us in our loungewear. Otherwise known as basketball shorts and no shirts.

Holding the coffee mug in one hand, I turn the knob with the other and wrench it open.

There standing before me is the most perfect, beautiful sight in the entire world. Everything around me is drowned out — the noise of the video game, the sounds of Carver and Lance yelling at one another — everything else is non-existent.

We stand there staring at each other for several minutes. Hell, it could be hours. All I know is that I can't take my eyes off her. And she seems to be just as entranced with me by the way her eyes dip down my chest, over the bulge that is starting to tent under the scrutiny of her gaze, and then back up again to my lips.

"Maybe I should charge for the show."

"Huh?" She asks, flustered and embarrassed as a red streak blossoms across her cheeks. "Oh, yeah. Sorry. I just wasn't expecting you to answer the door half naked."

"And I didn't expect to answer the door to find the girl of my dreams standing here."

I might be laying it on a little thick, but fuck it. If I'm only given this one last chance, I'm gonna make it count. I'm gonna pull out all the stops, say exactly what I feel, and go hard in the paint.

Ainsley steps forward but I don't make a move to retreat or move aside. She's inches from me and I can smell the sweet orange-blossom of her shampoo. I drag in a deep inhale and let it go just as she lifts herself up on tiptoe, grabs the back of my head and pulls me down into a scorching kiss. She tastes like cinnamon and coffee. The kiss doesn't last long enough, much to my chagrin, but gives me ideas of dragging her into my bedroom and stripping her naked.

But I don't want to foul out too early, so I take what she gives me and hope there's more of that to come.

I finally concede and step back to allow room between us. She glances up through her thick lashes, the sapphire so intense it makes me breathless. Or maybe that's just from her kiss.

"Can I come in and talk?"

Playing it casual, trying to act cool, I throw my arm out in the direction of my bedroom, prompting her to lead the way. Inside, my heart is thundering, beating a hundred miles per hour against my rib cage. She can probably see it if she looks closely enough.

We head back into my bedroom, passing the guys who give me sideways glances. Lance throws out a *"go get her, tiger"*, which Ainsley quirks her eyebrows at. I shrug and keep on walking. Nothing is going to stop me until I have her behind closed doors. And at that point, it's debatable whether I'll ever let her back out.

Once inside, instead of sitting down on the chair or the edge of the bed, Ainsley walks over to my bureau, her back to me while she runs a hand over the numerous awards and trophies I have on top of the furniture. My curiosity is at an all-time high and my patience is running out fast. My brain is just trying to keep up with what's going on.

"Remember the first time I was here?"

My cock perks up. Indeed, he definitely recalls every time she's been here. But that first night, my birthday party, was a very good night. She allowed herself to open up to me that night. She was fun, was cool with my stupid friends, and seemed to have a good time.

"Yeah, of course I remember. It was our first date. I had to coax you to come over."

"Maybe I'm a little stubborn…"

I harrumph. "Ya think?"

She turns with a big smile on her face. It does something crazy to my stomach, which has been in knots since she arrived.

"That night…I didn't sleep with you. But I wanted to really bad." She says with a sheepish expression, as she glances coyly at the floor through her long lashes. "But I didn't want you to think I was like any of your other girls. I wanted you to know that I was different and didn't just want you for your basketball celebrity. I wanted to distinguish myself as somebody more than just a groupie."

Moving forward, I take her wrist and gently yank her into me so that our torsos touch. I feel the small pebbles of her nipples against my naked chest and my cock decides he wants off the bench.

"Ainsley," I say with gentle assurance. "You've always been different than anyone else. Never did I once think of you as a groupie. I was the one who chased you, not the other way around. I knew you were special from the moment I laid eyes on you."

She laughs. "I know. You were extremely tenacious."

I stroke the inside of her wrist with my thumb. It's soft and smooth.

"And I got what I wanted." I kiss her hand.

"You did," she agrees. "But then I realized being different in your world can cause problems. I don't have the same time to allocate to going to parties, and joining you on the road for away games. Or even coming to watch every home game. I have responsibilities that interfere…my sister…"

"She needs you," I interrupt, walking her back toward the bed so we can sit. "I understand that, baby. And I want to be there for you and Anika. You need someone to take care of you, too. I want you to let me do that for you. And for some reason, you have it in that beautiful, stubborn head of yours, that I need to party-out the rest of my college life…well, I don't. Sure there might be some fun events in the coming few months, and if you schedule time to attend with me, that'll be awesome. But if you can't, then I'd rather spend a night in with you over a night out with a bunch of people I don't care about."

She drops her chin, but I tip it back up. I place a gentle kiss on her lips to show her how much I truly mean it.

"I just don't want you to get to the end of this school year and look back with regret because you missed out on it because of me."

Wrapping my arms around her, I tug her into my neck so she has no choice but to lay her head against me. Our hearts beat in rhythm. It feels right. Perfect.

"Listen to me, Ainsley, because I'm only going to say this once. The only thing I would ever regret is losing you. When I look back at the last few years, before I met you, I can't believe how empty my life was. It was filled with endless parties, girls, fans, and basketball. But none of that really made me happy. It all leaves a bitter aftertaste. That's because the sweetest thing I've ever had is right here in my arms. And now I'm kind of hooked on your sweetness."

Her small hand runs the length of my chest, circling its hard planes, dragging her fingernails across my bare abs, as I feel her warm breath flutter across my skin on an exhale.

Without Ainsley, my life would be meaningless. If we were opponents on the court, I know we'd be evenly matched. And unlike basketball, I want our game to continue forever. That would be the sweetest thing ever.

"I want you by my side, forever and always, baby. I love you."

She smiles, the one that lights up my life.

"I love you, too, Cade."

"Good," I say, stunning her when I flip her back onto the bed so she's flat on her back. A giggle erupts from her chest. "Now, let me taste some of that sweetness again."

Sweetness

The End

ACKNOWLEDGMENTS

Although completely fictional, the premise of this book came to me a few years ago while I was visiting my late uncle before he passed away. He was well into his nineties, but due to the limitations he lived with, my aunt had to arrange for his round-the-clock care. I'm so thankful that I could visit him several times while he lived in the adult-family care facility prior to his passing. It was during those visits that I witnessed firsthand the tremendous amount of effort the nursing home staff had to give their residents on a daily basis. Some of the staff were exceptional, others not so much. But for the most part, they treated my uncle with the dignity and respect he deserved. So for that, I thank all those working in this very underappreciated field. These individuals in your care rely on your service, dedication and help as they live out the remainder of their lives.

This book is dedicated to my Uncle Burt. I miss him every day and cherish the time I had with him.

Simon Forsberg (Cade's fictional grandpa) is named after my late father-in-law, Sam. He taught me how to play cribbage and always offered me a "beer and a bump" when I lost to him afterward. Sam did such a wonderful job raising his youngest son - my husband – to be a kind, generous and thoughtful man. So for that, Sam, I thank you. Rest in peace.

Thank you to my author PA, Keyanna Butler, The Indie Author's Apprentice. She's just fabulous and has provided me with amazing support and assistance throughout the last few months. I love her bubbly personality and creativity. She's just 'awesome sauce'.

To the WOTR crew, Jillian Jacobs, Angie and Melinda from Twinsie Talk Book Reviews – I'm so blessed to have found you all and been invited to attend the inaugural author con in Illinois this summer. I learned so much from so many of you and had a lifetime of fun. Way to Rock the Boat, ladies! Hope to see you all again in the future.

To my girlies, Stephanie Elliot and J. Nathan – two authors extraordinaire and my good friends. Thank you, as always, for your wisdom, encouragement and support. Love you both.

Giselle at Xpresso Book Tours – you're the best! Always on top of things and so professional.

Thanks to Jeff and AnnMarie for allowing me to give a shout-out to their Tempe pizza shop, Hungry Howies. Next time I'm in town, I'll stop by and have a slice!

Leigh, my librarian editor and lifelong friend of my niece, Steph, thanks for helping me out on such short notice. I appreciate it! You done well, my girl.

And to all the readers who have read my books, either on purpose or by accident, I can't tell you how much I appreciate you. Thanks for taking a chance on this indie author and encouraging me to continue to pursue my passions. If you liked this book, I'd be forever grateful if you'd place a review on the site that you bought it, or Goodreads.

Xoxo

Sierra

Stay tuned in and sign up for my newsletter by going to my website: https://www.sierrahillbooks.com

ABOUT THE AUTHOR

Since writing and releasing her first book in 2014, Sierra has found her creative passion writing about the fictional characters that live inside her brain, who constantly shout for their own love stories to be told.

Sierra frequently indulges in what some might consider to be an unhealthy dose of reading, dark chocolate goodies, and way too much coffee. She hates cold weather, scary movies and reality TV shows, and frequently finds herself traveling around the U.S. to see her favorite musicians.

Sierra resides in the Pacific Northwest with her husband of twenty years and her long-haired, German Shepherd. She is currently working on her next book.

Sierra Hill

Made in the USA
San Bernardino, CA
26 August 2016